The Garden

By Hollis Summers

Fiction

The Garden
The Day After Sunday
The Weather of February
Brighten the Corner
City Limit

Poetry

Start From Home
Sit Opposite Each Other
The Peddler and Other Domestic Matters
Seven Occasions
Someone Else
The Walks Near Athens

The Garden

Hollis Summers

HARPER & ROW, PUBLISHERS
New York • Evanston • San Francisco • London

FIRST EDITION

STANDARD BOOK NUMBER: 06–014174–3

LIBRARY OF CONGRESS CATALOG CARD NUMBER: 72–79713

Designed by C. Linda Dingler

for
Laura, Millie, Hank

Contents

From   3

Through   105

To   197

From

She had waked first. At home, in Athens, Ohio, Tom would have waked first. She pushed the covers away from her. She moved to the end of the bunk; she climbed down the little ladder awkwardly—she was glad no one watched her. It was terrible to be awkward.

Lewis was all right. He slept, beautiful, on the lower bunk, a tight bundle. In the next stateroom Tom snored. She could hear Tom's snoring above the engines of the ship. Or perhaps the engines had stopped. Perhaps Tom's snoring moved them over the water. They were moving all right.

She eased her suitcase, the dark blue, from underneath Lewis's bunk. "Ssh," she said to herself as she pulled the zipper, up, across, down. It was a good suitcase, light, easy to manage; the zipper was quiet: Lewis did not move. Tom had been wise in his choice of their luggage, the pale blue for Lewis, the dark brown for himself, the tan for Incidentals. Lewis liked to say "Incidentals." But she was tired of living out of suitcases. It was impossible to believe that three weeks ago they had been at home in Athens, Ohio. In Syracuse, day before yesterday, Tom had suddenly decided to leave the bus tour. He had been reading about Malta.

She lifted her nightgown over her head. She folded the gown carefully before she began to put on the clothes she had hung on the hooks by the washbasin: pants, bra, slip, sweater—heavy sweater.

It was a lovely cabin, a dollhouse cabin with its narrow bunks and the tiny mahogany clothes closet—without any hangers—and the print of a smiling Romney lady, elaborately framed, over the little chest by Lewis's bunk. The chest held two china chamber pots, sprigged with roses. "What are those things, Mamma? What on earth are those things?"

Lewis was a good traveler. And his face in profile was beautiful enough to be placed in the most elaborate frame in the world. Nobody would notice the frame.

Wool skirt—her heaviest skirt.

Tom was right. Lewis was a good traveler, and travel was good for a child, for all of them. Lewis would remember this trip. He remembered everything. Already he said, "Remember the boy on the *Raffaello*, Mamma?" "Remember those big waves?" "Now that I live in Taormina . . ."

In a month, in five weeks, they would be home.

She knelt to close the suitcase. It was like praying.

Her grandmother had kneeled beside a cherry spool bed, every morning and every night. They had moved a desk and chair and the bed to every place they lived. The other furniture changed from house to house. "They're not worth moving," Grandmother said of chests and chairs and tables. "We'll pick us up something just as good, better maybe, probably. But not my desk and office chair—or the bed." Grandmother kneeled by the bed, muttering sometimes, sometimes quiet.

It was too early to close the suitcase. She hadn't brushed her teeth yet. There were toothbrushes, and the washcloths, her makeup bag—and the clock. Toiletries were not Incidentals; they were Personal Luggage, Tom said. Tom's brother and his wife had teased him about the luggage categories.

She stood, smoothing her hands down over her stomach, around to her hips. The cabin was warm, as warm as the bedroom in Athens. She had been cold ever since they left home. She hugged herself, relishing the warmth. Lewis moved, but he did not open his eyes.

She had dreamed of her grandmother again, and a house in Waterford, West Virginia, a cold mean little house.

She placed her hand on the top bunk. She stood on tiptoe. It was strange that she had not looked out yet. All night she had kept looking out. Last night the moon was full. It shone in a circle of clouds; the clouds made a dome; the moon centered the top of the dome. "A circle of clouds doesn't mean anything," she had kept telling herself, half dreaming. Old people would say a circle of clouds meant something. Bad weather, maybe, nothing more than bad weather.

She saw Malta first. She was the very first member of her family to see Malta. "Malta is honey-colored," she said to herself. "Malta is the color of honey. We will be happy here."

Malta stretched under the sun. Last night the moon was full.

We will be happy here.

Malta lay like a background for a religious painting; it was a bright Nativity background on a Christmas card.

"Tom! Tom!" She knocked hard against the side of the cabin. Her knuckles shook the picture of the Romney lady. "Tom! We're there!"

Lewis sat up. "We're there, Mamma? We're there again?"

"Good morning, good morning. And it's beautiful, Lewis. It's gold-colored."

Tom was turning the doorknob. The Romney lady smiled still, but she did not tremble. "Let me in."

"I'm here. I'm here, Tom." She turned the key in the lock.

Tom blinked behind his glasses. He fumbled at the cord of his disreputable flannel bathrobe. "It's only a quarter of six."

A door opened down the hall. "Come on in. Don't stand out there."

"They said we wouldn't get in until seven-thirty. Isn't that what they said? Or seven. Was it seven?"

"You're still asleep."

5

"We're there, Daddy. We're there again."

She closed the door after Tom. The room was crowded. Tom kissed her cheek. Lewis was kneeling in the bed. Tom rubbed his hand over Lewis's head.

"What do you know about that?" Tom picked up the travel clock from the chamber pot chest. "It's seven-thirty. My watch stopped and I slept over. I'm really on vacation. What do you know about that?"

"We have plenty of time."

He moved around her to the door. "I've got to make tracks."

"We can stay on the boat until eight-thirty, that's what the maid said. Look out the window, Tom. Look out the porthole."

Lewis had climbed to the top bunk. "Look, Daddy. It's gold, all right. It's all made of gold."

Tom placed both hands on the bunk. "That's fine. We're just fine. Sure, sure. That's fine."

Tom was out of the room. The door of his cabin slammed.

"No, don't help me. I can dress by myself."

"Of course you can."

Lewis's hands were skilled.

"You can pack my pajamas because we are in a hurry." He kicked his pajama pants into her hands. "We are just fine, aren't we? And we're lucky, too."

"Yes. Yes, Lewis."

It was important to remember how fine they were. And lucky. She was pleased with Tom for changing his mind in Syracuse.

It was a time to walk carefully and make magics—that was Grandmother's talk, too. "Walk carefully and make magics, Caroline." Caroline had been elected vice-president of the junior class at Waterford High School, she had received the scholarship, or she had made straight A's, she had been employed to teach in Athens when she had finished at the university.

In fifteen minutes they were lucky again at the police passport check. They walked into the second class dining room just as one of the three policemen at the back table called Tom's name.

6

"Your passports. Good morning," the fat policeman said in Italian.

"That's all?" Tom was frowning.

The thin policeman motioned them away, calling another name.

"Bagalja," an old man in dirty blue overalls asked as they stepped out of the dining room.

"I thought they spoke English here."

"They do, Tom. They will," she said, not sure if she should have said anything.

As usual Tom insisted on carrying the heavier bags, the dark blue and brown. He walked fast ahead of her and Lewis and the old man with his cart. And then at the customs shed he tipped the old man more than enough for the four suitcases.

Tom had seemed afraid of the customs in Naples, too. "I am in It-a-lay," Lewis sang, hopping around them. "Quiet, Lewis. Be quiet. We're at customs." Good honest Tom acted as if they smuggled heroin or diamonds.

But they were lucky again. The mustached customs man asked if they had anything to declare, scrawling chalk marks on their bags even as he asked. *"Buon giorno,"* he said, as the mustached man in Naples had said *"Buona notte."* They could have been the same man.

She reached for the tan and the pale blue. *"Grazie,"* she said. "Thank you very much."

"I'll help," Lewis said.

"They aren't heavy, Lewis." Tom was already out of sight. "You carry my purse. It's heavy enough."

"I want to carry my own suitcase." It was too much for him. The pale blue held not only his shoes, and clothes for all seasons, but the toys Tom had allowed him to bring: the Lincoln Logs, the first two volumes of *My Book House*, the skates he hadn't mastered yet. Tom had skated and read *My Book House* and played with Lincoln Logs when he was a boy in Athens, Ohio. "What is Incidental? What are Incidentals?" she was saying to herself.

7

"My, you're a strong boy," she said.

"It's not any heavy."

The air was cold. But the day was bright.

They were lucky. Tom had found a taxi whose driver spoke English. Or perhaps they all spoke English.

"He says there's not anyplace to check this stuff." Tom was frowning. She wished he wouldn't worry.

"He can take us to a hotel then. We can stay in a hotel while we look for a house. That's what you said, you suggested."

"There's surely someplace to check stuff here at customs. The idea!"

"No place to leave your luggage," the man said. He turned. He was talking to another man and woman: they wore gloves, they both held canes in their right hands. "Beneath the gloves . . ." she thought. The couple was old.

"Now, look here. You said—"

"There is room for everyone, sir." The driver was taking three black suitcases from a porter in blue overalls, a different man from the one who had helped them.

"O.K. O.K. O.K. We'll go with you," Tom said, but he was upset.

The trunk of the car was too small for all of the suitcases. The man tied both blues to a rack on top of the car. He worked quickly. "Careful," Tom said.

Lewis and Tom rode in the front seat with the driver. She huddled in the middle of the back seat, trying to make herself small, between the old man and the old lady. "It's a lovely day," she said.

"Beautiful day," the old woman said. She was not American. The old man coughed.

No one spoke again until the taxi stopped in front of a gray hotel.

The driver was helping the people out of the car, first the old man, then the old lady.

The woman turned, steadying herself with her cane. "I hope you have a pleasant holiday." Her face was made of lines.

"The same to you." It was a foolish thing to say. She sounded like a foolish American.

The hotel said Paradise or perhaps the name was Paradine's. She had not heard the old people give the name of their destination. She had not even been watching the streets they had passed through. She had looked at the back of Tom's head, his navy blue beret set squarely, his ears like handles. Lewis slumped in the seat. She could see only the button on top of his cap. Across the street was water, a blue bay; boats bobbed on the water.

"Do you want—" she said, and Tom spoke at the same time: "There's not any point—"

"I'm sorry," Tom said. "What were you going to say?"

"Nothing." She had forgot. She couldn't imagine what she had been going to say.

"Go ahead," Tom said.

"I wondered if Lewis wanted to sit back here."

"I like it up here."

"You were saying, Tom?"

Tom had placed his arm on the back of the seat. He was looking at her hard, as if he had something very important to say, like "The world is on fire," or "I love you, I love you."

"There's not any point in getting a hotel and then moving right away. It's plenty early. We have all day."

"Yes. Yes, of course."

"We'll find us something today, this morning. It's out of season. There are plenty of places. That man in Syracuse said houses and apartments are going begging."

"That's fine. That's just fine. Yes. We'll be in our very own place tonight."

"O.K. Good enough."

She had spoken well. She leaned back. She must have been

9

sitting straight and uncomfortable ever since they docked, ever since Taormina, or Naples, or New York, or Athens, Ohio.

"But we need breakfast first, don't we, boy?"

"I'm hungry," Lewis said.

"And a bank. We'll have to find us a bank, and get us some Maltese money."

"Maltese," Lewis said. "My goodness."

"Take us to the *centro*," Tom told the driver. "Don't spare the horses," as his parents had probably said before him, his grandparents.

"Valletta?" the driver asked.

"Yeah. Yeah, sure."

"Maltese," Lewis said. "My goodness."

It was a lovely ride, the sea on their left, a bay, another bay, a park; on the right, hotels, and apartment houses, and then little stores with names she felt comfortable with: Fair Deal, Harris's, Kendall's; another park, a statue. It was like a small town, and it was like a city, too, like a place she remembered: but it wasn't like Athens, and it wasn't like Columbus, or Waterford, or New York.

They were passing huge stone walls. She had never seen such walls. "Look. Look, there," she almost said. But Tom was talking to the driver. Tom was telling him about Athens, Ohio, and the store, and about the trip over, and Taormina. "Cold as the mischief," Tom said.

The breakfast was delicious. Tom ordered without even checking the prices or asking for a menu: real orange juice, eggs, bacon, toast, orange marmalade. And she drank three cups of coffee.

Tom said, "You better take Italian money, or you don't get any. The cab driver took it all right."

"Of course," the waiter said.

And the bank was comfortable, like the bank at home. Tom cashed a hundred and fifty dollars in American Express checks.

"It's mighty good to be hearing English again," Tom told the girl at the wicket.

10

"Look here, Lewis. Look at the size of this money." Tom spoke loudly. But it was all right.

"Try this on for size," he said, handing Lewis several coins. "The big ones are pennies. What do you think of that?"

"My goodness."

The girl smiled. Her lips were pale; her eyelids green.

"Taxi, taxi," Tom shouted, and a taxi appeared from the narrow street beside them.

"He's driving on the wrong side," Lewis said.

"I was wondering when you'd notice. That's the way they do things over here." Tom was very jolly.

"Where to, sir?"

She sat alone in the back seat. The driver and Lewis watched Tom while he explained their situation. "We're on vacation—holiday, you folks call it. But we don't want the Hilton, not anything like that. We want a house, or an apartment—a flat, a flat, that's right, isn't it?" Lewis and the driver nodded. "We'll probably be here a month. We want to live here. *Live.* Like anybody. And we don't want to pay a lot. We want a real house."

"Here in Valletta?"

"No, not Valletta, not the capital. And not Sliema, that's worse." Tom had studied well. "Too many tourists. We're not just tourists. I'm not sure we want this side of the island, anyhow."

"We have many tourists," the driver said. "But this is not the Season. I know of a very nice place, not too far. Perhaps you will like."

"O.K., you can let us out when we get there."

"I will speak to my friend about—"

"No, you just let us out. If we take the place, I'll tell them you sent us. You can get your cut."

She wished Tom hadn't said, "You can get your cut." He didn't mean anything by it. Tom was good.

Lewis and the driver turned their heads, and the car started.

They were moving through the same street they had already traveled, past the same park, but no flowers bloomed. The flower beds stood empty. "Malta's warmer than Taormina. And cheaper," Tom had said. Flowers bloomed in the cold of Taormina: narcissi, and jonquils, and hyacinths spilled down the terrace outside their uncomfortable little apartment. Perhaps the jonquils were already gone here. And there would be flowers later. A man leaned over a bed of something, lilies, maybe. And there were trees—she would have to ask somebody the names of the trees.

It was cold. The driver's window was opened. She thought of asking him to close the window. She turned up the collar of her raincoat, hoping the man would notice her in his mirror. Perhaps he noticed her, but he did not close the window. She was glad Lewis sat protected between Tom and the driver.

She looked for the gray hotel where the old people had stopped. She hoped they were in their room by now. The old people had surely unpacked. Surely they rested in their room, lying on twin beds, talking quietly to each other.

The car slowed. Tom was saying, "You'll let us out at some place where my wife and son can wait for me."

She almost said, "I thought we'd look with you, Tom." She leaned forward. But she had known, surely, that she and Lewis would wait. Tom knew what they wanted. He had studied well. One whole section of Incidentals held the lists and travel books and maps and dictionaries.

"The Essex Bar. It's not very far." The man had made a rhyme. She wanted to laugh. She wanted Lewis to laugh. Lewis loved rhymes. They should have laughed together.

"Women and children—they are allowed—they go to the Essex Bar?"

"Of course," the driver said.

But she was the only woman in the bar, Lewis the only child.

Tom and the driver deposited their suitcases beside one of the first tables lined against the wall. Tom spoke to the man behind the bar. The room was as cold as the taxi. Plastic ribbons waved at the open doors.

12

"One coffee, one chocolate?"

The barman said, "Of course."

"And it's all right about our suitcases?"

"Of course, of course," the man said. He was as fat as the policeman at the passport check.

"See? We're fine," Tom called to them. "You see, this is our situation. . . ." The barman smiled and nodded.

Tom brought the drinks to their table, although the barman protested. The drinks were in tumblers.

"I forgot to say *black*," Tom said.

"That's all right. That's fine."

"You just enjoy yourselves. I won't be long."

The room had been quiet, as still as death. She had not been conscious of the quiet until Tom pushed his way outside through the plastic ribbons, and the noise began again.

Two boys played at a pinball machine: *Miss Atlantic City*, the machine said; a girl in a blue bikini smiled among flashing lights. On their heads the boys wore dirty handkerchiefs, knotted at the corners. They were very young; they shouted at each other. But Maltese sounded like anger—Tom had read that. "Don't be afraid of how they're going to sound," Tom had said. "It's a funny language."

Three tables down, an old man sat alone, talking to himself; there were five men at the table beyond him, three boys at the next. At the bar two men drank from beer bottles. Flies hung over the bar, circling, like a mobile. An archway led to another room, where dark men and boys sat drinking coffee from glasses, speaking to each other.

She tried to hear what somebody was saying. But nobody spoke English.

That was all right. That was good. Tom would like Malta—it was foreign enough, the most foreign place she had ever imagined. But they spoke English, all of Tom's guidebooks said so.

"This isn't so very terrible good," Lewis said.

"It's good and hot, though. It's good for us." She took a gulp of her coffee. The glasses were clean. Surely they were clean. She wasn't going to be a fretful mother. A person had to take a chance on cleanliness, even at home. Drinking a glass of anything was an act of faith, anywhere.

Somebody put a coin into the jukebox at the edge of the arch. Lewis jumped when the music started. His mouth said something but she could not hear his words. She reached over and patted at him. He moved back in his chair.

The music went on for a long time, drums, and electric guitars, and singing—men were singing. They sang English. They said *sweet* and they said *baby* and *please;* she couldn't understand the other words. She smiled at Lewis, but he wasn't looking at her.

"That was pretty loud, wasn't it?" Lewis said.

"Goodness, yes. I wonder—" Another record began, or perhaps it was the same record. The boys in their knotted handkerchiefs made lights flash around *Miss Atlantic City.* The barman smiled, nodding to the music.

When the record ended the barman came to their table. "You are all right, O.K.?" He was a handsome man, but older than she had thought at first. His black hair was combed in careful waves.

"Fine, thank you. We appreciate your letting us stay here. I feel we should order something else, but . . ." She was being silly; she shouldn't let herself talk too much. "Could I have another cup, another glass of coffee? It's delicious. And Lewis?"

"No, no, no, no." Lewis shook his head more vigorously than necessary.

But the barman did not mind. He patted Lewis's head. "Fine boy."

When he brought the steaming coffee, gray with milk, he refused to let her pay for it. She fumbled, holding out a five-hundred-lire note. "My husband should have left me some English, some Maltese money. I'm sorry, this is what I have, and you, you understand. . . ."

"You are my guest. We do not often have guest from the

United State of America. My brother—he's an America. He work in Detroit."

"Please, I insist."

The man waved his index finger back and forth in front of his nose. "No, lady. My guest."

There was no use. She drank deeply. "Delicious," she said, and the man began to tell about his brother in Detroit.

Tom came. Tom finally came. He rubbed his hands together. "We're on our way."

"This man, this gentleman, he wouldn't let me pay, Tom. Really, I—"

"My guest," the man said, nodding.

"That's mighty nice of you, that's mighty nice. Thank you. I've got two good leads. We don't know where we're going to settle yet, but we'll see you again, we'll count on that. If you wouldn't mind calling us a cab?"

"Cab, of course. Cab?"

"Taxi, taxi, taxi," she said. She was too silly. She should have said taxi only once.

"Taxi, my pleasure. My friend, just up the street."

"Now, this is our situation," Tom began, to the friend.

She was afraid Lewis would join in the words of the explanation. Maybe Tom wouldn't have minded. He was so pleased with his activity, he might have been pleased with Lewis.

But it would have been terrible if she had joined the recital. "Not the Hilton," she said to herself. "We're not just tourists."

The sun had gone. The air was sharp. Again the driver drove with his window open, his elbow resting on the ledge. He talked a great deal, but the wind took his words away—or she did not really try to hear his words.

They were out of the city section now. Malta's houses, flush with the pavement, were buff-colored. But the *galerrias* and divided doors and window frames of the buff-colored houses were painted bright: green, lemon, peach, blue, lavender. To herself

15

she read the names of the houses—almost every house had an engraved namestone set in the wall by the doorway. The car raced down the narrow streets, past the named houses.

They were in the country. Stone walls, heavy boulder walls, separated tiny plots of ground no bigger than the side yard at home. A few wild flowers grew in the fields. Alyssum? Candytuft? She would have to ask somebody. Five goats grazed in a pocket-handkerchief field—they wore halters of rope—of straw?—red and green and white.

Stores again, the houses with their names, the stone-walled fields.

The second bar was named Redemption.

But Floriana was too much like home, like the apartments in Lakeview Manor, Tom said. They waited for the barman to telephone for another taxi.

"Maybe you could have the next man wait for us. For you," she said after the third taxi, or the fourth.

"But I get leads this way, honey." Tom was almost offended. "I got two leads back there. The policeman. He couldn't have been nicer."

"I know. I know, Tom. But it's . . . We feel a little strange."

"You don't mind waiting, do you? I'm going as fast as I can. The people are certainly nice in the bars. Malta's famous for how nice the people are. Malta's not like Naples, honey." Tom would never get over her having had her purse stolen in the Naples hotel.

"But at home . . . You wouldn't go in the places where Lewis and I . . ."

"But we *aren't* at home. Isn't that what you kept saying before we left? 'We mustn't be disappointed if it's not like Athens.' Isn't that what you said? Didn't you keep telling me that?"

The third bar was named Swiftly. Their luggage seemed larger in Swiftly than in Essex or Redemption.

"I don't want any more cocoa," Lewis said. His lips were blue. "I don't like cocoa."

16

"Of course you do. But we'll try a soft drink. I bet they have Coca-Cola."

In the fourth taxi, or the fifth, or the sixth, he sat snuggled against her in the back seat.

"Are you cold?"

"No, not any."

"That's the boy." Tom stopped talking to the driver for a moment. The driver had said, "I'll take you around. I do not know a house to recommend to you."

"What about Żurrieq?"

The driver corrected his pronunciation.

"Żabbar? Hamrun?"

They were cross-stitching the island. She recognized a Shell station, a garage named My Nest.

Under the dark sky Malta was the color of old institutions, grade schools in Ohio and West Virginia, or the hospital where Grandmother died.

"Let's sing something," Lewis said.

What could they sing? She could not remember the tune of a single song.

"The houses have names, Lewis. Have you noticed? There's Ave Maria, Ave Maria, Joe Anna, Maria again."

What could they sing?

"Lily, Rose, Saint Peter," she read aloud. "Starfish, Shark—how would you like to live in a house named Shark? Winner. O.K. View—that's a funny one, isn't it?"

"Let's live in O.K. View." Lewis was trembling.

"Are you hungry?"

"No, not any."

"Mister, I'm sorry. But would you mind closing your window? It's cool—it's cold back here, it's very cold." She spoke quickly.

"Yes, madame." Slowly the driver rolled up his window.

It was raining now. Small rain fell against the windshield.

"What about the possibilities of Saint Paul's Bay?"

17

"It is on the other side of the island, sir." He was a taciturn driver, but he was not unkind. How many taxis had they taken?

"Sure enough." Tom was apologetic. "I was holding my map the wrong way. What do you think of that?"

"Tom!" Her voice was loud. "We should stop and eat, shouldn't we? It's after one o'clock. Soup, or something? We ought to have soup and a sandwich, maybe. Tom!"

"How about Birżebbuġa?" Tom asked.

"This is Birżebbuġa, sir," the driver said, correcting Tom's pronunciation. "That is Pretty Bay. That is the name of the bay."

It looked like the others. Rain pocked the bay.

"Pretty Bay. That sounds good. We ought to be able to find someplace here."

"I am not familiar with the village," the driver said. He was a young man. She had not noticed before. And he was growing a beard. The fuzz on his chin was like baby's hair. He wanted to look old. She wanted to say to him, "There's plenty of time."

"Picka, picka, picka bag o' cotton," she sang into Lewis's ear. Lewis giggled.

"It is siesta time. I am not familiar with the village."

The street was shuttered: Tony's Saloon, C. and S., Maria's. But the Courageous Bar was open. "The Courageous Bar," she said, surprised that she spoke aloud.

"How about letting us out here, fellow? 'The Courageous Bar on Pretty Bay.' That sounds pretty good, doesn't it, Lewis?"

The driver helped Tom pile their suitcases by a table against the wall. A jukebox played. A boy in a knotted handkerchief stood at a pinball machine. Flies hung over the bar. The room was crowded. No women, no children.

The barman stood at their table. He looked a little like Tom. Maybe he did. But he was dark. Tom was sandy-colored under his beret.

Tom was terribly proud of his new beret. He was right. The beret made sense. He could carry it in his pocket. But it was too small for him. It didn't have any give. It made his face as round

18

as the moon. He looked like a jack-o'-lantern in a skullcap. That's exactly what he looked like. She wasn't ashamed of him. It was wrong to be ashamed of somebody you loved.

She thought of the word *love*. She loved Tom.

No, the barman didn't know of a place to rent, not for sure. But the sister-in-law of the man's wife at the chemist's, just down the street—she had a property. It was rented, but maybe the people were moving out—Air Force people at Kalafrana.

No, he didn't have any soup. He was sorry. "Sandwich? You like ham sandwich?" The dark man smiled. His mouth was full of gold.

"Three ham sandwiches. Coffee for us, cocoa for the boy."

"No, no, no, no."

"You need something hot, Lewis."

"Not any."

"He's all right, Tom. Let him alone. We'll have something later . . . when we get in . . . our own place. We'll have something."

She studied a dirty plastic rose in a green vase on the table in front of her. "It looks almost real, doesn't it?" She did not watch the barman; she did not want to know how he prepared the sandwiches.

"I don't think it looks very real." Lewis scooted down in his chair. Only the top of his head was visible. His fair hair shone.

"Come on, boy." But Tom was not annoyed. Tom relished making arrangements. This was a good day for Tom.

The sandwiches were wrapped in waxed paper. She was relieved.

"Delicious," she said.

"I forgot to say black coffee again. Do you want me to send it back?"

"It's all right. Maybe we'll learn to like it this way. . . . You know I keep thinking . . ." She was not listening to herself. She wanted to hold Tom at the table.

But he was leaving. "I won't be gone long."

19

She reached toward him. "Anything will be all right, Tom. It's just for a little while."

"We want it right. We'll find something. Take care of your mother." She was silly. Tears came to her eyes.

Tom had been wearing a hat that first night when he drove her home from his brother's house. Tom looked good in a hat—it lengthened his face; it gave him a kind of distinction.

That first night she said, "What a handsome hat." It was a trim gray felt. She spoke naturally; she wasn't just making conversation. At first she had said everything naturally and right.

"I'll be changing before long. Dad was particular about hats. You put on your straw on May fifteenth and your felt on September fifteenth—that's what Dad said."

"It's funny, isn't it, about customs? I couldn't wear a cotton dress until the first of May, no matter what the weather was like."

"Ralph makes fun of me. He doesn't even own a hat. I keep telling him we need to show off our merchandise. But Ralph's all right. He and Ellen are all right."

"I had an awfully nice time tonight. I like your brother and his wife. The twins are wonderful."

They were at the big curve on Mulligan Road. Athens lay in the valley to the right. She leaned forward to look down into the valley gathered around the lighted spires—Galbraith Chapel, the Methodist church, the dormitories. Tom stopped the car for a moment; he leaned forward, too.

"It's beautiful, isn't it? It looks foreign." She laughed at herself. "I don't know why I say that. I've never seen anything foreign."

"Me either." Tom was smiling at her.

She was smiling, too.

She had not felt uncomfortable in the silence.

Outside the rain had stopped.

"Go on and eat, Lewis," she said. "Eat your sandwich."

"I don't like it."

"It's perfectly delicious. Go on, Lewis."

The boy wearing the knotted handkerchief put another coin

into his machine. It was named *The Derby*. Two men in overalls passed their table, bowing to them. Three men. A man in a suit, with a flowered tie.

The barman came to talk to them. He had an uncle in New York. The uncle had invited him to visit. "You live in New York?"

"No, no, I've just been in New York twice."

"You live in Detroit? Los Angeles?"

The man was kind. "Near there. Not too far." The man was very kind. She was ashamed of herself. "You have a very nice place here. We appreciate—"

"The boy? He don't like ham?"

"Of course he does. He just eats slowly."

A new customer stood at the bar. "You be happy," the man said.

"Eat. Eat, Lewis," she whispered, ashamed of herself.

A new customer started the jukebox.

She did not know how long Tom had been gone. Time had stopped. What if he had met with foul play, and . . .

She almost laughed at herself. It was important to laugh at herself. Grandmother was always expecting foul play. Tom could take care of himself.

"Finish up, Lewis. Go on, honey. Here, I'll eat part of it."

"Why doesn't Daddy come back?"

"He'll be back in a minute, in a little while. It takes time."

The rain had started and stopped and started again before Tom returned. His beret and the shoulders of his topcoat were black with rain: water dripped from his eyebrows. But he was ebullient. He should clip his eyebrows. There was no reason for him to go around looking shaggy. And he hadn't shaved well this morning.

Tom rubbed his hands together. Tom spoke loudly. Anybody who could speak English became a confidant of Tom's success. The barman stopped drying a glass to smile and listen.

The man at the chemist's had just been locking his store. He was late closing because he had to fix some medicine for somebody's baby. The people were moving out of his wife's sister-in-law's house, sure enough; as a matter of fact, they had moved out this morning, a man and wife and five children. The sister-in-law's own home wasn't very far away, just around a couple or three blocks. He and the chemist had gone to get the woman—the man had a car. He couldn't have been nicer. They were lucky. The place was right smack *at the middle of* Pretty Bay, just up the street. It cost a hundred dollars a month, sheets included, maybe utilities, too, he wasn't sure. They would have to straighten that out. A hundred dollars was more than the man in Taormina had said they should pay. But they were lucky, anyhow. There were a lot of service people left over from when the English ran the island. Tom didn't exactly understand the situation. But they were lucky.

"Does the house have a name? Is it named anything?" Lewis pulled at Tom's hand.

"I didn't notice, but we'll see."

Tom pulled away from Lewis's hand. He was at the bar, shaking hands with the barman. He was being cordial. There wasn't anything wrong with Tom's being cordial. He shook hands with the two men who stood at the bar.

"Would you mind helping us here?" Tom said to the boy in the knotted handkerchief. And because Tom was a kind and cordial tourist the boy stopped his Derby game and picked up the dark blue and brown bags.

"Thank you. Thank you," she called. "Hurry, Lewis. Run between the raindrops." She pushed at Lewis, her purse banging against her legs. Tom and the boy were far ahead.

"That's silly," Lewis said.

"Yes, of course it is. But hurry."

The water of Pretty Bay sounded loud, as if it said something.

Two buff-colored houses with double doors painted lavender, yellow. A street crossing. Lewis would have to be careful if he crossed the street alone; she would have to explain to him carefully about the right-hand traffic—the left-hand traffic? Which was it? An advertisement in a wooden frame beside a front door, front doors: a Western movie: a man stood with a gun aimed: Indians rode over a mountain.

Tom and the boy had disappeared through dark green doors. The door handles were brass, round as tea saucers; brass dolphins, door knockers, leaped against the dark wood. There was a doorbell button high on the right doorframe. "They put them high so the kids can't put pins in them," one of the taxi drivers had explained. "Kids can be mischievous."

"It doesn't have a name, Lewis," she said in the little vestibule. "But that's all right."

"The name of this house is O.K. Home," Lewis said, taking off his cap.

Tom and the other boy stood in the dark living room, among the suitcases.

"Thank you, sir," the boy said, stuffing into his pocket whatever coins Tom had given him. She hoped Tom had given him enough.

"Good-bye, madame."

"Good-bye, good-bye."

"This is O.K. Home," Lewis said.

"It's not home exactly." Tom's voice was tentative. Dear Tom. "We'll fix it up. Your mother can fix it up."

"It's fine, it's very fine." Her eyes had difficulty adjusting to the darkness. It was difficult to speak in the little living room, whose ceiling was almost too far away to see. Two chairs and a bulbous couch surrounded a little oak coffee table. The walls were light blue, probably. The crouched furniture was slip-covered in cretonne: blue and maroon and yellow fans faded into each other.

Tom moved in front of them to a light switch by the door. The room seemed darker. The shade over the naked center bulb was blue with white painted daisies. Two footstools, like nail kegs, stood beside her. A scratched console table against the wall held an orange glass vase with two plastic roses. It was impossible to imagine what color the roses had been. Above the table hung a picture of Christ with lowered eyes. Probably somebody had cut the picture from a magazine a long time ago. Somebody's child. Glass covered the picture. Black tape held the glass and the picture neatly together. Somebody had worked hard on the picture. Around the shade of the light bulb hung glass beads; each string of the clear glass beads ended with a red marble.

"It's the best place I've seen for the money," Tom said.

"It's nice, Tom. It'll be just fine."

"It's all cleaned. It's just been cleaned. Sheets on the beds and everything. They're going to bring us a couple of heaters. The man's working on the geezer in the kitchen—*geezer*, that's what

24

he calls the hot water heater. The landlady's upstairs, I guess. She's upset, I guess. She's found some things broken."

"Fine, Tom." They waited stiffly together.

"What do you think of us?" Tom rubbed his hands across his chest. His hands were dirty. So were her own hands. The three of them stood filthy in the freezing house. "We got to Malta this morning, and we already have a house of our own. What do you think of that?"

"We're some speeders," Lewis said.

The landlady, a great mound of a woman dressed in black, waited suddenly among them. Hair grew from a wart on her chin. Behind her stood the chemist, a trim little man in a black turtleneck sweater. He stepped forward. He was lame. His right shoe was built on a platform, three inches, four inches.

"My sister-in-law does not speak so good," the lame man said. "Maybe you need something."

"We . . . we, we, we . . ." She was stuttering. "We just came in. We haven't seen the house."

"You husband, he see the house. You see the house." The lame man was smiling.

It was a preposterous house.

The dark landlady led the way. Behind the living room, through a door curtained with the slip cover material, waited a vast hall. Stairs, with a wrought iron railing, soared. The room looked like a cathedral. Far above them a skylight shone murkily behind a grille, behind a flapping piece of plastic. Rain fell on her head as she moved under the skylight.

"Nice," the landlady said, drawing out the word.

The landlady turned on the center light in the dining room for a moment. A table, a multitude of chairs, two buffets, a china closet full of glass dishes the color of the vase in the living room; two vases bulged with plastic roses; a refrigerator. It would be good to have a refrigerator again. In Taormina the kitchen was a closet without any refrigerator.

For almost two weeks in Taormina Lewis had gone with her

25

to market every morning. He had been frightened of the marketing at first. He pulled at her. She stood in line with the phrasebook in her left hand, practicing. *Sogliola*, that is sole; *pomodori*, tomatoes; *arance*, oranges; *pane*, bread. A chocolate bar for dessert. She had prepared herself for Sicily, a little. She knew some of the words. The English names here would be strange, too, not American words.

"Kitchen," the lame man said.

"Niiice."

"Backyard." The landlady threw open the double doors that led from the dining room. Rain fell: small rain fell on the minuscule concrete courtyard. "What a good backyard," the lame man said.

"It's cold, isn't it?" Lewis pressed against her.

"A little bit," the lame man said.

"Niiice," the old woman said.

A dog appeared beside the dining room table. He was a huge Labrador, wagging himself. But she was frightened, too. It was the suddenness of the dog. Nobody could blame Lewis for whimpering and holding on to her.

"Come on, Lewis. Cut it out." Tom was embarrassed.

"It's all right, Lewis." She held tightly to the boy's shoulder. "He's a friendly dog, sweet."

"He belong to the house before you belong," the man said.

When the landlady saw the dog she yelled out. She chased the dog with her black scarf, shouting something, slamming the front door after him.

"Not nice," she said when she came back.

"You're all right, Lewis, you're just fine, honey."

"You follow my sister-in-law," the lame man said.

Six steps up the stairway, a turn, a landing. Eight steps up, a landing, a turn. Six steps. She slid her left hand against the iron railing; Lewis clung to her. Ahead of them the dark woman breathed heavily. How many steps walked upstairs in Athens? She couldn't remember.

She tried to look at everything carefully. But she didn't want

26

to see everything; a person should save some of the details for surprises, for later; the glass-covered magazine pictures framed with black tape: somebody's child had been very busy once; windows, walls.

There were three huge bedrooms: chests, armoires, mountainous beds.

Light on, light off. "Niiice."

"This room for you, Lewis. This for us," Tom said. "This room's left over."

The bathroom held a basin and a long tub, like a coffin, a very narrow coffin. Tom would find it difficult to sit in the tub.

"A commode? A toilet?" she asked.

The man opened a door. A toilet stood underneath a winding stone stairway. The toilet crouched. The steps of the stairway were like petals, three inches, four inches wide, not wider than the man's shoe was tall.

"You have a nice roof up there. You see all over. Good sun. You see the roof?"

"Another time, later," she said, her teeth chattering.

"It is a very nice roof. Your clothes get dry in pronto."

"It's all so big," she whispered to Tom.

"It's not bad for the money."

"You will need?" the man said.

"Need?" They stood in the long upstairs hall.

"You want something?"

"The heaters," Tom said.

"And a lamp or two. I didn't notice any lamps." She felt efficient. "Lamps to read by." She was proud of herself. "My husband and I will make a list."

"Of course, madame. Certainly. Everything, madame. And food. You will want some groceries to eat."

"Yes, we must get groceries. And the water's all right to drink, isn't it? From the tap? Of course. My husband's books say the water is all right to drink."

"Delicious," the man said, kissing his thumb and forefinger.

27

His movement was graceful. "The groceries is open at tree o'-clock. Almost dab right next door to me shop, my brudder-in-law. Tree o'clock. In a minute or so, a while."

It would have been terrible if she had said, "At tree." Tom was frowning at her.

"At three." She did not laugh. "Thank you. Thank you very much."

It was tree, it was long after tree. She stood at a window again. In the tiny dark kitchen she leaned against the primitive counter with its ridiculous little box of a sink, to look through the single dirty window to the black courtyard.

Her mind was using too many adjectives. She should think nouns and verbs. She was all right. Everything was all right. She wasn't just "holding on." "Hold on, Caroline," her grandmother said a thousand times, about menstrual pains, or a final examination, or an interview. "Think nouns and verbs."

Once they got straightened out she would be busy.

But even in Athens she could stand in the sun room and watch the oak tree for minutes at a time. The tree was two hundred and fifty years old—that's what the tree surgeon said. It was barely born, compared to Taormina, and Malta. But old is old. Old is old is old. She felt very old.

"Moony," Tom would say in Athens, but not unkindly. "My, what a moony girl I married."

Last night the moon had been full, pulling at the tides.

"Niiice," she said. She was sure she had not spoken aloud. The kitchen was warm. She had lit all the burners and the oven. It was a nice little stove.

Dark green leaves grew against the high wall of the house next door. They flapped heavily in the rain. Ivy? No, the leaves were oval, leaves she had never seen before. Bougainvillea? There had been bougainvillea in Taormina, and the oranges were as red as tomatoes, stretching down to the turquoise sea. But the weather was cold there, too. Anyplace was cold in January. People who wrote travel folders had to make their living. They had to say "Sunny, bright, delectable." Everybody had to say "Paradise."

"We'll move," Tom said in Taormina." We'll take a tour of Sicily. I've been reading."

She could not have been more surprised. Tom almost never changed his mind. But she was glad to leave the cold of Taormina and the childless couple in the next flat who really didn't like children.

"Lewis will be happier in Malta," Tom said. "He'll have a lot of kids to play with. We'll get us a house, a big house, on a beach."

"Fine, fine, Tom. That's a good idea. We'll get to see more of the world that way."

In Malta hail fell, real hail. It was popcorn bouncing among the oval leaves, against the stones of the backyard.

"It's hailing," she whispered.

Of course Tom did not answer. He was upstairs unpacking— he knew where everything belonged. Or he was in the living room, reading a guidebook. Or he stood at the front doors to watch the hail bounce against the street and Pretty Bay.

"Pretty Bay is the name of it because it is a pretty bay," Lewis said before he slept.

"It's hailing."

At least Lewis slept. Upstairs in the bedroom next to theirs, Lewis slept under four tattered blankets. But they were clean. "It's not very cold," Lewis said.

"They'll bring us heaters. We'll be toasty warm tonight."

She held to the edge of the sink. She wanted to run from the kitchen, through the vast dining room, the cathedral hall, up the thirty steps to where Lewis slept. Her knuckles were whiter than the hail.

She wasn't going to be silly. Lewis was all right. She had promised Tom she would stop being silly. "Lewis is a fine healthy sturdy adjusted boy," Tom said. Tom used too many adjectives, sometimes, but he was right. Lewis was fine.

29

Above the popping hail, the water across the street said, "Flush, flush," or, "Hush, hush, hush."

In Taormina they were too far away from the water to hear what it said. "It's cold. The books lie to you. And they can't understand you. Sicilian isn't Italian. Even the Italians can't understand them." Tom had worked hard on his phrasebooks.

"Good, Tom. Whatever you say."

Tom knew what they wanted. Tom is good, she said, but not aloud.

The room exploded with light.

"Tom. Oh, Tom!" She pressed her hands against her mouth.

Tom was laughing. "I didn't mean to scare you. It'll be a great picture. I got the hail, too, I think. Through the window."

Even if she had been looking at him she could not have seen him. Tom was being a caricature of himself. The lights from the flashbulb splashed against her eyelids.

"Don't. You shouldn't do that, Tom."

"I should have been taking pictures of you and Lewis—in all those bars. Open your eyes, honey." He held her shoulders. "Look at me, sweetheart."

"Tom."

"What's the matter with you?"

She pulled away. "You scared me, that's all."

Tom laughed. "It's past time the store was open. You want me to go for the groceries? It'll soon be dark."

"Of course not. I'm going. I was just getting ready to go."

She stepped around him into the dining room.

"I'll be glad to go for you."

"I want to go." She couldn't remember where she had put her coat or her purse. "You'll check on Lewis?"

"Silly. Silly Caroline. You promised me you weren't going to worry."

"I'm not worrying."

"Look here. What are you going to buy? What about money?"

"Yes, yes. You'll give me some money. I'll . . . I'll get things."

30

"That's the girl." Tom was very jolly. "Now, look here."

Tom slowly removed his billfold and the coin purse from his inside jacket pocket. The coin purse was an old man's purse, a black pouch with a clasp. "You can't be too careful," Tom kept saying when he was planning the trip.

"This is a pound—that's about two dollars and forty cents now, two thirty-nine, call it two forty. This is a shilling—twelve cents, for all practical purposes. There are twenty of these in a pound. This is two and a half shillings, a half crown. A shilling, they call that a bob. A pound, another one. This is five pounds."

"I'll get along fine, Tom." In the vast room with its tiny bulb under the heavy blue shade she could barely distinguish the bills, the coins. "Just give me some. The people all speak English, anyhow."

"That's what you think." Tom was genuinely amused. "That's what it says in the books. Why, this morning I met of couple of fellows who—"

"I won't have any trouble."

"A lot of them speak English, but they don't think it. You have to be careful. This is a foreign country, honey. . . . Your coat. You'd better take your coat. And the umbrella. It's cold. It's still raining. The store's just up the street, a block and a half up."

"I know, Tom. Yes."

She reached to pull down a coat from the rack by the door. She didn't remember the rack, great curves of wood crossing each other. Tom must have hung up her coat. The knobs were like fists. Her purse hung on one of the fists. Lewis's coat looked pathetic, no, funny, hanging high against the blue wall.

"That's not your coat, sweetie."

She was wearing Tom's coat. He had ordered the coats from the store, His and Hers, lined, reversible, washable, identical—they were fine coats.

She ran to the grocery, not bothering with the umbrella. At the Courageous Bar she left the sidewalk and splashed into the street.

The wide doors of the bar stood open. Three men stood at the doors, not speaking English.

"*Ingliz?*" she said to the round-faced woman behind the counter that ran around two sides of Saint Mary's Grocery. The woman had a sweet face, like a woman attending Mary in a painting, one of the paintings.

"*Ingliz?*" Tom had said to every taxi driver.

"Of course, sir."

"Yes, madame," the woman said.

Blessedly they were alone together in the store.

"We're just new here. We rent from your brother, your sister-in-law? I don't understand the relationships exactly. We're just up the street, at Twenty, on Pretty Bay. We're here on a long vacation. My husband has a store, too, a clothing store, a department store." She was breathless, but she wanted the woman to know about Hutton's in Athens. "Your . . . the chemist was very kind. We'll be here maybe a month. We need things, food. There's a child, Lewis. He's four—he's almost five. He'll be five the twenty-seventh of next month."

The woman was kind, too. She was interested. "Yes, yes," she said. "You will want bread and milk and cheese, I imagine. Matches. Matches for the stove. Fruit. We have oranges today. And bacon. We have unusually good bacon. And eggs. The greengrocer is just around the corner."

"No, I want to get what we need for tonight. Here. Tomorrow I'll buy vegetables."

"There's a peddler with fresh vegetables every morning. A butcher's shop is down the bay, not far from your house."

The woman moved slowly behind the counters.

"Yes. Yes, yes."

The milk came in a long, thin bottle with a gold cap; a pint, it was probably a pint. "Eight pence," the woman said, "and six pence deposit on the bottle. Instant coffee, five and four, Maxwell House. If you do not care for any of these items . . ." She spoke

32

beautiful English, like an actress in a moving picture about a time a long time ago.

"I want all those things." She was breathing more easily. It was comforting to see brands she recognized. She did not try to figure out the cost. "Quaker Oats. Quick Quaker Oats." The box was flat instead of round. It made good sense to have flat boxes—they would fit better in the cabinet. "And the water is all right to drink here, from the tap? That's what I've heard."

"Perfectly, madame. Butter? This is Anchor, from New Zealand, one and nine. Or from Australia, one and eight."

"That one. The one without the kangaroo." She laughed. She had not meant to laugh so loudly. She was comforted. "And that, the Oxo cubes. And that . . . that box. . . . Yes, the steak and mushrooms." Even if she didn't recognize the brands, she could read the labels. "Three and six? I'm used to thinking in lire now, almost used to thinking in lire. When we were in Sicily . . . We had a couple of rooms—it was a kind of *pensione*, we could eat there when we wanted to. But I cooked, too—we had a funny little kitchen in a closet. When the weather was decent—almost decent—I fixed picnics at noon. Lewis loved the beach. But he was the only child at the *pensione*, and the other people . . . well, they didn't have children. Not that Lewis—"

Two dark figures entered the store; a woman and a young girl. They wore scarves on their heads. They were copies of each other.

"Children—they enjoy picnics." The woman nodded to the dark figures.

"Three and six?"

"That's forty-two cents in your money. Food is not expensive in Malta."

"That can of rhubarb. And some cookies. The Triple Top, two packages. Thank you. Thank you very much."

She wanted to get away from the dark figures and the woman with the beautiful voice. They all breathed heavily. She was ridiculously conscious of their breathing. She reached into her pocket for all of the money Tom had given her. The woman added some figures on the edge of a newspaper on the counter.

"Here. Five pounds. Is that enough?"

"Do you have less? Something smaller?"

"This. Here. I have these."

"It is one pound thirteen," the woman said, taking a bill and coins from her hand as if she waited on a child who wasn't bright. "A basket? Do you have a basket?"

"No, no. I should, shouldn't I?"

"These are two pence each. I am afraid you will need two of them."

"Fine, fine. Just fine," she said in Tom's voice.

The woman packed the groceries carefully into two plastic sacks.

The dark woman and the dark child spoke to each other.

"Thank you," the clerk said. "Bye-bye."

"Bye-bye," she said, feeling foolish. But they all said Bye-bye, even the taxi drivers and the policemen and the men at the bars. "Bye-bye, bye-bye," she called over her shoulder.

She walked slowly. It was good to carry the heavy plastic bags through the rain. Each of the white bags bore an inscription. Under the street light she stopped to study them. In a green square, on a red square, in white letters, both of the bags said *7 Up*.

She did not leave the sidewalk at the Courageous Bar. Men and boys stood in the doorway. She threaded her way past them, through bicycles and motorcycles.

Rain fell against the poster of the Indians and the man with a gun.

Tom and Lewis met her at the door of 20, Pretty Bay.

"There's another one in the dining room, and the kitchen's toasty warm." A coal oil heater burned in the living room. Lewis held to Tom's hand, dancing. "We have a nice house, Mamma."

"You call it paraffin. The paraffin truck comes around every morning." Tom's face was flushed. "And there's a peddler comes around with vegetables."

"I didn't know I'd been gone so long. But I'm glad. I'm glad about everything. Here, Tom." She pulled the money from her pocket. "I came home with more than I started."

"Keep it, silly. You'll need money. Let me take those bags."

"O.K. Fine."

She moved into the hall to hang her coat on one of the fists.

Tom and Lewis smiled at her. They did not say that the landlady sat in the dining room, counting the dishes in the china closet. "Good morning," the old woman said. "Air Force robbers. Almost true."

Tom set the bags on the huge table.

"Almost through. She's almost through," Lewis said.

"Hello. Good morning." She was embarrassed. She stepped back, bumping into Tom. She was sorry the landlady sat muttering in their new house.

They stood in the hall again.

"What all did you get, Mamma?"

"Sh, sshhh. I'll tell you. I'll show you everything, in a minute, in a little while."

"The man brought the heaters right away." Tom was smiling.

"He lighted the geezer, Mamma. Daddy knows how to light it now. We got hot water. All over. Upstairs and downstairs, as hot as it can be."

"I didn't know I was gone so long." She whispered in spite of herself. "I'm glad about the heaters, and the water."

"We're going to have somebody to help clean. The landlady's niece. She'll come in every day to help out."

Tom couldn't have been more pleased with himself. She didn't want to hurt his feelings, but she said, "No. No, Tom. Please, Tom."

"Isn't that niiice, Mamma?"

"I don't even like to have Mrs. Lovell at home, not two days a week. I won't have anything else in the world to do here, Tom. Please, Tom."

"The girl could shop for you."

"I don't want anybody. I like to keep house. I've told you. I've told you a thousand times."

"But the floors—look at all these tile floors. And they don't have things to clean with—appliances."

Tom was being firm. She was determined to be firmer, this once. She tried to keep her voice low. "You're sweet, Tom. I appreciate it. But I'm just not going to have somebody else in the house every day."

"But, Caroline . . ."

She did not say, "Don't 'But, Caroline' me." She said, "This is our house, Tom." It was a good thing to say. "A few days . . . one day a week. All right? You understand?"

Tom shrugged. "One day, two days, as long as it takes to get the heavy work done."

"Fine, Tom. But not for a week yet. Everything's clean now."

Lewis was watching them carefully, turning his dark eyes from her to Tom, to her.

"That's settled," Lewis said and they laughed together.

At last the landlady was ready to leave. At last.

"Your niece. Clean. One day a week. Not six days a week." Tom sounded like an Indian chief in a movie. "Your niece. One day. Not six days. A week from today she will come. Next Tuesday."

The landlady comprehended. "One day." She raised a twisted finger. It hurt to look at the woman's old hand.

"And the laundry. The washing?" Tom and the landlady were making arrangements.

"I can do our things, the wash-and-wears."

"Good morning. Good morning," the landlady said.

Finally, finally they closed the doors behind the old woman.

They laughed together as they unpacked the 7 Up bags on the dining room table. Tom whistled. Lewis tried to whistle. He

36

didn't whistle very well yet, but he would learn. Lewis was going to be all right.

And it was a fine meal: omelet, the marvelous bacon, toast, fruit, the cookies, and it was easy to cook in the strange kitchen, even with Tom and Lewis watching her. The place was remarkably well equipped: spatula, tongs, everything.

Tom and Lewis complimented the food. "This is delicious, Caroline."

"Delicious, Mamma. We ought to have these at home sometimes, in Athens home."

"We do, Lewis. It's just an omelet. You're both hungry. That's what's wrong with you. We haven't eaten today, not properly."

"We'll help with the dishes." Tom was yawning.

"I'll carry in and out." Lewis yawned, too.

"You'll do nothing of the kind. I won't be a minute." She did not move from the table.

Tom lifted his arms and stretched. His stomach bulged under his sweater. He was getting too fat. "I'm pooped."

"Me, too. I'm pooped, too." Lewis yawned and laughed at the same time.

She did not want them to leave the table. She wanted the three of them to sit together warmed by the kerosene heater, warmed and filled, forever.

"It's not seven o'clock yet. It's not quite seven."

"We have a lot of exploring to do tomorrow." Tom patted his stomach.

"There's plenty of time, Tom."

He stood suddenly. "Pictures. We got to take us some pictures."

She pushed herself up from the table. "Tomorrow will be plenty of time."

"No, right now. The first night, our first night."

"You've taken too many of me already. You take Lewis. I'll just finish up here."

"Come on, Mamma."

37

"What's the matter with you, Caroline?"

She and Lewis sat on the fans of the cretonne couch cover. They leaned against the dining room table. She stood in the kitchen, on the first landing of the stairway, the second landing. Three plastic elves' heads hung on the stairway wall—she hadn't noticed them before. "Cheese," she and Lewis said to each other in the gaunt third bedroom that overlooked the black bay. They said, "Cheese," in Lewis's bedroom with the picture of Jesus in a boat speaking to three men and two ladies; they sat on the wicker chairs in the big bedroom, Tom's and hers, with the four suitcases at their feet.

"Please, Tom. Let me take one now," she kept saying. "I know how to do it. I'm an awfully good photographer."

But he allowed her to snap only one picture. "O.K., one. Just one. Here. Take me here."

Tom opened the door to the toilet off the bathroom. He stood halfway up the stone stairs. He made a face. He was pretending to be a monkey on a ladder.

"Look. Look at Daddy!"

She was startled by the flash, even when she held the camera.

"I hope I didn't blink my eyes," Tom said. "That's enough, I guess. We've got all day tomorrow. And the next day, and the next."

"Yes, Tom. Yes, of course." She was tired. She was almost too tired to speak.

He put his arm around her shoulders. "You're feeling good, honey?"

"Just fine. Yes." His arm was heavy.

"We're going to like this place. I have a feeling."

"You and Lewis go on to bed. I won't be a minute."

She was many minutes, more than an hour.

She washed the dishes over and over. She saw herself in the dirty window. She looked like herself. She would have recognized herself anywhere.

When she finally finished, she hung her Athens apron on the

doorknob. She turned out the kitchen light. The courtyard was darker than sleep.

She turned out the dining room light, the hall light. She felt her way up the steps, remembering the house.

She turned on the light in the upstairs hall. Lewis slept. His covers hung straight, but she straightened them.

In their new bed, Tom slept, his arm flung across his eyes.

He said something. Perhaps he only mumbled. Mumbling sounded like "Marie." Marie had been dead for almost two years, for twenty-two months.

Caroline Hutton had not even thought of the real Marie when she read the names of the houses to Lewis—Maria, Ave Maria.

In the bathroom she brushed her teeth carefully. She was not jealous of Marie. If Marie were alive, Caroline Thaxton would not be standing in a dim bathroom in Birżebbuġa, Malta. Tom and Lewis and Marie would be sleeping in Athens, Ohio, where Marie belonged. All of the Hutton blood, for a long time, had belonged in Athens.

But the three of them would not be sleeping yet. Athens was five hours earlier than Birżebbuġa, five or six. It was afternoon in Athens, Ohio. Maybe there was snow. The branches of the oak tree held snow. The shadows of the branches were blue, or lavender. Lewis sat on the living room floor; the sun flooded Marie's wheat-colored carpet. Lewis lined up his Disney figures, talking to them. Tom should have let him bring the figures on the trip.

Marie sat in the white leather chair, watching Lewis. Her hair shone in the sunlight. Tom wouldn't be home from the store for three hours yet. The telephone rang. It was Tom calling Marie. Tom generally called at three o'clock, at tree. "How are things?" Tom asked. "How's Lewis? Everything fine?"

"Everything's fine," somebody said into the little mirror.

Tom had opened the windows. The wind was louder than the waves. She closed the windows as quietly as she could. Tom moved, but he did not wake.

She shook with the cold. She held herself tight, to keep from shaking.

Before she slipped into Tom's bed, she stood at the windows and looked into the courtyard. There was nothing to see, but she looked for a long time.

"Caroline," Tom said when she was beside him, but he did not wake.

When he woke up he couldn't remember where he was. That hadn't happened to him for a long time, not since when he was a kid, visiting someplace, Uncle Dave in the country, or his mother's folks in Louisville. He had been dreaming, too, about when he and Ralph were kids and going to grade school, and about Marie, too, except she was grown up. He was grown up, too, part of the time in the dream. He and Ralph and Marie were having an argument.

It was a funny thing. He never dreamed at home. Caroline was right. There was something about being away from home that made you think about all of your life all at once. Caroline said her dreams were heavy and thick; thick-textured, that's the way she expressed it. But Caroline was always having dreams. She had nightmares sometimes, too, poor girl, even at home.

He was in Malta, by golly: area, ninety-five square miles; population, 317,000. It was just a flyspeck on the map. A lot of maps didn't even show Malta. But 317,000 other people were waking up on the flyspeck. And there was lots of room around him. A car honked. He thought about the little narrow streets running back and forth across the island. He felt good. He had discovered Malta all by himself. Nobody had ever said, "Tom Hutton, you ought to visit Malta." He had acted on a hunch, and he was proud of

41

himself. Ralph and Ellen had never once thought of going to Malta.

It was cold. It was really cold. But the windows were closed. Caroline must have closed them when she came to bed.

She slept on her side with her hand under her cheek. She looked tired, poor kid, even while she was asleep. Her hair spread out on the pillow. Her hair was black as ink. It was a pleasure to look at Caroline.

But it didn't seem quite fair to watch people when they didn't know you were watching.

He eased out of bed and put on his warm bathrobe and the fleece-lined house slippers—he'd almost not packed his house slippers. Nobody had said anything about how cold it could get on the Mediterranean, not Ralph or Ellen or the travel agent or any of the books. But Ralph and Ellen always stayed at luxury hotels where there was always heat and thick carpets and everybody spoke English. As a matter of fact his brother and Ellen had not really been abroad. Staying at the Hilton was like not leaving home. That was interesting to think about.

As quiet as anything, he took the glass jar out of the heater. They hadn't used too much last night, but he filled it anyhow. He took out the burner. He turned the controls, the red disk, and the black knob. He waited, timing himself by his wristwatch, just as the lame man had told him to. The house was very quiet. Caroline didn't move. He lit the stove. The flame came full and neat. He replaced the burner. The lame man was proud of the heaters— he had a right to be. The room would be warm when Caroline woke up. Lewis could dress in their room. He would be toasty warm, as Caroline would say.

He opened the door into the upstairs hall. Caroline was really sleeping. The walls were thick, even thicker than in their house in Athens. It was a nice stairway, like a stairway in an old movie. Yesterday a lot of Malta reminded him of someplace he'd been before. It was like someplace left over.

He lit the heater in the dining room, and then the burners and

42

the oven in the kitchen. He left the oven door open. It was cold as cold. But he was still glad that he hadn't taken one of the Lakeview type apartments.

The kitchen was mean. They didn't make kitchens for wives over here. They made them for servants.

He was sorry Caroline was so set against having a maid. But he was proud of her in a way.

He filled the teakettle with water. He got out the Maxwell House instant coffee. He went into the dining room and got two cups and saucers from the big china closet. He could remember when the store carried those orange glass dishes. His mother had had a china closet, too, before she did over the dining room. Marie didn't like the house. "These cabinets are ridiculous. Dumb. Ostentatious," Marie said, but they never got around to changing them.

He brought a chair from the dining room into the kitchen and closed the door. He sat down to wait for the water to boil. There was a tiny little table in the kitchen. They could all eat there, in a pinch. The chair was bentwood, like the chairs in the ice cream parlor on Washington Street, a long time ago.

A traveler ought to be a traveler. You shouldn't have steam heat if most of the people didn't.

You had to take a chance on being dumb if you wanted to learn anything. Caroline was afraid of taking a chance. She had a good ear for languages. She talked French to those people on the boat without a bit of trouble, just what she remembered from college. Language was like anything else, like business. You had to be willing to be dumb to get smart.

The vacation was the best thing that ever happened to them. There came a time in a man's life when he had to change a little, or decide that he wouldn't ever change. Ralph wouldn't ever change.

"Tom?"

Caroline was at the door. She didn't open it. She stood outside

43

in the cold dining room and called, "Tom?" He got up to open the door for her.

She was already dressed. She had on her green sweaters, and a green headband. Her hair hung straight down. She didn't look much older than Lewis.

"Well, who looks pretty?"

"Silly."

He put his arms around her. She leaned against him, shivering. She kissed him. He was a lucky man to be married to Caroline.

"Sleep well?"

"Wonderfully. It's so quiet here."

"Not like Naples, is it, Lady Caroline?"

"Wasn't that a dreadful hotel?" She pulled away from him.

"You slept well?" He had said it before. Sometimes it was hard to think up things to say, even when they were being very friendly. He thought about saying, "Sweet Caroline," but he didn't.

"Coffee water on, how nice. And it's so warm." She hugged herself, holding her elbows.

"You're glad we came? You're glad we left Sicily?"

"Of course. The water's ready."

He got another chair from the dining room and closed the door again.

"Maybe we ought to leave the door open a little. In case Lewis calls. He's sleeping."

"He's a lucky boy." But he left the door closed.

Caroline started to make the coffee.

They were standing in a little kitchen in Birżebbuġa, Malta, because he had been filling in for Jean Grady at the notions counter and Mrs. Fontaine had asked for two yards of elastic. Mrs. Fontaine had been his mother's best friend. He couldn't imagine his mother ever being so old.

"My, you're looking old, Thomas," Mrs. Fontaine said. "And you, with a young wife. How old are you now, Thomas?"

"I'm going to be thirty-nine, Mrs. Fontaine. Week after next."

He stuffed the elastic into the pink and silver sack that said

HUTTON'S. The new sacks and silver wrapping paper had been Ellen's idea.

"And how old is young Lewis?" Mrs. Fontaine said.

"He's four, Mrs. Fontaine."

"I suppose your mother would be proud of you. She was a very proud woman. She was my friend, of course." Mrs. Fontaine took the sack from his hand. "You know, Thomas, I used to be so much older than you were.

"Good morning," Mrs. Fontaine said.

But it wasn't only Mrs. Fontaine and the elastic.

And it wasn't only Caroline's losing the baby.

Caroline was a real soldier. "It wasn't a baby," Caroline said. "It was a fetus. We can probably have other children, Tom. Later. But I'm glad we haven't prepared Lewis for the baby. He would be terribly disappointed. No, Tom, don't touch me. Not right now."

Caroline had cried herself to sleep the night before Mrs. Fontaine came in to buy the elastic. "It's not anything," she said. "It's just that time of the month, leave me alone, Tom."

And that next week he had gone to sleep at the Rotary Club dinner. It was Rotary Ann night. He wasn't tired, exactly. He'd had a good night's sleep. Dr. Graham was showing his slides on the Holy Land. The room was hot. It must have been ninety degrees in the hotel dining room.

And he had argued with Ralph over not anything—a new line, or how much they were going to pay a clerk: Ralph believed in starting them low and raising them immediately. Ralph was probably right.

And before that, and before that, and before that . . .

They stood in a kitchen in Birżebbuġa.

Marie had not killed herself. She had been determined to play in the Easter Championship at the club, that was all. She would have gone to the doctor after the tournament. If she had got through the tournament. Nobody would think of blaming any-

45

body for having a ruptured appendix. Peritonitis wasn't something anybody would expect in this day and age.

Marie was a modern woman. It was crazy for her to die of something as old-fashioned as appendicitis.

He didn't think about her. He almost never thought about her. Tell the truth and shame the devil, his mother said, excusing herself for being outspoken.

"Lewis is a lucky boy," he told Caroline.

She smiled. "We'll have oatmeal. And the oranges. We're almost out of milk. I wasn't a very good shopper last night. But there's still the wonderful bread. I can toast it in the oven. I really like oven toast, we all do. I don't know why I never fix it at home."

She was chattering the way she used to, before she lost the baby. It was pleasant to hear her, and to watch her move. She kneeled down to put the toast in the oven. He thought of patting her bottom. But he didn't touch her. They were getting along fine. Maybe they would have intercourse tonight. Maybe tomorrow night.

"Why don't you go wake up Lewis? He won't take his nap if he sleeps too late. Tell him breakfast's ready."

"It's morning. It's morning already?"

"Sure enough, Lewis. It's morning already." He was a good-looking kid. "Your mother has breakfast almost ready."

"Mamma?"

Lewis had called her Mamma easily, right from the first. Caroline was a good mother. Marie wasn't a good mother.

"We're in Malta, aren't we? We're in Birżebbuġa, Malta."

"That's exactly where we are."

"I better get up in a big hurry."

"Let me help you."

"I can dress by myself, Daddy."

"Good boy."

It was a fine breakfast. "Delicious," Lewis kept saying.

"I have to shop. I have to get things." Caroline's cheeks were pink.

"Why don't you let me go for you?"

"No, Tom. I want to go. I like to."

"Whatever you say."

"You and Lewis take a walk, or something. Walk on the beach." Caroline was beautiful in her green sweaters and the green headband.

"Let me go with you, Mamma."

"You and Daddy. You'll explore while I shop. You'll wrap up."

"Come on, Lewis. We'll have a game."

The boy wasn't very good at ball. But he'd learn.

"Catch. Here it comes." He threw the red and white ball. Lewis missed it. They weren't four feet from each other.

"I didn't catch it again."

"That's all right. Throw it to me."

The boy threw pretty well. "Good one. That's the boy. Now watch out, here it comes. Good fellow."

Once at the Redmons', in the Redmons' kitchen, Ralph said, "You're attracted to cripples, Tom. That's what's the matter with you."

Ralph had been drinking. Ralph drank too much.

Caroline had lost the baby.

He didn't know what Ralph meant; he still didn't know. But he had wanted to hit Ralph in the mouth.

"What do you mean?"

"Nothing. You're a good fellow, Tom."

"God damn you, Ralph." That's what he had said. He was surprised at himself. The Huttons almost never cursed, not even Ralph. Cursing was something their mother had really been against.

Ralph acted as if he hadn't heard.

"Good fellow."

47

"I caught it. I caught it, Daddy."

"Good fellow. Great. Now, watch."

But Lewis dropped the next one.

He caught the next and the next.

"Can we stop now, Daddy?"

"Once more. Three's the magic number."

But the boy didn't catch the third ball.

"It doesn't matter. We'll walk a little. Your mother will be back soon."

A man in shorts waded in the bay. He held a net in his hand. It was hard to imagine a man wading in the cold water.

"You want to take my hand, Lewis?" He didn't know what made him say it.

"No, thank you." Lewis skipped ahead.

Normally he would have asked the man what he was trying to catch. But maybe the man didn't speak English.

"What's the man doing?"

"I don't know. We can ask him."

"Don't ask him, Daddy." Lewis reached for his hand.

"You wait here. I'll go across the street and get the camera. I'll take your picture and his, too."

Ralph and Ellen made fun of tourists and their cameras. But you had to be sure of what you saw. A person's eyes got tired. If you had a picture you could remember what you might forget.

"Mamma'll be here in a minute," Lewis called.

"I won't be a minute. You wait right there."

"Say 'Cheese.' Look at me, Lewis."

It would be a good picture. Behind Lewis's head the man lifted his net.

"Another one. Hold still. Smile. O.K. Fine."

"Now what do you want to do, Daddy?" Lewis twisted the toe of his sneaker in the sand. "What do you want to do now?"

"We could walk some more. We could play some more ball."

Sometimes he felt embarrassed with Lewis. It was a funny feeling.

"The sand's dirty, isn't it, Daddy?"

"Well, now that you mention it, yes. I guess they clean it up in summer, when people go in swimming."

"What's all that mess?" Lewis pointed to the seaweed piled against the wall. A piece of newspaper started off across the beach. It looked alive, or like a machine.

"What's it for, Daddy? I'm talking to you."

For a minute he was mad at the boy, hot under the collar. But there wasn't any reason to be mad. "It's seaweed. It's a part of the sea."

"I don't think it looks very nice."

"Sorry about that."

The sun disappeared. It was colder than Christmas. The wind went right through you. You might as well be naked. But the man in shorts kept wading around as if he didn't mind.

"Here, Lewis." He took the ball out of his pocket. "Catch."

The kid missed the ball. It plopped into the water.

"Oh, my goodness."

"Don't try to get it. The waves will bring it in."

They did, but they took a long time. And Lewis got his sleeve wet clear up to the elbow. He tried to dry his sleeve on his pants.

"Now look what you've done."

"It isn't very wet."

"You're sopping wet. Come on. Let's go back and change." He grabbed Lewis's hand. "You'll catch your death of cold."

The boy's teeth were chattering. "Your mother will never forgive me if you catch cold."

He set Lewis down on a dining room chair by the heater while he went upstairs to get the dry clothes.

It was only nine-thirty. By this time at home he would already be at the store. Everybody would be there, the counters uncovered, the clerks standing around looking fresh and smiling. Except Ralph. Ralph wouldn't straggle in for ten or twenty minutes. "I got a little behind." Ralph would walk down the far right aisle. "Good morning, Mr. Hutton," the girls would say to Ralph.

Nobody, not even the old ones, said *Ralph*. Several of them said *Tom*. "Tom, can you help me a minute? This cash register's stuck," or "Tom, will you O.K. this check for me?"

He would be as busy as a bird dog until ten-thirty or eleven, when he went next door to Heath's for coffee, and a doughnut; maybe he'd be having a doughnut this morning. He didn't go home for lunch; and a man could get pretty hungry, running around all morning. At three he would call home to see if everything was under control.

It seemed a long time to three, or six. It was always after six when he got home.

Lewis was trembling. The heater wasn't much force.

He felt sorry for the boy. He rubbed him down with the dry part of the sweater—he'd forgot to bring a towel.

"It's not very cold any more," Lewis said.

"That's a boy."

He turned the black knob on the heater, but it didn't help.

"I know what we'll do. We'll sit in the kitchen and learn us some Maltese."

"That's good. That's a good idea, Daddy."

Lewis caught on fast. It was amazing how the boy caught on.

"Bongu, kif int? Good morning, how are you? You say *Bonjoo, kif int?"*

"Tajjeb hafna, grazzi. Very well, thank you. You say *Tayep hafnah, grattsi."*

"Is that the right way to say it, Daddy?"

"Sure, of course." He hoped he was right. A penny, *sold—salt;* shilling, *xelin—sheelen.*

"That's funny, isn't it? *Salt. Sheelen."*

It was a sight how the boy caught on. Lewis was good company, all right. They'd been together more the past few weeks than they ever had before.

After Marie died—that wasn't a good time. But Mrs. Lovell had helped for a while. And the Thompson girl had been almost like a mother to Lewis. Ellen was fine, too.

50

It was almost funny, crazy to think about. At first it was painful to be around the boy, but he had got over that. A person could get over things in a hurry.

When Caroline came back from shopping, when she finally came, Lewis said, *"Bongu, kif int?"* For a minute he didn't know what the kid was up to.

"We talk Maltese now. Daddy and I do."

Caroline put two big straw baskets down on the table. She kissed Lewis on the forehead.

"Bongu, kif int, Mamma."

"My goodness, how smart you both are."

"How did you get along?"

"Marvelous. I had the most marvelous time. Wait until you see. These straw bags, first. Aren't they wonderful? And the bargains. I'll never be able to shop at home again."

She had to show them everything, the black currant jelly, the lemon curd, and the canned ham, and lettuce, and olives. She showed them every single item in both baskets. Lewis seemed really interested. "Wow," he kept saying, and "Oh, boy."

"It's not like Sicily. You buy a rottolo's worth, not an etto."

Caroline was flushed. She was like a person who had had too much to drink. He was glad Caroline didn't drink. It was nice to see her so happy.

"And I'm in love with the butcher, I may as well tell you. These marvelous lamb chops, four and nine. And liver, just look."

"Oh, boy."

He didn't mean to look at his wristwatch. He was just wondering how long she'd been gone.

"Oh, Tom. I've been too long, haven't I? You need to go to town, don't you? I didn't mean to stay so long, but . . . it's just marvelous. Everybody's so nice to you. And they speak English, they really do."

"I thought I'd explore around a little. And I need to stop at

51

the bank again. We don't have much money left, not since I paid the rent."

"There's a bank here. But it's just open on three days a week, and then only in the mornings. It's open now, though."

"Since I've already been to the other one, I might as well . . ." He didn't want to get away from Caroline and Lewis. It wasn't that. He was used to being busy. At Taormina he had sat in the bars almost every morning and afternoon, for a little while, drinking coffee, an occasional beer—you didn't have to drink alcohol in bars abroad. He didn't approve of drinking, not really.

And somebody always talked to him. They liked to hear about America. And you learned a lot, too. And the men, the old men particularly, they liked to have their pictures taken. "I won't be gone too long."

"You'll not be home for lunch?"

"I'll get something downtown."

Sometimes he wished she wouldn't be so nice about everything. Marie would be having a fit.

"We'll have lunch, Lewis and I. Lewis will have his nap."

"I think I am almost too old to take a nap any more."

"The idea! The very idea!" Caroline said. She was a good mother.

He caught the bus in front of Tony's Saloon, right up the street, not ten yards from their house. He was wearing the dark glasses Caroline made him buy in Syracuse. He felt like somebody else behind the glasses. "You'll ruin your eyes," Caroline said. "The sun is brighter than you know."

It was a funny bus. A lot of the windows were open, cold as it was. There was a driver, and a boy who took your money. It was only eight cents to Valletta, or six cents. He didn't count his change. The guidebooks said you could trust the Maltese.

He took a seat in the middle of the bus. The driver sat in a little glass booth. The glass behind the driver's head had some words printed on it. Underneath the words there were a couple of pictures of Elvis Presley, and a photograph of the very bus they were riding in. There was a shrine, too, at the curve of the booth. It was a box of a thing, a plaster head of a young Jesus in a fancy crown. The box was edged with plastic roses and little Christmas tree lights. It was a sight.

The bus was old. It rattled like anything; you wondered why the windows didn't fall out. It didn't make any speed at all, except on the little stretch beyond someplace named Ghar Dalam. Maybe the shaking was good for your liver.

It took about forty minutes to get to Valletta, but he didn't mind. There were lots of things to see. He had all the time in the world.

In the country the fields weren't any bigger than the backyard at home. And there were rock fences everywhere. In one of the little communities he saw a couple of young girls in their bare feet sloshing water over the steps and mopping up. It was a wonder they didn't catch their deaths of cold. He took some pictures from the bus window. Several people on the bus smiled and spoke to him.

He carried his pen and notebook in his right inside coat pocket, with the passports. He'd started the notebooks on the boat; he'd already filled three of them.

The Rotarians, the men's group at church, maybe some of the ladies' groups around town, were sure to ask him to show his slides. They always asked people to give talks when they came back from a big trip. He was keeping good notes. He wasn't going to be like some of the fellows who couldn't remember where the pictures came from.

Maybe he would start a notebook on "The Businessman in Malta." That would make an interesting speech.

He hoped Lewis's cold wouldn't come on. But he was a healthy boy. There wasn't any reason to worry over him.

He hoped the Huttons hadn't been darn fools for deciding on the vacation.

They were adjusting well. They managed to keep warm enough. And already she was used to the waves. She didn't hear them for long periods of time.

It was only the flies that bothered her. She wasn't afraid of them. They weren't like rats. She wasn't compulsive about them. She did not imagine their bodies magnified.

She had known there would be difficulties in living abroad. "I'm not expecting good plumbing or central heating."

"That's the girl," Tom said.

The plumbing was good, the refrigerator was fine. But she hadn't been able to find a fly swatter at the C. and S., or Joe's, or Saint Mary's.

The third day the older woman at Notions asked, "Fly swatter, what is that? Bamboo? I hear about it. Somebody else ask me. I saw one."

"For flies. We have so many flies."

Above the woman's head, on the top shelf, she saw the two spray cans, Shelltox. It was a beautiful name. She was so pleased she almost hiccuped. "Shelltox. Two. The two cans."

"Madame is bother."

"I'm sorry. I don't mean to be a bother."

"The bugs, madame. Oh, I beg you."

She did not mention the Shelltox to Tom. But in the afternoon, before he came home, and at night, after he and Lewis had gone to bed, she sprayed. She moved the bowl of fruit from the buffet to the china closet; she cleared everything from the counters beside the sink, and sprayed. "Children, let us spray." That was one of Lewis's jokes. She sprayed almost prayerfully. She was waking early these days. She would have time to get downstairs before Tom and Lewis appeared, to sweep up the flies.

Time was of a piece in Malta. Already they had settled into the time.

Tom was a good man. He kept busy. He was as busy in Malta as at home. Maybe Tom bustled. He didn't mind taking infinite time and pains in bustling. He was staking out Malta for them, he was lining up the things they should see. Most days he ate lunch downtown, learning; he walked a great deal; he was looking marvelous. He had found the British Council and brought books home to her—mysteries. She told him she was just ready for a mystery binge.

They ate breakfast an hour later than at home, dinner an hour later. But they kept the time intervals of Athens, Ohio. The Huttons always lived a planned day. Tom knew what he was going to do a week from now, a year, and the rest of his life. She was grateful for him, utterly grateful. She loved Malta already. And they had not quarreled.

Tom said, "You're sure you don't want to go in town today?"

"We will, Tom. We will later, when Lewis is good and well."

"He just has the sniffles. My goodness, Caroline."

"I know you're right. I'm silly. I want to be a positive thinker."

"You're all right." Tom looked at his watch. "I'm meeting the fellow I told you about. The Maltese, the one who went to Indiana. He wants me to see the armor at the palace. We'll all go again. Lewis will like the armor, won't you, boy? You'll remember it."

"We'll go later." Lewis seemed pleased to be staying at home. Lewis was an utter joy.

55

"I'll get a bite downtown."

"That's fine, Tom, that's just fine." She was tired of saying "That's just fine." Lewis sneezed.

She said, "Maybe it's an allergy, the seaweed or something."

Tom said, "Probably."

"I don't have very much cold."

"You're ever so much better." She leaned over to kiss Tom. She felt guilty about not going with him, but not very guilty. "We'll see you at dinnertime."

"Sure. Bye." He patted her arm.

"Lewis and I will take a good walk. We'll find a nice walk. I hear the bus. Don't miss it."

"Bye, honey. Bye, Lewis."

"Bye-bye, Daddy."

He made the bus all right. They stood at the door and waved to him.

She felt good. It was going to be a lovely day. She luxuriated in the thought of the day. She had no reason to feel guilty over luxuriating in the thought of the day.

They left the house at ten-thirty. They walked casually, turning right because the sun shone on a honey-colored wall, turning left because a donkey brayed; circling, doubling, right again, and left, and circle—a little black dog: Lewis wasn't afraid of the dog; another bay appeared and a fishing boat with high ends started from the land: the boat was called a *dghajsa;* a vegetable cart— she bought artichokes, four cents apiece, and stuffed them into her knitting bag. She had money. If they were lost, and they weren't lost, they could find their way home. She could call a taxi. "Twenty Pretty Bay, please." And the driver would be willing to take them straight to their house. "How much to Pretty Bay?" she would ask. Tom would want her to be efficient.

The place had a name. There was a wrought iron archway with words spelled out in spidery iron letters, like old-fashioned handwriting. The letters held the arch together. There were plaques on the pillars beside the archway; one had an inscription—she would read it later—the other a medallion: a queen, or a saint, some woman. To the right and left rose great stone walls.

"My, what high walls. How high do you guess they are, Lewis?"

"About a dozen." Lewis sniffed.

"Do you need another Kleenex?"

"I have a lot, a plenty."

Lewis held her hand, but he did not pull her through the archway. They went together down the broad path between the orange bougainvillea hedges. The hedges were as tall as the gate. But the path was wide.

The ticket booth must have been three hundred feet, three hundred yards from the entrance. She was no good at gauging height or width or distance, but she kept wondering about them; she wanted to remember the details of the place, to tell Tom.

"My, my," she said.

"My, my, my," Lewis said.

The ticket booth stood at the end of the path. The bougainvillea hedges on either side must have been fifteen feet high, maybe twenty feet. She would tell Tom, "The booth was like any ticket booth, like at a state park at home. And the paths went to the right and left of the booth, between the hedges, twenty-five feet high, maybe that high."

In a paved semicircle around the booth stood tricycles, shining in the bright sun. The sky had been clouded when they had started their walk, but now the sun was bright. At home weather wasn't very important, but it mattered in Malta, away from home.

The window of the ticket booth was a half circle. Beside it hung a sign, typed on white paper, as if the sign were made new every day, like the menu in a *pensione.*

Hours: 10 A.M. until Sunset
Daily

Admission 1/
Children Free

Tricycle Rental: 1/

NO BICYCLES ALLOWED

CHILDREN NOT ALLOWED UNLESS
ACCOMPANIED BY PARENTS

Welcome!

"What do you think of this, Lewis?"

"What, my goodness?"

"They have tricycles for rent. A shilling apiece."

"A *sold?*"

"No, for rent." She laughed. "Oh, I see what you mean." She could hardly control her laughter.

A man waited inside the booth. He almost frightened her. She jumped, ashamed of herself.

The man was smiling. He could have been any age. He had a sweet face, like a woman's face. He was somebody you could trust forever, with everything. She would tell Tom, "He had a very kind face."

"One ticket. And one tricycle. I'm not going to ride."

They were all three laughing together. Lewis coughed.

The man stepped out of the booth. He was surprisingly tall, six feet at least. Most of the men she had seen in Malta were relatively short. But she would not mention the man's height to Tom. Tom wasn't short, but he wasn't tall, either.

"How will this one suit Master Lewis?" the man said in his beautiful English voice.

"How do you know what my name is?"

"I heard your Mums speak to you."

"What's your name?"

"Lewis, no. You don't . . ."

The man answered his name, but she did not hear it; it was a Maltese name.

"It is just your size. It is just right, Lewis."

The seat was red leather; it looked like real leather. The spokes of the wheels were silver, like real silver.

"My, my," Lewis said, and then he said, "Thank you," very politely.

"Bon boyage," the man said.

"Yes, yes. Wait, Lewis, wait."

"He will be all right. He will always return here. He can ride anywhere within the enclosure."

"It's beautiful, utterly beautiful." She did not know exactly what to do. She didn't want to follow Lewis; the man must not misunderstand her; she wasn't a fluttering mother. But she did not want to keep talking with the tall man in the bright sunshine.

"I'll stroll a little." She sounded affected. "I'll take a little walk."

"There are benches throughout. Your son will appear."

"It's large. The park is large."

"Within the enclosure we have almost a mile of paths, madame. This is not our busy season."

She took a few steps to the left, in the direction Lewis had disappeared. Then she marched to the right, firmly. "Thank you. Thank you very much. It's beautiful," she said over her shoulder.

She did not go far, just out of sight of the man and his booth. She stood against the hedge, trying to hide herself, waiting.

Lewis appeared.

"My, what a quick trip."

"Oh, boy," Lewis said, because Tom said "Oh, boy," because people had said "Oh, boy" for a long time.

"Wait. Wait for me, Lewis."

"Hurry, Mamma."

She was jogging. The man did not appear at his booth. Fortunately. She was fortunate.

Jogging was good for a person. She needed exercise. It was important not to get fat. A person had only to look at her grandmother, only to have looked. Her grandmother would have lived

59

longer if she had not been so fat, longer than seventy-nine years.

The path was smooth and soft. It was tanbark, something like tanbark. But it couldn't have been tanbark. Malta didn't have trees, not many.

"There are no rivers in Malta," she had read. She thought about rivers, the Ohio River running past Pomeroy, Ohio.

"Wait. Wait for me, Lewis." She did not have the breath to say, "Your daddy must come with us. Wait!"

Lewis stopped pedaling. He was a good driver. "Isn't this nice, Mamma?"

She was breathing too hard to answer.

"You sit down a little. Why don't you sit down?"

"Really, Lewis." But she had a stitch in her side. She couldn't remember when she had had a stitch in her side from running. She felt very young, silly young. She had yanked off her headband. Her hair had flown in the wind.

They were between bougainvillea hedges again, or they had not left the hedges—she had been too consumed with running to notice.

A green iron bench, exactly like park benches at home, waited beside her. A square had been cut out of the hedge for the bench to fit into. If Lewis had not called her attention to the bench, she would have missed it.

"You won't go far? You'll come back for me in a minute?"

"I'll go a little way up, and a little way down, and I'll come back for you." Lewis cocked his head. He was playing coy with her. He was handling her.

"Don't be smart-aleck, Lewis."

She had never said to him before, "Don't be smart-aleck." She was surprised at herself.

Lewis straightened. "I'll just go a little ways." He was not offended. They had a good relationship. She loved the boy, dear God.

He disappeared.

She could be anywhere. She could be in a dream where the air was warm. She stood to take off her top sweater. She stretched, conscious of her breasts, of the pull at her stomach. The sun was a benediction, on her face, her bare arms. And there were no flies. She would have expected flies buzzing in a public garden. In Bir-żebbuġa. But surely they had walked clear to another village.

The air was sweet. Narcissi, or hyacinths—narcissi and hyacinths grew somewhere near. And roses. Roses wouldn't bloom in Athens until June. And there couldn't be flowers; the flower beds in the parks had been empty.

She took a few steps, ten, twelve, in the direction Lewis had disappeared.

The hedge stopped. The man at the ticket booth might have been telling the truth, almost a mile of paths. But the park was a city block, two city blocks. If she listened carefully she could hear the sounds of traffic. She could hear the sea. A person was never far from the sea.

The hedges only circled the park, opening to paths, leading to the gardens.

Narcissi moved in the wind. Roses nodded. There were iris, beds of iris. A dozen? Twenty? From where she stood she could count . . . how many beds of flowers? And she couldn't see them all, or name them. There were little trees, too; orange and lemon and even grapefruit. She must tell Lewis to look at them carefully. She would tell him to look at everything carefully.

And there was a pond.

At first she had thought it was a circle of tender grass.

The pond was green with algae. Only at the center could you be sure the place was water.

For a second she was repulsed. Water should be water. Grass should be grass. But the pond was beautiful. It was the color of imagined grass.

She shivered.

She was ashamed of herself. The pond was beautiful. Around it grew narcissi and hyacinths.

Lewis appeared on the other side of the pond. At first she thought he rode in the water.

"Lewis!" She did not mean to sound alarmed. "Hello! Hello, there, Lewis."

"Here I am, Mamma." He stopped moving. He waved. He seemed very far away; perhaps the park was larger than she had imagined. In the bright sunlight Lewis's body was a small black stick figure, hanging above the silver wheels. The figure raised its arm again.

"I see you, Lewis."

"I'm here, Mamma."

"I'm here, Lewis." She was happy. She was determined to remember how happy they were together.

She turned from the park before Lewis moved again, back to the aisles of hedges, to the bench where Lewis had told her to wait. She was reasonably sure she had found the right bench.

She sat carefully.

She thought about opening her knitting bag. But it wasn't worth the effort. She needed to make her mind blank. She brushed at her skirt. Her mind was full of lint.

She loved Tom. She loved to live with him, with Tom and Lewis.

Her mind imagined a door opened to a garden. She imagined a knocking at an opened door. She was being silly. Nobody knocked at opened doors, not if the person belonged in a garden.

Lewis appeared. His face was red.

"You don't want to get yourself too tired, honey."

"I don't go clear around. I just go for little trips." His feet tapped impatiently at the pedals.

"Don't go too far."

"There isn't any too far."

"Yes, I know. That's all right."

"The flowers are pretty, Mamma. The man has lots of pretty flowers."

"Aren't they beautiful, though!"

"You want some, Mamma?"

"Of course not, Lewis. Lewis, no. We mustn't pick them."

He was gone again.

He appeared, and was gone, and appeared.

She imagined the door, determined that no knock should sound against it.

And appeared.

"My heavens. It's almost one. It's ten minutes until one. You must be starved."

"Once more. Just one more time." Lewis held up his index fingers.

"Just one more time."

He was not gone long.

They left the tricycle in front of the ticket booth. "Thank you very much," she said into the opening of the booth. She knocked lightly with the back of her hand against the counter. "Thank you." The sun was too bright for her to see into the booth. She was sure the man was not there. Anyhow she said, again, "Thank you very much."

"That was fun. Oh, boy, that was fun."

"Now, let me see. Which way?"

Lewis stopped his song. They were at the iron archway with the curling letters. "This way and that way and this way." Lewis wagged his hands.

"You funny darling," she said, but she did not reach down to hug him.

He was right.

This way, and that way, and this way. They found their way to the house as they had found their way to the park; right, to buy an ice cream bar—it was pasteurized, the wrapper said so, and it wouldn't spoil Lewis's lunch; left, to a bay where an oil tanker had docked; circle, right, and left again.

They were on Pretty Bay.

"There's our house. There's where we live." Lewis ran ahead of her. She did not call to him to be careful. The street was empty.

63

Lewis held her knitting bag while she unlocked the door. It was pleasant to open the heavy doors into the vestibule, to turn the graceful brass handles of the inner doors. The glass lace curtains were frayed, but they sparkled. A person needed to open only one of each of the doors, but, with her hands free, it was a pleasure to sweep into the room, like a lady in a play. She wouldn't have made such an entrance if Tom had been watching, but Lewis was delighted. He giggled until he started coughing. He dropped the bag, but it didn't matter. He sneezed.

The house was colder than a tomb. That was all right, too.

"Let's hurry to the heater. Let's hurry to the nose drops. It's aspirin time."

"You're funny, Mamma."

The dining room was cold, too, even with the heater; and dark, dark as sleep. She turned on the center light. It didn't help much.

"You need something around you. It's a funny house, isn't it, Lewis? You take off your clothes when you go out, and you put on clothes when you come in."

"That's funny."

If he wasn't better by morning, she would get a doctor. But she didn't trust doctors, not really. Doctors attended you at death.

They had tomato soup from a can, and cheese sandwiches toasted in the funny broiler above the stove. They ate in the kitchen with the door closed into the dining room. Lewis didn't want her to put her cardigan around his shoulders, but he didn't complain much.

"This is good soup, Mamma." He dribbled soup on her sweater, but she didn't mention it. He was full of cold.

If Tom had been at home when they came in she would have told him about the park, the garden, whatever its name was. She had not meant to keep the park a secret.

But Tom didn't get back from Valletta until after five. Lewis was up from his nap, drinking hot lemonade out of one of the orange glass cups. They sat in the dining room in the wicker chairs from the hall. And Lewis seemed better, he really did.

Just before Tom arrived the lame man had brought a floor lamp, a thin wood column with a vast silk shade, fringed; the switch was centered on the wood column.

"It's nice; it's very nice," she told the lame man. "And a bedlamp? You were going to give us a lamp for the bed."

"Bet lamb?" The man smiled. Perhaps they spoke of dodoes.

"A lamp for the bed. To read by. We read in bed at night sometimes. Bedlamp. *Bed lamp.*"

"Of course, madame. You will tell me what you want. Bed lamb. My wife's sister-in-law. Agreeable, very agreeable."

"We don't want to be trouble."

"It is a beautiful day."

"Good-bye, good-bye, thank you. Bye-bye."

Tom was full of himself. The tourist bureau had given him maps and folders. He had talked for a long time with the young man at the counter. The boy was going to school at the university and he worked part time. The other fellow, the fellow he met, was named Joe Manduca. He was an engineer. Joe was up to his ears in work, so he was a little late coming to the bar, but he was very nice. Joe took him over to the palace, where all the armor was displayed, the best armor collection in Europe. Joe told the man at the desk to look out for his friend. "You just can't imagine all that armor—and not very big, the men weren't very tall. I didn't look at anything too hard, though—I'm saving it for when we all can go. I was just checking."

She wanted to lean over and pat Tom. She was angry at Joe Manduca. He had slighted Tom. She was angry at Tom, too. He shouldn't have put himself in such a position. But Joe Manduca shouldn't have left Tom to wander alone among the suits of armor. Tom was . . . Tom was guileless.

"And then what?" She was furious, but Tom didn't notice; he

was unfolding one of the maps; he probably wouldn't have noticed, anyhow.

They sat in the wicker chairs, close around the dining room heater.

Tom had been to Saint Paul's Cathedral and then Saint John's Co-Cathedral. "Beautiful. You never saw anything so ornate."

"We took us a big walk," Lewis said.

"Good boy. You've got to get over that cold in a hurry. We've got a lot of sightseeing to do. Come over here. Here, get on my lap."

"He's better, Tom. I think he's ever so much better, just today."

"There were flowers and everything."

"We can go with you day after tomorrow, Tom. Day after tomorrow."

"That's the boy. I want to show you something." Lewis settled himself behind the map. Tom looked at her over the child's head. "I went to that bar for lunch—I had cheese cakes again, three of them, and two meat cakes." Tom sounded apologetic. "They're not like anything we have at home. I didn't catch the name of them. I want you to try them. They're delicious."

"Wonderful. How fine, Tom."

"You're all right, aren't you?"

"I'm marvelous. We've had a lovely day." She laughed. She leaned over and kissed Tom's cheek.

"I didn't mean to abandon you. I don't mean to."

"Abandon. It's what I want you to do. You must keep on going out. Every day. You need to find out what we should see."

"We had a good walk. I'm all well." Lewis patted at Tom's cheek.

"Golly." Tom was pleased.

Two of the men at the bar had been particularly nice, Tom said. They had taught him how to pronounce the names of the villages.

"I don't exactly remember this one, but this is Mdina—you

66

pronounce it Med-ee-na. That's the old capital. We'll go there. And this, this is Tarxien. There's a ruin there. Let's see. I don't exactly remember this one. Or this. X-g-h-a-j-r-a. Here's Hal Far."

"How far to get to Hal Far?" Lewis giggled.

"What a joke, Lewis," she said. "You've made a funny joke." Lewis said his joke three times.

"That's funny, but that's enough." She was ashamed of herself. She sounded like a schoolteacher. But Lewis wasn't offended.

"Where are we, Daddy?" Lewis waved his hand over the map. "Here. Right here."

"That's niiice."

"I almost forgot. Down you go. I have a surprise for you in my raincoat pocket. From a stationer's. They don't seem to have stores around here like Hutton's."

Lewis was flushed. Maybe it was only because they had been crouched around the heater. She felt flushed, too.

"Daddy has a surprise. Oh, boy."

She thought, "Sick Present," but she stopped herself. Almost a year ago—they were just married—she had bought Lewis a Sick Present at the grocery, a plastic puzzle, a train with yellow wheels and a red smokestack. "Sick Present, Lewis." They stood by Lewis's bed upstairs. She couldn't imagine why Tom was suddenly annoyed with her. His voice was cold. At dinner that night —Lewis ate from a tray upstairs—Tom said, "Caroline, I don't mean to be critical, but you don't get presents for being sick. It makes being sick attractive. We don't believe in that."

"We don't? *We?*" Back then she had been too open. Tom meant Marie, of course. But they did not speak of Marie. Tom kept saying there was no reason to speak of Marie. "This is our life now." He was right, of course.

But she said, "Who is we?"

"I mean we. All of us."

She had cried. Back then she hadn't known how to keep from crying. Tom had been upset. He couldn't stand for her to cry. She had learned. She almost never cried now.

67

She was learning. She wanted to learn.

Tom had bought three paperback books, about engines and horses and clouds.

"What a fine present, Tom."

"Read to me, Daddy. Read the one about the sky."

"Maybe I can help your mother."

"Of course not. You settle yourselves, toasty warm." But Tom insisted on getting out the mats and the silver.

She worked well again. Lamb chops, carrots, the artichokes.

How many evenings had they sat at the pink dining room table in Birżebbuġa, Malta? They were getting along terribly well.

Tom's voice was comfortable. He read matter-of-factly, not as if he were an adult reading to a child.

"Let's try this one."

"I like the other one best."

The melted butter with lemon juice in the little custard cups. Milk for Lewis and Tom. The bread. Napkins. Frayed linen, but real napkins. Salt for Tom.

She served the plates, the biggest chop for Tom. The other chops would stay warm in the funny broiler. She had been in the kitchen only twenty minutes, twenty-five, twenty-five at the most. She was lucky.

Before she went into the dining room with the plates she stood a moment looking into the courtyard where hail had once fallen. She was lonely. It was silly to be lonely. She wasn't homesick for Athens, it wasn't that. She was glad she stood in a kitchen in Malta. "I am happy with my being," she thought. It was a silly sentence.

Her voice broke a little when she said, "Dinner. Dinner's ready."

But the dinner was good, everything went off well. Lewis had never eaten artichokes before.

"I'm not sure I'm going to be crazy about artichokes."

"Of course you are," Tom said. "Watch me." He broke off a

68

leaf and dipped it into his cup of butter and lemon. "Oh, boy, delicious. Go on and try it." Tom always insisted that Lewis eat everything. Tom was right.

Lewis dribbled. But he ate the artichoke leaf.

"That's pretty much fun, isn't it, Lewis?" Tom was pleased. "Maybe your mother's the best cook in the world."

"Don't be silly."

"No, I mean it!" Tom's glasses caught the light of the blue-shaded bulb over the table. His eyes were two circles of light. "Somebody taught you mighty well. I wish I could thank your grandmother, or whoever."

"Oh, Tom." She went into the kitchen for the other chops. Her grandmother had been an excellent cook, really, a natural cook. Cooking had been a joy for her. Maybe it was the only thing Grandmother honestly enjoyed. The other activities—her teaching, the housework . . .

A person shouldn't think about the dead too much. A person could break her heart, thinking about the dead and the little joys of the dead.

Tom and Lewis helped her clean up. Tom talked some more about the bus, and the men in the bar, and the statue of Queen Victoria in front of the library with all of the pigeons in her lap. Lewis laughed and said, "In her lap?"

Tom went upstairs to move the heater into the bathroom. Then they sat together in the wicker chairs. She got out her knitting.

"You've done a lot," Tom said.

"A lot?"

"On the sweater. You're going to have yourself a good-looking sweater, Master Lewis." Tom said Master Lewis, as the man in the park had said. For a foolish moment she expected Lewis to say, "How did you know my name?"

"We better read us a book again," Lewis said, pushing himself into Tom's lap.

"In a minute."

They talked together. Tom talked mostly. They would take the bus to Valletta and see things. They would have cheese cakes downtown for lunch. Joe Manduca said Malta was on its way. It was going to be *the* place on the Mediterranean in a little while. Malta had been independent just since 1964. It was a young country, and at the same time, older than anyplace. The boy at the travel bureau had said . . .

If she listened carefully she could hear the sea beyond the hall, the living room, the vestibule, the street. A voice sang, a radio, or somebody walking past. A horn. A ship's horn? Surely not. A car, a truck maybe, passed outside. It was raining again. The wheels passed through water.

Tom read.

Tom had finished reading. "That's about it. That's it. It's nine o'clock."

"Just one more, Daddy. The one about the sky, because it is such a good book you bought me."

"We've finished. That's it, Lewis."

"Just once more."

"It's time to take your bath and go to bed."

"You could read the sky book again, couldn't you? I'd like to hear that one again, too." She had dropped a stitch; she was unraveling, two rows: she concentrated on the little loops, popping up between her fingers. She had forgot to concentrate on being invisible, like a maid, or a piece of furniture.

"It's nine o'clock." Tom stood up quickly. Lewis did not fall to the floor. Not exactly. Tom was holding his arms. But the boy almost fell.

She was angry. "Really, Tom!" She had almost said, "I am his mother. I have a right." She was not the maid. She was not a piece of furniture.

"What's the matter?"

"Nothing. Nothing at all, Tom." She folded the knitting carefully. She stood. She looked hard at Tom. If she looked hard enough she could . . . Looking at him she did not think about looking at him.

"What's the matter, Caroline? It's time for Lewis to go to bed. He needs his sleep. He doesn't need a doctor, he just needs rest."

"That's what you always say." This morning Tom had said, "He doesn't need a doctor." Perhaps he had stood in the same spot all day, saying the same words. Tom had a lot to learn, for all his goodwill and friendliness. Tom didn't belong here. He belonged in Athens, Ohio, hustling through Hutton's department store, being nice to people he didn't know very well, like the boy at the travel bureau, and Joe Manduca, and . . . just anybody.

"Do you want him to stay up? How late do you want him to stay up? Ten? Eleven? Twelve?"

"It's time for bed, Lewis," she said over her anger. "Up we go."

Tom spoke easily. "You need some help?" He didn't believe in quarreling. "We won't quarrel, will we, Caroline?" he said the night he had asked her to marry him. "I love you. I'll remember that, Caroline. I can't stand the idea of quarrels." It was as close as he had come to criticizing Marie. "I love you, Caroline." She had cried, back then. She was a damn fool. She had a long history of being a damn fool.

"You stay here and . . . read? Whatever?"

"Oh, shoot," Lewis said, but he kissed his father good night.

" 'A kiss and a peck, and a hug around the neck,' " Tom said, and Lewis said the words after him.

"I can bathe myself all right," Lewis said.

"Go ahead then, Mister Independent. Just go right ahead."

She stood and watched him. He did a pretty good job. She stood in the doorway. He was a graceful child.

"I can dry myself all right."

"Nobody's stopping you."

But after he was in his cold bedroom, in his cold bed, he reached up to her. "I wish you would tell me a story."

"You haven't said your prayers."

She had cried the first night they were in Tom's house together. She and Tom had stood by Lewis's bed. She had been surprised when Tom said, "Your prayers, Lewis."

Every night she had prayed, for as long as she could remember. "Help me, oh, God, help me."

That first night Lewis said, "Bless Daddy, and me, and Mamma."

In Malta tonight he said, "Bless Mamma, and Daddy, and the garden. Good night."

"Once upon a time," she began, "there was a beautiful garden, with bougainvillea hedges and spring flowers; iris and roses and . . ."

She had only begun the story, and Lewis was asleep. She was glad. He was tired. Tom was right. And she hadn't known what the story was going to be about.

She creamed her face carefully. She bathed slowly. She turned down the heater, but she didn't shut it off. She hurried into bed. She heard Tom moving around downstairs. He was putting the house to bed. She would get up early tomorrow. She would make it a point to wake up the house.

"You're through down here, aren't you?" Tom called.

She did not answer.

When Tom came up she pretended to be asleep.

Tom bathed in a hurry.

Lewis had said "Good night" instead of "Amen." She thought of telling Tom about Lewis's funny prayer, but Tom was asleep.

After a while, after a long while, she slipped out of bed. The moon was bright enough for her to find her robe; she picked up a blanket from the foot of the bed. Tom did not move.

Hunched over the dining room table, she finished one of the

72

mysteries. The light was terrible. The book was marvelously dull. She was yawning.

Tom had been almost pathetic, bringing the books. Dear Tom. He took a foolish pride in her reading, whatever she read. He respected her for something that didn't deserve respect.

The nephew did the murder. She had known all the time.

$\mathcal{S}$he had dreamed of somebody named Bertha again. She spoke, her lips moving, about to say a word. Bertha. Or Mother. She had probably been about to say Bertha. Her mouth was dry. She ran her tongue over her lips. Tom slept like a baby. She had not spoken aloud. Tom lay on his right side, facing her. Without his glasses, in the moonlight, Tom didn't look like Tom.

She propped herself on her elbow to study Tom's face.

Of course it was Tom.

There wasn't anything to be afraid of. A person needed to control her thoughts. It was wrong to let your thoughts fly out in strange directions.

The difference between sanity and . . . and not being sane was a short line. Everybody knew that. People let themselves go crazy, allowed themselves. Grandmother blamed Uncle Fred for his condition. "Fred never learned to control his thoughts," Grandmother said again and again.

Caroline Hutton would protect Lewis.

Bertha. Grandmother. Mother. The words were very much alike.

Bertha was somebody in the third grade. Her parents were divorced. She lived with her father. One day—it was winter—Bertha Cole and Caroline Thaxton sat at a cafeteria table together; they ate from lunchboxes. The sandwiches were clammy. Their tin boxes smelled of bananas. Bertha and Caroline teetered forward on their chairs, whispering to each other.

Bertha was giving a great confidence. Bertha was her very best friend. "This is the third day." Bertha turned her head back and forth. Her neck was dirty. She pushed her thin hair behind her ears. She wore earrings, tiny pale spots on her fat earlobes. "And I'm going to wear them forever." Bertha leaned so close their faces almost touched.

"And I'll tell you something else, if you promise not to tell. Cross your heart."

"And hope to die."

"I pretend my mother is dead. I write her letters in heaven."

"My mother really is dead. My father, too."

She almost never thought about her parents. She must have been six or seven when she got around to asking about them. She must have been a very slow-witted child. It embarrassed her to remember.

"Golly, you're lucky," Bertha said.

"They were killed at a railroad crossing. They were taking me to the hospital because I had a fishbone stuck in my throat. I was bundled in a blanket. I was thrown clear."

Her grandmother had said very matter-of-factly, "You were thrown clear. The bone dislodged. You landed in a snowdrift. It was like an act of God." Grandmother sat sideways in her golden oak chair, in front of her desk. "I'm surprised you haven't asked before."

She had wanted to laugh.

She didn't tell Bertha about the bone's dislodging. She would have been furious if her best friend had laughed.

"That's a very sad story. I'm sorry for you."

"Thank you." She had almost said, "I am a kind of a miracle."

That is what she had said to Grandmother. She had been pleased with the words.

"Of course you're a miracle. But no more than anybody else.

Everybody's a miracle," Grandmother said. "Your father was not a good driver. I say it even though he was my son. You might as well know the truth. And the truth shall set you free."

She told Bertha, "My father was so worried about me that he killed himself and my mother. I wasn't even three years old. Maybe not even two and a half."

Bertha said, "My!"

"It's a secret. Cross your heart."

Bertha crossed her heart. "My goodness, Caroline."

That other night, in winter, by the gas grate, her grandmother said, "Do you have any further questions?" She had taken off her glasses to tell the story. She held the glasses by the right shaft.

"No, I don't guess so. I guess not."

"You have something to do, don't you? Have you done all your Numbers?"

She told Bertha, "My grandmother says we should all try to live up to being miracles."

Bertha said, "I think you ought to write letters to your mother. You could hand it in for an Extra."

"Maybe. And I'll let you read it, Bertha."

Bertha smiled. She placed her hands over her earrings. Perhaps Bertha's earrings weren't opal at all. Pale blue? Could anyone remember childhood? The earrings were pink, shell pink.

The Huttons were always saying, "Remember when . . ."

Tom and Ralph and Ellen remembered together. A lot of their stories were humiliating: somebody embarrassed the family, told a confidence, acted up. But the Huttons were not humiliated. They remembered together. Memory fed on memory, other people's versions of fact. A single child had very little to remember.

She did not want Lewis to be an only child.

Her essay, two pages, was named "My Mother's Face." She wrote it in her bedroom.

She told of her mother's looking down at her while the roaring train approached. "My mother's hair was golden. Her eyes were bright blue. My mother said, 'Miracle.'"

76

She imagined Bertha's eyes reading the Extra.

But she hadn't been able to wait for the next day.

She stood by her grandmother's chair. It took Grandmother a long time to read the two pages.

Grandmother said, "Your penmanship is improving."

"Thank you."

"The story isn't true, of course. That's permissible, I guess, in fiction. Your mother had brown hair, much lighter than yours. Her eyes were yellowish. She was a rather pretty girl, though."

Grandmother handed her the two pages. "That's very nice, even if it isn't true."

Caroline tore the two pieces of paper into twos, and fours, and eights, and sixteens. She flushed the scraps of paper down the commode. Three times she pulled the handle in the cold bathroom.

Bertha moved away before spring. Her father was a railroad man. "He's been bumped again," Bertha explained. It must have been late February. "I'm sorry to lose you as a friend."

"I'm sorrier, Bertha. But we'll write each other letters. You know my address, one two seven Maple Street." She spelled Maple for Bertha.

"I'll send you my address as soon as we get there."

But Bertha had not written.

After a while Caroline Thaxton stopped expecting the mailman to bring a letter.

In the next town there were two fourth grades. She did not have to be in Grandmother's room. She could remember the name of the town if she tried. Elsonville. That was the name of the town.

She had not been unhappy.

She could remember dozens of happy times in the houses where she and Grandmother lived together. And good times at school. And church. A social, a marvelous evening at a Valentine party in a church basement.

And she had picked out her own wallpaper for that bedroom

in Elsonville. She adored the paper, white, with little nosegays of rosebuds and bachelor buttons.

Once, somewhere, Grandmother's Sunday school class arranged a luncheon: fifteen old ladies and Caroline. The ladies gave Grandmother a corsage of pink carnations. "For me? Imagine!" Grandmother said. She was wearing a flowered voile dress.

Grandmother sewed beautifully, even though she claimed to dislike sewing. She had made a red jumper, corduroy, for that Valentine party at church. And a white nylon blouse with full sleeves that buttoned tight at the wrists. The sleeves felt glorious. When Caroline came home from the party she stood in front of the mirror, lifting and lowering her arms. She hated to take the outfit off.

"Are you still up, Caroline Thaxton? Don't you know what time it is? Tomorrow is a school day."

"I'm just about to go to sleep."

She was telling the truth. She was almost telling the truth.

She crossed her heart.

"Tomorrow. We'll go with you tomorrow. I can't wait, Tom."

"Fine. That's fine, Caroline."

After Tom left she finished the small household chores, the dishes, the beds, a little dusting, a lick and a promise. She and Lewis shopped. Lewis was much better; Tom was right. They could have gone into Valletta, but she was glad she had been firm. She thought about the cold, damp churches. And it was tiring to drag around all day, even for an adult. She wanted Lewis well, really well.

On impulse she stepped into The Electric Shop. The young woman at the counter was fascinated by the idea of someone's making a bedlamp. "How clever of you," she said. "What a smart mums you have, young man!"

There was a discussion about the length of the cord. The woman said, "We do not want it too short, do we? This socket, or this one? A pull chain or a button? A button. We must be very careful."

"I'm taking too much of your time."

"Ridic. I will arrange the wiring. I won't be a jiff. But you will be careful. One doesn't fiddle around with two twenty volts when one is accustomed to one ten, does one?"

The woman disappeared behind a curtain. It was pleasant to be fussed over. "Oh, boy," Lewis said.

The woman refused to take any money for her work.

"I insist. Please."

"Don't be ridic. Let me know how you fare."

At the Notions she bought three wire coat hangers.

"My mamma is making a bedlamp," Lewis said.

In the kitchen drawer she found pliers. In her zeal she broke one of the hangers. But she needed only two. She covered her creation with three layers of aluminum wrap.

"That's good, Mamma."

She was delighted with herself.

"Are we going to lay down and read now?"

"*Lie* down. Of course not. We'll take a walk. The sun will do us both good. It's a lovely day." She did not mention the park.

And the park appeared.

She had, honestly, not been looking for the park. It waited for them.

"Good morning, madame. Good morning, Master Lewis," the tall man said. Today he waited outside the booth. He held a wire broom. When they appeared he stopped raking at the gravel circle around his booth. He leaned the broom against a palm tree.

The sky was suddenly gray. She had not been conscious of what was happening to the sky. But it had been this way in Taormina, too; sudden sun and sudden rain. And sun again.

"This is your vehicle, I believe, Master Lewis."

"That's my trike," Lewis said, although no one could have been sure under the gray sky.

79

"Do you think it's going to rain?" She fumbled in her knitting bag for her change purse.

"Possibly, but not likely. But the trees will serve as shelter. And it never rains for long in Malta."

"Of course. I know." She did not know for sure. But she knew, too. She felt comfortable with the kind man.

"Good-bye, Mamma."

"I'll wait up there."

They had made a pattern, as she and Tom had made a pattern.

She sat on the bench in the bougainvillea hedge—she was almost sure it was the spot where she had waited the other day, yesterday, or the day before. It couldn't have been only yesterday.

She sat quietly. "Sit down and compose yourself, Caroline."

She thought about . . . She didn't think about anything. Athens, maybe. Maybe about how strange it was to be Mrs. Thomas Hutton of 20 Pretty Bay. Maybe about the child she had lost, the fetus. She would probably be able to bear other children. Dr. McConkey had said, "Probably. It's not anything to worry about."

If she thought about anything, she thought about Athens. It was ridiculous to dwell on her girlhood and Grandmother. The dreams were at fault. They kept dragging her back to when she was six, and eleven, and fifteen, before Tom. She was glad to be Mrs. Thomas Hutton of 20 Pretty Bay.

She stood up. She walked to the hedge's opening to look into the garden. She waved to Lewis, who waved from the other side of the green pond.

She returned to the bench. She took out her knitting. She had started the blue-green turtleneck for Lewis on the boat. She had finished only the back. She felt she had been knitting on it forever. She shouldn't be tired of the sweater already.

Purl knit. It was a pretty stitch.

She could not say—one could not actually remember if she and Lewis had seen other people in the park the other time, that other time. Yesterday? The man at the booth, of course. "It is not our busy season." But surely there had been other people. It had been a perfect day, the other time. She had dreamed about the garden.

She was straightening herself out. Everybody had complications. "There are complications," Dr. McConkey said.

She had asked him pointblank. "Probably," he said, and then he had explained everything all over again. She barely listened.

She had been foolish in her excitement over being pregnant. She had wanted too much too soon. Life played tricks on people who were too eager. Purl. Count. Count your blessings. My God, dear God, she was blessed. Purl six. Knit one.

She hadn't expected to get married. She was so lucky she was almost frightened of her good luck, all of the time. A person needed to remember to be frightened.

She smiled at her knitting. Perhaps they should try starting the new baby here, in Malta. A baby for Lewis. And Tom would be pleased when she told him. Doctors could be wrong about complications. If she could not bear a child . . . There were greater burdens.

The park shouldn't be empty. Dozens of mothers should be walking in the park. The sun shone. For the last two mornings Birżebbuġa had been full of prams and strollers. Older children walked beside their attractive mothers, touching the carriages, getting their directions from the movement of the carriages. They were sedate and beautiful children.

When she shopped she tried not to peer into the carriages. At home she was always peering. Sometimes the young student wives on Court Street stopped and smiled at her. "He's asleep," they said sometimes. Or a baby looked up at her and gurgled. "She likes you," one of the young women had said, smiling at the pregnant friend who walked beside her.

Yesterday afternoon she had seen two shapeless old women pushing pathetic carriages—a green tin cart with a dirty linen canopy, a battered wicker buggy. "Grandmothers," she explained to herself.

But the carriages did not hold babies.

81

She had almost cried out when she saw carrots and onions and bread in the stroller. The wicker buggy held pans of fish, their throats cut, their eyes staring everywhere.

Old women sold produce from their carriages. A pram was better than a cart for an old woman.

The Maltese children were beautiful. They lay in their carriages, smiling, like paintings of children.

The woman wheeling the carriage down the tanbark path was thirty-five—no, older, forty, older maybe. But there was surely a baby in the carriage, not onions or fish. The child was a menopause baby. The woman had waited almost too long. The pram was made of dark blue canvas. Dirty white fringe edged the bonnet.

The woman stopped. She stared at something beside the path. It would be nice to know what the woman stared at. A person could check, later, after the woman had passed.

In a hushed voice Grandmother spoke of menopause babies. "You must remember to be careful, Caroline. They're either geniuses or idiots. A woman has to be very careful."

Uncle Fred had died in an institution; but he wasn't sick, not mentally, not at first. Grandmother talked about Uncle Fred while she was dying. She had taken a long time to die.

The dirty little boy who appeared out of nowhere belonged to the woman, too. "Watch out!" he shouted. He was an ugly child with fat cheeks and straw-colored hair, like a cartoon child. "Watch out!"

"Watch out yourself," the woman said.

The boy on the shining tricycle almost hit the woman.

"You little bastard." The woman's voice was terrifying.

The woman had borne the boy when most women had finished with their children. He should have been old enough for junior high school; his mother should have finished with PTA, with being the Corresponding Secretary. But the boy was no older than Lewis, maybe not so old.

The woman stopped again. She moved a step, another, still staring at whatever lay beside the path.

She was a fat woman. Her shoes were house slippers. Her skirt was too short for her heavy legs. Two buttons were missing from the neck of her bright green blouse. Short-sleeved. It was too cold for a short-sleeved blouse. Her hair was dark, dyed probably, cut short as if in anger.

But her eyes were lovely, pale blue—glassed over or very deep; a person couldn't tell which. It was silly to say that eyes were shallow or deep. A person couldn't be sure. A person couldn't be sure that the well behind Grandmother's Elsonville house was bottomless. Maybe it wasn't. Maybe people just told children that to keep them from fooling around. Still, you could throw a rock into the water and never hear the sound of its landing.

Tom teased her for attributing too much to eyes, and hands, and voices. Tom said you couldn't be responsible for what you were born with. At first he had teased her. She was careful what she said now.

The woman's eyes were blue as blue.

The woman was leaning toward her, looking down at her with her blue blue eyes.

"We've met someplace, I know we have."

The invisible baby in the canvas carriage began to cry. It was a baby, all right.

"Animal, vegetable, mineral?" they had asked each other at the church parties, a long time ago. "Animal. Oh, yes, of course, animal," they said to each other. "You have just nineteen questions left."

The woman's face was steady. With one fat hand she began to jiggle the buggy. She placed her other hand, her left hand, on Caroline's shoulder.

Caroline Thaxton moved her eyes. She pulled her eyes from the woman's eyes.

She had only glanced at the woman. She had surely not stared at her coming up the path, pausing, moving the little distance from the path to the bench set in the bougainvillea hedge.

The woman's hand was square. Her nails were short. There was dirt under the thumbnail and under the middle nail.

"Where on earth have we met before?"

Caroline Hutton coughed. A long time ago she had stared into the bottomless well for minutes at a time.

"Are you upset, honey?"

"How do you do?" She did not mean to shrug her shoulders. But the woman removed her hand.

"You're upset about something?"

"I'm fine. I don't think we have met. We just got here. Monday. Last Monday. Or Tuesday?"

"Someplace else, then. We've met someplace else. Billy and us, we've been all over."

"We're from Ohio. We just arrived. We were in Sicily for a couple of weeks, but I'm sure—"

"No, not Sicily. I'm from Nebraska. Lincoln. But no, someplace else. I've seen you more than once. You're so pretty. I remember your face."

"No, really." She was embarrassed. She was only nice enough looking. "You're nice enough looking," Grandmother said. She thought about Grandmother's silly little verse. She was saying the verse:

> "If a lady shirks her duty,
> Whate'er her face, she hath no beauty."

"That's a riot. That's funny." The woman laughed until her gums showed. "Wherever did you hear that?"

"My grandmother. I've been thinking about her so much lately. I guess it's being away from home. And dreaming a lot. I don't know. She's dead. She died two years ago."

"My name's Clar. It's short for Clara. Not Claire, but Clar. Give me time. I'll think. I'll remember. I never forget a face, but I'm terrible at names."

84

"My name is . . . I am . . ." Sometimes it was difficult to say one's own name. "Caroline Hutton."

"I'm Clar Tate. Mrs. Tate."

"Really?" She laughed. She wasn't really embarrassed. "Those were my initials. Before Tom and I were married. I was named Caroline Thaxton—that was my name, for twenty-nine years." She was being silly. It couldn't matter to the strange woman how old Caroline Thaxton had been when she married. "I'm thirty now. Almost thirty-one."

It was only that the park had been quiet and beautiful. She had been owning the park and the sky and the heavy-scented air. She had been asleep, maybe. Maybe she had been almost asleep when the woman appeared.

"That's good. You know what you're doing by then. We were too young, both of us. But I'm older than Billy. Twenty months. I should of known better."

"I was Caroline Thaxton."

"That's a coincidence, isn't it?" The woman said coincidence. "You're always running into coincidences. I came across myself in the telephone book in London, and I called myself up. You don't mind if I sit down?"

"Please."

"When the person answered I didn't know what to say. I said, 'This is Clara Tate.' I called myself Clara over the telephone. The other person said, 'So is this.' She sounded a million years old. She asked me to tea, but I couldn't go. That was when we were moving here." The woman had an easy laugh; it was not unpleasant. "I guess there aren't many people all over the world sitting together, talking, with the same initials. Isn't that something to think about?"

"Lewis. I don't know where Lewis is." She stood. Her knitting bag dropped, but she did not bother to stoop for it. "My son. On the tricycle. He should have been around by now. I wasn't thinking."

She staggered, like a drunk person.

She looked to the left where the path curved, to the right where the path rose a little. She took four steps, five, six, to look at the green pond. Lewis wasn't in sight. She came back to the woman. "He's not out there."

The woman was laughing again. "He's all right, honey. He and Buddy, they've found each other. They're having fun together, on the trikes. Sit down. Mercy! I said you looked upset." The woman laughed genuinely. "You don't have any reason to be upset. They have miles of paths around here."

"No. I . . ." She looked into the woman's blue eyes. "He's my husband's child. I . . ."

"Sit down." The woman was pulling at the hem of her skirt.

"I have to find him. I have to make sure."

She heard the tricycles before she saw them.

"Oh, boy," Lewis called. "We're having a race. We'll be back."

The other child, the cartoon boy, did not speak. His face was crimson.

"Buddy's slow," the woman said. "You wouldn't believe he's already five."

"He's . . . he's a nice child." She sat down.

"It's good for them to have each other. Buddy's been lonesome here. My God, so have I. I hate this place."

The baby in the carriage cried, and stopped crying.

"Another little boy? You're lucky." She leaned over to look into the carriage. She could not imagine why she had not looked into the carriage before.

The child slept. He was a vast child.

"No, that's Becky. She's slow, too. Sixteen months. She could walk if she wanted to." The woman laughed. "She's too fat for her own good. For my own good, too. How on earth do you keep such a lovely figure?"

"I don't. I don't know." She wasn't making sense.

"I always say 'Good enough.' About them being slow. They'll come out of it. Maybe they're easier to take care of when they're slow."

86

The woman's, Clar's, face was round. It was not an unpleasant face.

"She's a big girl."

"As a matter of fact I'm awful glad to meet you. Generally this place is empty as a graveyard." Everything was funny to Clar. "Of breathing people, I mean. Sometimes on Sunday you'll meet people, but not too much. But Buddy likes to come."

"I don't mean to be foolish about Lewis, to worry about him," she heard herself saying.

"You can't afford to, honey. My God!"

The woman settled herself heavily on the bench. She spread her legs. She pulled at her skirt. "My God!"

"It's turned out to be a nice day after all."

"Sun sure feels good, doesn't it?" Her huge legs were veined. "Yes. Yes."

They spoke as if they had only begun a conversation.

"We're supposed to have central heat in our apartment, but you wouldn't know it. My God."

"It's been quite cold. For six days, anyhow. We've been here six days, I think. Or seven. It's hard to keep track."

The woman breathed heavily, almost as if she slept. From her sleep she said, "It doesn't matter whether the boy is yours or your husband's. I wouldn't worry about it. A kid is a kid."

"What? Yes." The woman was not looking at her. Clar sat placid in the sun, like a turtle. "He's like my own child. I love him —that way. I didn't mean anything by what I said."

She thought of saying, "I'll take my knitting bag back. Thank you for holding it." She thought of saying, "We'll no doubt meet again." She thought of saying something polite.

"This morning I called Billy a goddamned fool. I almost forget what the argument was about now. Isn't that funny? He said I was one, too, a goddamned fool. He picked up his briefcase and he whammied out the door. He always carries a briefcase now. He works in the telephone accounts department, and he carries a briefcase. That's Billy for you. He was working for a construction

87

company when I met him in the States. Billy's done everything."

"Tom has always worked in the store."

Lewis appeared. The other child appeared.

"Lewis!"

"I'll be right back."

"I followed Billy to the door, but I didn't open it. I said, 'Are you coming home for lunch, Billy?' He didn't answer me. But he was standing in the hall, all right. I could hear him breathing. The elevator didn't come and didn't come, and I could hear him breathing."

The woman should have sounded outraged, or hurt, or sorrowful. Think nouns and verbs, Grandmother said.

"I just leaned against the door and waited until the elevator came. We have terrible service. Then Becky started crying. She'd dirtied herself. She can't stand to be dirty for long. I ought to of left her that way for a while, but I didn't. I was laughing. I kept hoping the elevator would stick. It sticks a lot of times. We have terrible service."

The sun shone. A fly buzzed. A sparrow swooped to the path, picked up something, flew away. There were no sparrows in Malta, somebody had told Tom, somewhere.

No, that was in Sicily. But people told Tom wrong. In Taormina she had sprinkled bread crumbs on the railing of the balcony. Sparrows came for the crumbs. And a wren.

"Me, too. That's another coincidence. I'm almost thirty-one, I mean." The woman shifted her cumbersome body. "Two people, girls, almost thirty-one years old, sitting on a bench in Malta." The woman laughed.

She did not say, "No, surely not." She said, "Yes, yes." She did not dare to ask the woman's birthday.

"Billy has always kept his Maltese citizenship, wherever we've been. He's crazy about Malta. A lot of places we had trouble with the papers, but Billy manages, the son of a bitch."

"We've kept our citizenship, too," she said, to cover the silence or the woman's words. She had almost never thought about the

88

word *citizenship.* An application blank? A certificate? When they applied for their passports?

Tom had taped a map to the kitchen wall. The map stretched from Ohio to Sicily. Oceans hung on the kitchen wall, deeper than any wells.

"I guess I hate men," Clar said. "But I guess we couldn't get along without them." Clar laughed at everything. "Is your husband any good. Any good?"

Caroline smoothed at her skirt. She was not sure she had heard the woman correctly. She was not sure she understood what the woman meant. "Yes, yes."

"Oh, well, a lot of women don't like to talk about it. Myself, I get tired of it. At night I say, 'God damn it, Billy, keep your hands to yourself.' But he can't keep his hands off me. There's Becky to prove it. You don't happen to have a match on you?"

"Match? No. No, I don't smoke."

"I have a lighter here, someplace." Clar pushed herself to her feet. She leaned over the carriage. Becky began to cry. "Shut up, for God's sake."

Becky shut up. Clar found her lighter. "Cigarettes are a lot cheaper here. They're terrible in England." She inhaled deeply. "Becky almost died when she was six months old. Pneumonia. I was worried sick. That's funny, too, isn't it?"

She thought of Becky's dying. She was cold suddenly. She could not imagine why she had sat listening.

"Don't be upset, honey," Clar said. "She got all right."

"Here I am, Mamma."

Buddy came behind.

"Hello, Lewis. Hello, hello."

"Guess who won?" Lewis was smirking.

"It's time. It's time we were getting home."

"Us, too, I guess. Billy'll be there. Mark my words. That man!"

"Good-bye, Buddy."

Buddy did not answer.

Clar dropped her cigarette. She ground at it with the heel of her house slipper. She seemed angry at the cigarette, turning her foot again and again. "Smokey the Bear, that's me." Clar had a sweet laugh.

Caroline laughed, too. It was important to laugh with Clar in the park under the sun.

"We'll meet again," Clar said. "You all must come up and visit us. I'll get Billy turned around a little. And you come up. You got to handle Billy. We'll have a drink together, or supper. Supper would be better."

"That's very kind. Of you. To think about."

"We'll probably meet tomorrow here."

"I'm not sure. Tom wants us to go into Valletta. He has planned."

"God damn you, Buddy. Quit acting dumb."

"Come on, Lewis. We must turn in your tricycle." It was difficult to look at Buddy or his mother. She could not imagine what Buddy had done that was wrong.

The slow day slowed.

They stood together, two women, and a baby carriage, and two boys with their tricycles.

"We just leave the trikes," Clar said. "The man's not here. They have terrible service."

"Bye-bye, Buddy," Lewis said.

At the gate Clar said, "I go this way. But we'll meet. I'm always here."

She had waited until Clar said, "I go this way."

She took Lewis's hand. "We go this way. Good-bye."

She and Lewis set off in the opposite direction.

They got home all right. Tom was already there.

"Guess what?" Lewis said.

She could not imagine what Lewis was going to say. But there had been no reason to worry.

"Come upstairs, Daddy."

She stood in the hall and listened.

"Look what Mamma made. Mamma is a clever."

Tom said, "I'm married to a clever."

That night the lamp worked beautifully. With a little rearranging it didn't shine in Tom's eyes. Tom said it was better than their lamps at home, and she should go into business.

She started the second mystery from the British Council library, but she didn't get very far with it.

She turned off the light and thought about the day.

The morning was bright. The sky looked as if it promised a perfect day.

The Shelltox had worked well last night. She swept up half a dustpan of flies. She emptied the dustpan in the garbage can under the sink. She covered the mound of flies with two paper towels.

A fly buzzed in the china closet. It moved from one stack of ugly orange glass to another, from cups to saucers, to plates, to the fruit bowl, to the cups again. It was a vast fly, like an illustration in *My Weekly Reader*.

It wasn't so big as a bird, of course it wasn't. It was only a fly. She was crazy, thinking about a bird moving among the orange glass.

She was almost afraid to open the china closet doors. She wasn't afraid, of course.

She opened both doors. She chased the fly. She killed it with yesterday's *Times*, on the very center of the refrigerator.

She filled the sink with the lovely hot water, two or three capfuls of the liquid soap; she was lucky that Saint Mary's carried the soap.

She washed the fruit first, the apples, oranges, bananas, and placed them in their clean bowl on the buffet. She was ridiculous. She worked feverishly. Of course all day the flies would wander the fruit. But fruits were covered with their own skins. The world was made that way.

After the fruit and bowl she started on the bottom shelf. There were five shelves of dishes.

"Hurry, hurry," she said to herself. She was washing bowls she had never noticed. Tall glasses. The house was terribly well equipped. A person should be grateful for the dishes.

The second shelf. The third. The fourth.

She tried not to think of the fly, its hairy legs, its bulging abdomen, the eyes looking at her.

She was just finishing. She had almost finished the last shelf when Tom came down.

"What on earth are you up to?"

She should have told him. It was stupid to keep secrets which weren't secrets.

"I'm just being housewifely."

"What do you mean? My gosh."

"A lot of these things, we've never used, we've never touched them. Who knows what kind of ailments the Royal Air Force suffered from? I've just been washing up."

"You're a funny girl." Tom blinked behind his glasses.

"I was just getting ready to call you."

"You haven't even turned on the oven yet."

"It's not cold, not very. I was just going to. I hadn't realized. It's a lovely day. It's not even cold yet." She was sounding like Lewis.

"Silly Caroline." He put his arms around her. He kissed her neck, and then her lips.

"I love you, Tom."

A fly wasn't anything. It was just a fly.

"Caroline."

"Let me go, Tom. Go wake Lewis. I love you."

She was humming to herself.

A roach scuttled across the top of the counter. But it wasn't dark brown. It was pale. For all its speed it looked dead.

She almost fell, rushing to the buffet for the Shelltox.

She pressed her forefinger so hard against the button of the can that her finger felt frozen. The pale bug stopped moving at the very edge of the refrigerator.

$\mathcal{H}$ e was sad over Marie's death. Of course he was. He'd felt terrible. But the funny thing about it, he hadn't felt as bad as people expected him to. They said things like . . .

Ellen said, "Poor Tom, how can you go on?" She was crying hard. He'd never seen her cry before. She was almost too ugly to look at, thin and tight—her face was like leather. She stayed out in the sun too much.

Marie's father was really broken up. He looked like an old old man. "I don't see much point in going on," Mr. Spencer said. "I never thought I'd say this, Tom. But I'm glad her mother's gone. I'm glad she's spared this." The old fellow was really pathetic. "I shouldn't act this way, Tom. I know it's your grief. But it's my grief, too."

"You were meant for each other," Ralph said. It didn't sound like Ralph. They stood in the funeral parlor by Marie's casket. She looked very pretty. But she still had that smirk on her mouth. Other people didn't notice it, evidently. Marie was always smirking—she thought she was better than anybody, she really did.

"She's so beautiful," Mrs. Fontaine said. A lot of people said that.

Ralph put his hand on his brother's shoulder. Ralph was crying, like a baby. Everybody cried. Naturally when you saw somebody else cry, your throat got tight. You got tears in your eyes.

"Poor baby," Ellen said, putting her arms around him.

Everybody touched him a lot during the funeral. He wasn't much of a toucher himself.

He and Marie had been twenty-four when they got married. Marie didn't want any children, not at first. "I'm satisfied with my life as it is," Marie kept telling everybody. It was almost ten years before she said, "Everybody has children. Everybody's a bore. We might as well be bores, too."

But she had had a hard pregnancy and delivery. "That's it, Tommy boy," she said when they let him in to see her at Sheltering Arms. He hated to be called Tommy. "I've had it. You've had it. You've had all your inheritors."

It was all right with him. At least he was able to be a father. He didn't want anybody unhappy over anything.

They had a good enough sex life. Not better than with Caroline, but different. Marie was rather wild. They had slept together before they were married. He didn't really like to think about it. It could have been messy. Being married to Caroline made you think different about things. He would hate for Caroline to know he and Marie had slept together before they were married—a good many times.

He wished he had a nickel for every time somebody had said, "You and Marie were meant for each other."

It was true enough.

Except he and Marie didn't have anything to tell each other. They knew everything there was to know, together: all their lives happened to them together, they hadn't needed to rearrange anything. They just kept on being themselves.

Marie was like part of himself dying, maybe, that was true enough. But you could do without a part of yourself every once in a while.

He didn't miss her. He hadn't missed her, not even at first. She was always out, at the club, or meetings. Or she always had people visiting. Marie had a lot of girl friends. Caroline didn't have many friends. That was funny to think about.

And Lewis got along fine with Althea Thompson.

"Mamma's dead. She's in heaven," he told Lewis as soon as Dr. McConkey called from the hospital. He didn't know what else to say.

Lewis was a soldier. "She won't come back?"

"No, but we'll get along fine."

And they had got along fine. He went back to the store the day after the funeral, even though Ralph had insisted that he take a vacation. "Why don't you go to the ocean somewhere, go to Virginia Beach or somewhere—Miami?" Ralph was always wanting somebody to go to the ocean.

"What would I do with Lewis? Take Lewis and Althea Thompson with me?"

"Why not? People would understand."

"Come on, Ralph. We're better off here."

"You owe it to yourself."

"Marie would want me to stay here." He said it just because it was something to say. It was what people were always saying. But it was a good thing to say. Marie wouldn't have cared. One way or another.

He had dreamed about Marie. They were on the front porch of her sorority house, on College Street. He was kissing her. It wasn't any different from kissing her on her own front porch, across town. That is what he had thought in the dream.

It was Caroline's fault. Caroline was always saying, "Guess what I dreamed last night?" "I was in the third grade, there was this girl named Bertha." "I was in high school." "I was working at the library, at the university." "I dreamed about your mother, Tom. And I never saw your mother."

"I dreamed a lot, too," Lewis said. "I dreamed about porpoises."

"I saw your mother so plainly—she looked like the snapshot, the one your father took on a beach somewhere."

He almost said, "Come off it, Caroline." But he didn't. It was good for her to be talking. After she lost the baby she had turned quiet. For a little while it had been hard to get her to talk at all.

"I dreamed about porpoises. What did you dream about, Daddy?"

"I can't remember. For the life of me I can't remember."

After Marie and the sorority porch, he was all of a sudden in that car his dad was so proud of—an old Buick with a lot of chrome. His father was driving. Generally Ralph sat up front and Tom sat in the back with his mother. But he was in the front seat. He was Ralph.

Somebody said, "Tommy is a prissy boy."

He wasn't prissy. He wasn't attracted to people who were prissy. Look at Marie. And Caroline wasn't prissy. She had almost shocked him when she said she was going to the doctor to be fitted for a diaphragm. "I'll have to have the little operation, too."

"The pill?" He didn't know what to say. Maybe it was because he kept thinking she was so much younger than he was.

"My new book says diaphragm." She spoke as naturally as anything. "You do want to have children, don't you, Tom? Pretty soon?"

"Sure, Caroline. Why, of course, honey."

"We're not getting any younger. We'll wait a little while. We don't want people to think you had to marry me."

"Really, Caroline."

"I'm being forward. You've made me forward, Tom." She leaned against him. They were standing by that old desk in her apartment. They were kissing. Back then, she had been more relaxed. Losing the baby, that was too bad.

"I don't mind sleeping where you and Marie slept," she said. Back then she mentioned Marie a lot, too much. "I'm not afraid of ghosts. Marie is Lewis's mother. I think she might like me, too. Wouldn't she? She would want you to get married. She'd like me, wouldn't she?"

She talked too much; but it had all been pretty easy.

96

"Everybody would be crazy about you," he said, and they were kissing again.

It had been easy to talk to Caroline back then.

"I don't put much store in dreams," he told Lewis. "We ate too much last night. Those chops were good, too good."

The doorbell rang. They looked at each other. Lewis was out of his chair.

"No, I'll get it."

It was only the mailman. His bicycle leaned against the wall. "Mr. Hutton. Mail for you. A letter from the States."

The young man was very polite. He had a nice way of saying your name.

"Thank you very much." It was a letter from Ralph.

The young man stood for a minute. He wore a dark suit and a dark necktie.

Tom wanted to do what was right. He felt maybe he should tip the fellow, or shake his hand, or invite him inside for a cup of coffee—something. You wanted to do what was right, but you didn't want to be dumb. He worried about it. But one of the fellows at the bar had said, "Of course you don't tip a mailman. You give him something at Christmas and you won't be here." It was a big joke to the fellow.

"Have a good day," he said to the mailman.

"What is it?" Lewis stood on his knees in his chair.

"A letter from Uncle Ralph. They forwarded it from Taormina. That's good service, isn't it?"

"Read it, Daddy. Read it to us."

"Isn't it funny?" Caroline said. "I'm always expecting some great news—I don't know what. Money. I've won a Nobel Prize or the Academy Award." She spread her hands. It was a pleasure to look at Caroline. She was just fine. "It's not that I'm not delighted to hear from Ralph."

It wasn't much of a letter, but it was pretty good for Ralph. He said they were having a great run on galoshes. "You should stay away for a year or two. We'd be millionaires. The store's fine.

97

Everybody asks about you. Tell Caroline we appreciated her letter. Ellen has read it around to several people. Seriously, enjoy yourselves. We had more snow, four inches, last night. I guess you can't imagine that."

Ralph signed the letter "Love," the way they had signed all of their letters, from camp, or college, or the service. "You always sign a letter to your family with 'Love,' " his mother said. "That's the way you sign letters to your family."

Even his father signed "Love" on postcards, from a New York buying trip. "The train was late. I got the same hotel room I had last time. Hope you are all well. Love."

But his folks never talked about love. Nobody would ever have said, "What is love?"

Last night, in bed, Caroline asked, "What is love? But I love you, Tom."

After they had had sex last night Caroline said, "I feel like crossing myself, the way women do at the shrine up at the corner." That is exactly what she said before she went to sleep.

Sometimes Caroline could be almost scary. Her eyes could turn bright, as if somebody had put lights behind them. Her eyes had been brighter than the moon. What could he say to her?

What did his folks talk about?

They certainly didn't talk about love, or sex.

They didn't talk about religion. They went to church. The Huttons had practically kept the church up, for years and years. A great-grandfather had been the first minister. They always had a blessing before meals. "Lord, we thank Thee for these blessings we are about to receive. Bless this food to our use and us to Thy service. For Jesus' sake, Amen."

He still said grace. The first night he and Lewis and Caroline had eaten together, after the little wedding trip to New York, he told Caroline, "We usually have a blessing. But it's all right. Either way."

"I'm glad," Caroline said. "We always had a blessing."

"It doesn't hurt any, I guess." He was embarrassed.

Lewis helped out with the blessing now. He liked to say it.

His folks didn't talk about money, not money as figures. His dad said business was good or bad. So did Ralph. You couldn't imagine Ralph writing, "We grossed such and such last week."

Now that he thought about it he guessed they talked about people mostly. Who came in the store, and who was sick or getting married or going on a trip.

The paraffin man came before they finished breakfast.

When they were through breakfast, he sat at the table and read Lewis the sky book again. He wished he'd never bought it; it was a dull book, about the sun and moon, and naming the kinds of clouds. Lewis liked the sound of the names of the clouds. That boy was the limit.

"One more time."

"That's plenty. We've got to get away from here."

Caroline stood in the kitchen door. She was through with ridding up.

"That was a good breakfast," he said, as he always said, though for a minute he couldn't remember what they'd had to eat. "I'll go down and get a paper, and then we'll be off."

"Off? Off?" Caroline looked dreamy. For a minute he expected her to say something about having sex last night—hint something. She wouldn't have said anything straight out, not in front of Lewis. She was very careful about Lewis. But she could have hinted something. He wished she would. But she never did. She was a funny girl.

"To Valletta. We're going to Valletta, aren't we?"

"No, no. I thought we said tomorrow. Those places. They're damp and cold. Don't you remember how it was in Taormina? That church, by the park, and . . ." She was hardly listening to herself.

"You're well, aren't you, boy?"

"I never was so well. But I like to ride on the tricycle, too."

She moved around them to the buffet, and stood with her back to them. She reached out and turned the vase of flowers, a couple of times. "I have to shop. The cleaning girl's coming tomorrow. I have to get ready for the cleaning lady; you know how I am." She turned, laughing at herself. "I couldn't be ready for a long time. I'd rather you went on."

"I'll wait. I'm not in any big hurry."

"No, really. I'd rather not. Tomorrow will be a better day."

"It may rain tomorrow."

"No, please, Tom." She sat down at the table. She was all right. She reached out and put her hand over his. "Not today. We'll count on tomorrow."

He could have insisted more. But there wasn't any point in having an argument. They had plenty of time for sightseeing. And he hated to wait around.

He bought the paper, and then he caught a bus at the stop up the street. All of the buses had the same words printed behind the driver's cage. Sometimes the letters were painted, and sometimes they were fancy decals:

VERBUM DEI

CARO

FACTUM EST

He should have been able to figure out what the words meant. He would remember to ask somebody. This time the shrine by the driver's head was a crucifix, very bloody, with the usual plastic flowers and the Christmas tree bulb.

There was an article in the paper on The Feast of Saint Paul's Shipwreck. Some doings were coming up, all over Malta. He wanted to read the paper, but there were too many things to look at. A fellow could keep busy with just looking around him. A box by the entrance said:

KAXXA GHALL

BILJETTI WZATI

BOX FOR USED TICKETS

He couldn't figure how to pronounce the words, but he wrote them down in his notebook.

ZOMMU MALTA NADIFA

KEEP MALTA TIDY

He hadn't dreamed about Saint Paul.

He didn't think about when he was a kid, not much. When he thought about the past it was about a time not very long ago. When Marie died. When he met Caroline that night at Ralph's, and the picnic out at Dow Lake. "When you're away from home, you're all the ages you've ever been." That's what Caroline said.

A big fat man sat down beside him. The man was up in years. The seats weren't very comfortable, and they didn't really have room enough for two grown men.

The man said something.

"Looks a little like rain, doesn't it?"

The man turned sideways, turning his head to the opposite window.

But the people were kind in Malta, generally.

He got off at Floriana and caught a bus to Saint Paul's Bay. He did it on the spur of the moment.

It was a pretty place and practically deserted. The waves were high, and all colors—blue and green and black and purple. He sat on a bench and looked at the bay for a good while. There was an island out in the water. He figured that the island was where Saint Paul landed after the shipwreck. There was something about snakes, too, but he couldn't exactly remember.

He caught a bus back into Valletta. The shrine on the bus had a silver Mary with Jesus on her lap; they were plastic. Mary looked very sad.

Through

It wasn't quite six o'clock. She was getting up earlier all the time; Tom was sleeping later. It was good for him. Tom had been working in the store forever; even in high school he had worked afternoons and Saturdays. It was wonderful the way he was able to adjust to Malta.

She dressed quietly, clenching her teeth to keep them from chattering. She put on pantyhose, and the long wool stockings, and her green and blue plaid suit. She carried her shoes to the second landing. Tom did not stir.

She loved waking the house. She could make as much noise downstairs as she liked. It was a strong, quiet house. Tom and Lewis couldn't hear her, no matter how much noise she made.

She turned the key to unlock the inner front doors. She undid the little latch. She pulled down the top bolts of the outside doors, pulled up the bottom ones. She turned the Yale lock.

She stamped back to the courtyard. She opened the shutters, but not the doors. She would open them later, when the front doors were closed. With both sets of doors open, the wind controlled the house.

You had to wake the house noisily. The latches, the bolts were old. The hinges didn't move easily. The house needed its sleep, and it needed to be waked.

Here, she never thought of going downstairs once they had settled in bed. At home she was always slipping down, for a glass of milk, switching on the kitchen radio to hear people talk in Chicago or Philadelphia, to walk about the living room, to turn the pages of a book, to straighten the magazines, listening to the purr of the furnace. The house at home never slept. Houses in Athens did not have to be waked or put to bed. They kept their draperies open, the furniture waiting for people, any time.

It was Tuesday. The house in Birzebbuga looked fine: the kitchen, the dining room, the hall, the living room. She had prepared for the cleaning woman. But she wouldn't be coming until nine. "Nine," the dark landlady had said. "Niiine."

She stepped into the street. The street was monotone. On the left side of the bay the colored doors were pasted on the monotone. Today the sky was clear enough, she was early enough, for a sunrise. It was blue and pink again, childish colors, and beautiful, the colors Lewis would choose from a crayon box for the sunrise.

Television aerials hung all over the sky, some as simple as crosses for a crucifixion, some as complicated as space machines. Tom had decided not to rent a television set. "No car, no television, no radio—we're going native." Tom was pleased with himself.

Other people were awake; they were even more comforting than the night radio voices of Chicago and Philadelphia. The girl from the C. and S. walked solidly down the street, her head lowered.

"Good morning, Natalie."

"Good morning, madame."

"Don't tell me you're going to open the store already."

"We almost never close. I wish somebody else would open the store. It's my aunt's doing."

"It's a lovely morning." She was sounding like Tom, but that was all right, that was good.

The girl looked surprised. "Yes. Yes, it is."

106

She was glad Tom was outgoing. She must remember that she was glad Tom was the way he was, particularly when they got back to Athens. When you made fun of somebody, you exaggerated whatever it was that bothered you. And the exaggerations turned out to be the truth, and you exaggerated more. She wasn't going to be like Ellen, and a lot of other wives. Making fun, satire, turned out to be as true as what you started making fun of.

Of course there wasn't time to walk clear to the park. She didn't really know whether she could find it without Lewis.

But there would be time, if she hurried. The gates would probably be closed. There wouldn't be anything but the gates and the medallions on the posts and the inscriptions under the medallions of the women.

Clar would not be waiting at the garden. Clar was in her apartment, in bed with Billy. If they were awake, Billy was thinking up something outrageous.

She passed the cobbler's and headed toward the church.

The sky was quiet. It had run out of pink and blue crayons.

She turned right.

"All right."

"Good morning." It was the lame man, the chemist. She couldn't imagine why he was out so early.

"Beautiful morning," the man said.

She was at Saint George's Bay. She turned so quickly that she almost fell. She was awkward.

She ran.

At the church she took the back street. She didn't want to overtake the lame man. She turned at Saint Anne's Lane. She came out on Pretty Bay. She almost ran into the lame man. But it was all right. "Exercise, all right," the man said.

"Yes. Yes, I need it." It was all right.

The doors had slammed shut. But she had taken off the lock.

Tom and Lewis were still asleep. She stood in the hall under the skylight and called softly. Nobody answered. But she was awake, and she had waked the house again.

107

Because Mrs. Lovell at home—because Marie's cleaning woman was old, she had expected the cleaning woman to be old. For Mrs. Lovell she planned little activities, polishing the silver, vacuuming the couch cushions. "Isn't this awful weather, though," Mrs. Lovell said, whatever the weather. "It makes me so blue. Sometimes I don't think I can stand it any more."

She had barely finished fixing the soup and sandwiches for lunch when the doorbell rang. "I have come to clean for you," a girl said. It was five minutes before nine. "My uncle sent me." She spoke beautifully.

"Good morning. I'm Caroline Hutton."

The girl said something.

"I didn't quite catch your name."

"Catch?"

"Your name. What are you called? What do people call you by?" She felt hopelessly provincial. She could not speak simply. "What is your name?"

"Agatha."

The girl was probably twenty-one. She was tall. Her black hair, parted in the middle, curled around her shoulders. She carried several string bags. She wore a scarf around her head, a blue uniform, a light blue sweater. Her hips were large. Perhaps her hips would grow as large as the hips of the Maltese Venus. But she was beautiful.

"What a pretty name. Come in. Come on in."

"I am named for the secondary saint of Malta."

"You can hang your things here, here on the rack in the hall. Agatha. It's a lovely name." She wanted to be pleasant. "You wouldn't want to be called Paul, would you, or Paula?" She wanted the girl to know she appreciated the history of Malta.

"Agatha." The girl frowned. She did not offer her last name. It was hardly fair for a person to give only a part of a name. "I have come to clean, madame."

"My husband and son, they are still asleep. We have new habits

108

in Malta. Generally Tom is out of bed by . . ." There was no reason to apologize for Tom's sleeping.

The girl waited.

"You've cleaned before? This house, I understand."

"The Air Force family. She did not want for me to clean very well."

"Not want?" She was sounding as if she spoke in translation. Perhaps she could tell someone about her foolishness, to make herself seem less foolish. Maybe Clar would think the conversation was funny.

"She did not want to buy materials."

"Materials?"

"For cleaning. The house is very dirty. The English lady possessed five children and a very dirty dog."

"You're welcome. To materials."

"Disinfectant. Brass polish. Scouring powder. Steel wool. Cleaning cloths. The other lady did not wish for the house to be cleaned well. I will be glad to fetch materials."

"You'll need some money." She walked around the quiet-voiced girl. She took her purse from the console table, under the picture of Jesus. "I have five pounds. I just have only five pounds."

"That is too much, madame."

"They'll give you change. Get what you need. Saint Mary's is opened." She spoke slowly and loudly, as if the girl were an addled old woman.

"I know, madame."

"Of course you do."

As soon as Agatha was out of the house she ran upstairs to wake Lewis and Tom. "Hurry, Tom. The cleaning girl's here." She pulled Tom's covers back.

Lewis sat up straight. "What's the matter? Is the house on fire?"

"Oh, Lewis."

In the other room Tom laughed. "Almost the same thing,

Lewis. It's cleaning lady day." Tom stood at the door. "You know how it is at home when Mrs. Lovell comes."

"Don't tease me, Tom."

But she didn't mind. It was one of their jokes together.

Lewis understood. He giggled. "At home I have to sit in the front yard all day." He was making a grown-up joke.

"You. You, Lewis." She tickled the bottoms of his feet.

They were a family.

She gave them cold cereal and fruit and milk. "There's not time for anything more."

"We know, we know," Tom said.

They were at the table when Agatha came back.

"Agatha, this is my husband. This is my son, Lewis." She was afraid Lewis was going to ask the girl's other name.

Tom got up from the table. He shook hands with Agatha. Lewis put his napkin beside his plate. He was standing up and shaking hands, too.

If she wasn't careful, she was going to cry.

"Now, let me see . . ."

"Your money, madame. I will show you." Agatha headed for the kitchen. There was nothing to do but follow. Tom winked.

The girl took the materials from her string bag, naming the cost of each item. "The price amounted to . . . From the five pounds I received . . ." She counted out the change, enunciating the name of each coin and bill. It was a pleasure to hear her speak. "Is that adequate, madame?"

"Wonderful. Why, yes, just fine. Yes, of course." She wished Tom and Lewis were not listening to her chatter.

Tom and Lewis had finished eating. Tom said, "I am disappearing. I'll see you tonight."

"Shhh."

"What did I say wrong? Do you want me to come back tomorrow night?"

"Oh, Tom." He was in fine fettle. He kissed her. It was a lovely morning.

After Tom had gone, she tried to be helpful. "Let me do something, Agatha. You tell me what to do."

"Rest, madame."

"Maybe I need to shop. Lewis and I need to do some shopping."

"I will be here."

It was a wonderful morning.

At the vegetable truck she stood in line behind a pleasant English lady. "And what is your name, sir?" The lady smiled down at Lewis.

At home he had been impatient standing at the check-out counter at Kroger's or the A & P. Often Lewis was tired and whining. At home she changed lines, changing for the worse: the person in front of her wanted to cash a check, or decided to run back for a can of tuna; the tape in the cash register collapsed. "I'll check with the manager," the clerk said, and Lewis whined, "Let's go home, Mamma. Why don't we go home?"

Lewis waited patiently. "My name is Lewis Thomas Hutton, Athens, Ohio," he told the lady. "But I really live at Twenty Pretty Bay."

"Lovely! Lovely!"

She didn't mind waiting. She studied the beautiful vegetables. She didn't know the names of all of them.

"Good-bye, Lewis Thomas Hutton," the lady said.

They moved forward in line.

Many of the customers spoke Maltese to the handsome young man who owned the truck—he was short, shorter than Tom.

"Cauliflower, please, yes, that much, yes a little more. And the beans." She was not in a hurry.

The park would wait, was waiting.

The vegetable truck stood comfortable under the sky. "And carrots. We haven't had carrots for several days."

He wrapped each purchase deftly in a cornucopia of newspaper. She placed the newspaper cones in her shopping basket.

A couple of evenings she had seen the young man standing in

front of the Courageous. He wore a light suit, a lavender shirt, and a purple tie; he looked decadent. Here, under the sky, in his Levi's and gray sweater, he was admirable.

"Cheerio, madame. Cheerio, Master Lewis," the young man said.

Agatha had attacked all of the house at once. The doors and windows stood wide open. The brisk air tore through the house. Tom's newspapers fluttered on the coffee table. The stair matting and the throw rugs hung on the line in the courtyard. In the kitchen Agatha scrubbed on her hands and knees.

"Agatha, my goodness!" She placed the groceries on the dining room table. "My goodness, Agatha."

The brass spigots of the sink shone bright enough for a church altar. But the house was full of flies.

"You're sure I can't help you? You should let me do something."

"I know the house, madame."

"You're marvelous. I feel helpless."

Agatha stood on her knees. She wrung out one of the new cloths. "Thank you, madame."

She had not meant to say, "The flies. But the flies."

Agatha smiled. Her hands paused. She looked like a religious painting, something in one of the churches.

"No difficulty, madame. I will attend to them before I leave."

"How? How?" She started to walk into the wet kitchen, as if the girl were offering her salvation. Caroline Thaxton was a silly goose.

"Before I leave, I will close the doors until only a fraction of air enters. With a cloth, a tea towel, I will direct the flies to the openings. That is all."

She imagined Agatha performing a ceremony. The girl would surely say something to the flies.

She was cold. She hugged herself. "But that's marvelous."

Lewis said, "I think I'm hungry again."

"They leave, the flies. They do not want to stay with you."

112

"That's funny," Lewis said.

"It's not time to eat, Lewis. We'll . . . we'll . . ."

There was no place to get away from Agatha. For a little while they sat on Lewis's bed, playing the naming game. "What is the name of a car, Mamma?"

"Let me see. No, I can't think." She loved the game, but she honestly couldn't think. *"Now, this is now. I must think now."*

They had started the game on the *Raffaello*. The deck was almost deserted when they saw the porpoises.

"What on earth are those, Mamma?"

"I think they're porpoises. They must be."

The porpoises jumped the horizon, like imaginary animals. She had been as excited as Lewis. "Careful. Hold tight to the rail."

A Frenchwoman joined them. She made kissing sounds to Lewis.

She was angry, no, sorry, that the woman had appeared. The moment of seeing the mammals under the bright sky, alone with Lewis, was a delicate moment. As a child, reading Genesis—for years she had read the Bible every day—she had asked herself what everything would be called if Adam had not done the calling first. "Porpoises."

Extending the moment into a joy she could hardly contain, Lewis asked, "What would they be named if they had some other name?" The child had read her mind. He couldn't read her mind, of course.

There were other people around now. "Look. Looka there," a man called.

She held tightly to the railing to keep herself from embracing Lewis.

"Impossible," the Frenchwoman said.

"What would you have named them, Lewis?"

"I say . . . *jumps*. Is that all right?"

"Yes, I'd call them that, too."

"Look at 'em go," the man shouted.

113

"What is a rabbit, Mamma? What is the name of a cat? I think a sparrow is named *spit*. Is that all right?"

"It is probably a very good name." *Now, now,* she told herself. Now Agatha appeared. Agatha was everywhere in the house. "I will come back another time."

"No, please. We're just . . . No, please."

They moved into the front bedroom. She had almost forgot that the front bedroom existed.

She had been in the room only once, twice: that first afternoon, and another time. She had rarely even looked into the dark room with the closed curtains.

The room was big and bright. Agatha had opened the French doors to the postage-stamp balcony. The curtains, the same cretonne fans of the living room couch covers, billowed into the room. Flies circled. A person should expect flies in a house without screens.

They stood on the balcony for a few minutes, looking down into the street: a baby buggy, a man with a ladder, a truck full of lumber, a cart and a horse, an old man with a cane. The bay was dirty blue.

"It's funny, isn't it, Mamma?"

"Yes."

"You don't have to hold my hand so tight."

"Excuse me."

She tried to imagine why Tom had not chosen the balcony room for Lewis or for themselves. The colors were terrible, of course. The armoire and the dressing table and the two chests were painted a dark lavender, with mustard yellow drawer handles. The walls were a sick yellow. But Tom wasn't particularly conscious of color. And none of the bedrooms was beautiful.

There were twin beds, army cots painted mustard. The pink mattresses looked clean, and comfortable enough. The flies moved slowly.

"You lie down there, and I'll lie down here, and we'll go back to the game."

114

She had not noticed the wicker baby basket. It was on the floor, in the corner, between the armoire and the wall. It was yellow. Its handles had been painted lavender.

She started not to notice the basket, at least not to mention it.

"They had five children, the English people," she said.

"What is a good name for baby?"

"The baby must have slept in here. With two other children. Over there in the corner. The basket."

Lewis sat up to look. "The littlest baby?"

She was pleased with herself for having been willing to point out the basket. She was relieved with herself.

"Five is a whole lot of children."

Agatha was at the door.

"Look, Agatha. We'll get out of your hair. Out of the way." She stood.

"No, madame, I wanted to ask a question of you. I do not like to ask the question."

"Of course."

The girl stood on one foot, her right foot behind her left ankle. She looked no older than Lewis. She held a cloth tightly in her hands.

"Yes?"

"My uncle told me I will receive ten shillings, for the work, for the time I am here."

"I think that is what Tom said. But it's not enough. I was planning to give you more. It will be fine with Tom. You clean so well. I'll talk to him."

"No, no, madame. That is sufficient. I want to ask. Will it be convenient . . . inconvenient? Will you give me six shillings and keep the four, when I come to clean, until your departure from Malta? Then I will have the fours together."

She couldn't understand. "Of course. I just don't see . . ." She was ashamed of herself for being stupid.

"If it's not inconvenient."

"Of course not. If you tell me . . ."

115

She wished Tom were there. He was always wonderful with Mrs. Lovell. Tom knew how to manage situations.

Lewis sat on his knees on the other bed. "Tell her," he said.

Agatha half raised her head and smiled at Lewis. "Thank you very kindly." She had a sweet smile. She turned.

"No, please."

Agatha still did not look at her. The girl spoke haltingly. She lived with her parents, who were old. The father was retired with a pension of ten pounds a month. She made one pound a week for cleaning at the bank; she had another cleaning job. Her parents demanded all of her money. She wanted to get married, to a carpenter, a splendid carpenter, Manuel. "My fancy," she called him. She needed at least eighty pounds. "A bride must have her furniture."

It was difficult to listen to the girl. She wanted to listen well. The student couple who had moved into Grandmother's apartment had offered to buy the desk for twenty dollars. She had given them the desk and chair.

"Eighty pounds? It must be very fine furniture." She was sounding like somebody she didn't know very well, or didn't like. It was dreadful to be a rich American. "I mean, I'm sure it will be very nice."

His mother would not let him marry a bride without furniture for the bedroom.

Funny Lewis was nodding, as if he understood everything.

"Madame. If it is not inconvenient, you will save the four shillings. Thank you, madame."

"Agatha." But the girl was out of the room. Her feet scuffed the stone stairs.

"Come on, Lewis. We'll take a nice walk."

"The tricycle place?"

"I don't know. We'll see."

Agatha was scrubbing the floor by the china closet.

"I've already fixed sandwiches, for all of us. There's soup to

116

heat. Whatever you want to drink. Lewis and I will take our sandwiches for a picnic. Is that all right with you?"

"Thank you, madame."

"Ham and chicken salad. I hope you like that. On the good Maltese bread."

"You have a bread card?" Agatha looked up at her. At least the girl was willing to look at her.

"Not really. The lady at C. and S. She orders for me, on her card. I don't really understand. At first I thought the lady said, 'Russian card.' I misunderstood ration, I guess." She was babbling.

"You must be careful." Agatha was solemn. "The men on the trucks, some of the shopkeepers, they have two prices. One is for the foreigners. I can shop for you, if you wish."

"Thank you, thank you, no. Everything is very inexpensive."

She was sorry the girl was suspicious of the Maltese. "Come on, Lewis."

"Good-bye, Mrs. Agatha," Lewis said.

"Your money. It's on the buffet. Six shillings. That's what you said. I'll save the other for you. And we'll probably be back before you leave. In case we aren't . . ."

At the door she turned right instead of left.

"This isn't the way to go, Mamma."

"No. Yes, of course." They turned.

She did not really pray to Clar. She did not really say, "Be there. Be there, Clar. Come to the bench, Clar." She did not say to herself, "Talk to me, Clar."

At the gate she had almost said, "We really shouldn't leave Agatha alone. We should go back."

"Good morning, Master Lewis. Good morning, madame," the man at the wicket said.

The sweater was coming along fine. She did not thrust her mind toward Clar's. "I'm always here," Clar had said.

117

But she had not expected her. She had honestly not expected her.

She did not pray to Clar. She did not say, "Come, come."

They ate their sandwiches on the bench. Lewis drank his milk from the Thermos bottle. He refused a cup. She did not press him.

"I'll ride a little more now," Lewis said.

"Maybe you shouldn't exercise so soon after eating."

"I'll exercise quiet."

Time was long.

Agatha still worked at 20 Pretty Bay when they got home.

She told Tom about Agatha after they were in bed. "What do you think, Tom? We could give her something. What do you think, Tom?"

"She's your project. Whatever you want."

The light from the bedlamp shone on Tom's hair. He was getting gray.

"But I feel, I don't know. I wish she hadn't said that about people cheating. I wish I could be sure she wasn't just . . . just playing me. I don't want to be dumb, Tom. I don't want to be sentimental."

He kissed her cheek. "That's what's wrong with all of us, I guess." He flopped over on his side.

"I want to be good. I don't want to be dumb-good. She's the best cleaner in the world. Maybe I ought to wait to see how she turns out."

"Maybe." Already Tom sounded asleep.

"That's cowardly, isn't it?"

"Not necessarily. Good night."

"Being a parent or a child or a grandchild, being any-body . . ."

Tom breathed evenly.

She was glad she had mentioned Agatha. She had almost kept the girl and the dowry furniture a secret. That would have been terrible. A person got in the habit of keeping secrets—of making secrets, even. In a while everything could become a secret, and you wouldn't have anything to say to anybody.

"Lewis is all right, I tell you." Tom was almost asleep. He was wearing his bathrobe over his pajamas. She wore her long-sleeved yellow sweater over her nightgown. They were a cumbersome pair. "We're not arguing. We're getting along just fine. We'll make out. You're a good girl, Caroline. We'll make out. We'll make out just fine."

In the next room Lewis slept. The Huttons slept easily.

"Come to supper," Caroline said once to Edie Bratton. "We may be low on meat, but we'll make out."

"Oh, what you said!" Edie clasped her hands over her mouth. "I didn't mean anything."

Caroline Thaxton had never dated much. She didn't like the word *dates*. Or *going steady. Making out.* She wasn't sure what the words meant. The words changed. Words meant for such a little while. "We'll make out," Grandmother said, when there wasn't enough money to last until the first of the month.

Ignorance was painful to remember. It was another word for stupidity.

It wasn't Grandmother's fault—you had to be fair. She had reared her granddaughter the way she had been reared herself. It was difficult to be reared in your own time, much less somebody else's.

120

When people touched, even when they allowed their words to touch each other, even if they had been born in the same century together, you ran the chance of being stupid.

In high school she told herself, "I love I. L. Murphree." They had necked, whatever the word, in the back seat of Tilly Craddock's car, out by Indian Rock. Tilly was with somebody named Walter.

"I love you, I. L.," she said, pretending not to notice his moving hands.

Tilly and I. L. were married that July the fourth. Tilly was pregnant. They were married in the Episcopal church. Tilly's wedding gown was full-skirted, but everybody knew she was pregnant. Grandmother refused to go to the wedding. Caroline had to go by herself. As chance would have it, she sat beside Walter.

Walter said, "It's really hot today, isn't it?"

She said, "Yes, isn't it?" She knew her face was as red as the carnations in the silver vases on the altar. Tilly had a red, white, and blue wedding.

But she had defended Tilly. "It was a lovely wedding, Grandmother. I'm sorry you wouldn't go with me. I felt silly, all by myself. Anyhow, this is the twentieth century."

"There is no shame any more. Promise me, Caroline. Before God. Promise your old grandmother you will never allow a boy . . . liberties."

"I won't, Grandmother. I don't think I will." She thought about I. L.'s hands. "But some things you can't promise, exactly. You never can tell, for sure, what will happen to you. I mean, what kind of situation you may be in. I mean . . ."

If her grandmother had asked about the night at Indian Rock, she would have told the truth. "Not anything, Grandmother. Not anything, really. But almost. Maybe almost." It was impossible to imagine lying to Grandmother. Lies were almost impossible to imagine. But secrets? Secrets weren't exactly lies.

They had quarreled. All of their life together had been a kind of quarrel.

"Promise me, before God! Whatever will become of you!"

"I'll turn out all right."

"I can only pray."

Grandmother shook her head and stalked into the kitchen to fix supper. It was baked potatoes, just right, and an herb meat loaf, a recipe Grandmother had made up. But it had been difficult to eat. If she let herself, she would remember the tines of her fork, toying with the meat loaf. Grandmother had saved Betty Crocker coupons forever to buy the stainless steel knives and forks and soup spoons and butter spreaders. She had saved coupons for eight of everything. "In case a lot of company drops in." But they never had a lot of company, not even after Uncle Fred went to the asylum.

Grandmother said it would be all right to ask Jerry Hawks for supper sometime, but Jerry never came. Twice, three times she had asked him.

They had gone out together to a hockey game and a basketball game. She had her own ID card, so she wasn't any expense to him. They had been to a play, too, *J.B.*

Clar Tate would not have given I. L. or Jerry a second thought.

Grandmother said, "She it is who is pure and clean, she it is who is the queen."

Clar would laugh at the rhyme.

"Whatever will become of you, Caroline?"

"Just what you want. Just exactly what you want to," she said, ashamed of herself.

In Athens they had changed their roles.

Grandmother had retired after her year's teaching in Coolville, the same year Caroline started teaching in Athens.

"Just exactly what you wanted."

She was the one going out. She was the one who came home to fix supper, to tell stories about the children. "Guess what Betty Pat Leach said today? You can't imagine the picture Karen decided to draw. Do you know what Henry Hornsby came up with in show and tell?"

Her grandmother's hands were like claws. Arthritis was a disease of the mind—that's what a newspaper article said. Her grandmother's hands were frozen claws. "I've done something to her," Caroline thought. "Dear God, forgive me."

"Guess what Laura Vimont told the class, the whole class?"

She had made up stories to amuse the old woman. Perhaps the old woman had made up stories to amuse her granddaughter, all these years, for all these years.

"Thank you, Jerry. It's been a perfectly marvelous evening."

She said, "I like you, Jerry. I like you very much. I want you to know that." They were her very words. They were not her words. She had read them in a magazine article, in a *Woman's Day*, from the A & P.

They worked in the library together. He was poor, poorer than she was. He came from Vinton County. "Good morning, little beauty," he said at first. "Who's sweet and clean and ready to be kissed?"

She was frightened of Jerry. And she had frightened him.

There had been an instructor in the history department, Franklin Quigley.

"Careful of him," Celeste in requisitions said. Celeste was thirty-five. She wore tight skirts, and her hair was a bushel of curls. "They say he already has thirteen notches in his belt, and it's not even Thanksgiving yet."

She had acted skittish. She had babbled. From the moment he had called at the rooming house until he brought her home she had not stopped talking.

"How did it go last night?" Celeste raised her painted brows.

She had cried. All of a sudden, there in the library stacks.

Celeste tried to comfort her. "I didn't mean anything. Poor baby."

"Please. Just leave me alone."

She had tried to apologize to Celeste. But she was awkward. "I'm sorry, Celeste. It was silly to cry."

Celeste had been cool to her for the rest of the year.

The instructor had not asked for a date again, but he had been pleasant when she checked out his books.

She loved her grandmother. Perhaps everybody felt guilty when somebody died. Maybe nobody was able to love enough to feel guiltless in the presence of death.

Bless us all. Bless Lewis and Tom and Becky and Buddy. Bless Clar.

She was tired.

She was tired of being anxious and tentative and guilty.

None of Tom's books said that you had to bring all of the past with you when you traveled. But you brought everybody with you, unsorted.

"I have a son," Tom said that first night as he had driven her home from Ralph and Ellen's. "He would have been here tonight except he has a bad cold. I got a sitter from the university. The girl who generally takes care of him was busy. She had a date. I expect she'll get married. Her name is Althea Thompson."

She had not imagined that Mr. Ralph Hutton's brother was married. "I . . . I didn't know."

At first she had not caught the name of the man sitting across the dining room table. She was seated between the twins. She had talked mostly to the twins, Beryl and Marilyn. She made little jokes. The girls laughed at all of her jokes. "Oh, Miss Thaxton," they said together.

Tom stopped his car in front of her place. "This is it?"

"Yes, thank you." She started to open the door.

"My wife died. Three months ago, four months. You didn't know?"

"No, no. Oh, I'm sorry."

"Yes, it's too bad. It's all right you didn't know. It was a nice evening, wasn't it?"

"It was a lovely evening."

"They are nice girls. Ralph and Ellen have a nice boy, too. He's in Oregon. He's with the Forestry Service. The twins say you've been their best teacher."

124

"My grandmother died in March. I was living with her; she was living with me. We lived together here. In half of the house, a little apartment."

"It's hard to take, I guess."

"Yes, it keeps being hard." She spoke naturally. She wasn't thinking up words to say.

The car windows were down. The air was sweet. From somewhere a radio sounded a slow old-fashioned tune.

He will ask me to marry him, she said to herself before she knew what she was thinking.

"We're getting along fine, Lewis and I. Everybody's been mighty nice. Lewis is a real soldier. It's remarkable the way people can adjust."

"You've been in a war?" she said, because he had said soldier.

"Not really. A desk job in Washington. I've been lucky."

"Yes. Yes."

They were too old to be sitting in a car together, in a soft July night.

She pressed her hand against the door handle.

Down the street a couple sat in a convertible, necking.

She had not walked down the street for a month.

In early spring she had taken walks every night, but she had been embarrassed by the lovers in the cars. She did not want them to think she was a lonely old maid, spying.

For two months she had walked back and forth on the little front porch, after her supper, after the light had gone.

"It's been a nice evening," she said.

"Very nice."

Tom was easy and genuine. "Here, let me help."

"No, don't bother. Don't bother to get out. I know my way."

She tried to imagine the child who belonged to the pleasant man. It had been impossible to imagine Lewis's face.

"I don't know when I've had a nicer evening," Tom said. He was out of the car. He walked up the steps with her. He waited

125

while she fumbled for the key. It was Grandmother's purse. The purse was practically new.

She felt like an old lady, fumbling. "All of the jokes they tell are true. About ladies' pocketbooks."

"I wish you could have seen my mother's." He was laughing.

She was sorry he had not said, "My wife's." He had said only, "My wife died."

The key appeared, as it always did, at the moment she was positive she had forgot to bring it.

"Thank you again."

"The thanks go the other way around." Tom was easy and clean and genuine.

"Thank you. Thank you for bringing me home."

The second time Mrs. Hutton invited her to dinner she had been surprised. The six-week summer session was over. In Athens teachers were invited to the students' homes no more than once a year, if at all. Twins. Perhaps twins were different. Mrs. Hutton, Ellen, said, "You must call me Ellen. I don't have patience with last names. The twins adore you, I suppose you know that." Ellen was easy. They were all easy.

The second time, Lewis came. They shook hands. "How do you do, Miss Thaxton." His hand was firm. Somebody had taught him well. She could have cried for the handsome, mannered child.

Lewis and Tom took her home. They walked her up the steps to the porch. She had bought a new pocketbook. She had placed her keys in the coin purse.

"Good night, Miss Thaxton." She and Lewis shook hands again.

She would be a good mother to the child, that is what she had thought. She was not ashamed of herself for thinking, "I would make Lewis a good mother."

But she had not set her cap for Tom. She was against women who set their caps for men. She had known only that Tom would ask her to marry him. She wasn't sure what she would say when

126

the moment came. She was easy. She said the right things easily. She admired Tom. She loved Lewis.

Tom made her say the right things.

She did not think of being silly, the way she had been silly with that boy in the fifth grade, or I. L., or Jerry.

She would always be grateful to Tom for not allowing her to make a fool of herself. You loved people who made you easy, she told herself after the fourth evening.

She and Tom had gone to Columbus for dinner and a play.

"Yes, yes, I would like to hear the lecture," she said, because it was true.

"Yes, I've been wanting to see that movie."

"Yes, yes."

You loved people who didn't allow you to make a fool of yourself.

She did not want to be a "buttoned up woman." That was Grace Young's phrase. "Buttoned up women make the biggest fools of all."

Tom did not consider such complexities.

She loved Tom.

"A picnic sounds wonderful," she said.

"I'll bring Lewis, if that's all right. We have a boat at Dow Lake."

"Let me bring the food." She spoke without thinking. It was a natural thing to say.

"That'll be fine. You bring the fixings, and I'll bring the steaks. Even Stephen."

"Whatever does even Stephen mean?" She was laughing.

"I don't know. It's just something we've always said."

"We've always said it, too. I never thought what it meant."

"Even Stephen," they said at the same time, laughing.

They both came for her. Lewis and Tom stood on the front porch.

"How do you do, Mr. Lewis Hutton?" She and Lewis were shaking hands again.

"How do you do, Caroline? That's what Daddy calls you. Caroline."

"That's my name. My name is Caroline."

Lewis giggled.

The lake was quiet. Tom rowed almost to the dam. He rowed well. The day had been ridiculously hot, a hundred degrees. The lake held cool shadows.

"We call this place Wendy Point. Lewis named it. I don't know what it means. But it's named Wendy Point."

The man's wife, the child's mother, could have appeared among them, the woman named Marie. But she did not appear.

"That's its name because of Peter Pan," Lewis said. "I like to name things."

She had leaned toward the boy.

When they were eating at a picnic table on Wendy Point, Lewis said, "I never did eat potato salad so good before, did I, Daddy?"

"It's my grandmother's recipe."

"Did you make the cookies?"

"Grandmother's recipe."

"Your grandmother was smart," Lewis said. Was, he said, not is.

Death was only one of the sudden clouds above them.

They laughed together.

"Marie didn't make any cookies," Lewis said.

Tom's hand stopped at his mouth for a moment, for a second of a moment. The sky stopped for a moment—she imagined the sky's stopping. A hawk hung in the sky. She should have said then, perhaps she should have said something. But she had not spoken.

When the little businesses of being the new Mrs. Hutton became complicated, she imagined Marie's standing, efficient in the next room, waiting. The telephone rang. Sometimes she waited a minute for Marie to answer. The telephone call was surely not for Caroline Thaxton. When she was very tired she even imagined Tom's mother in the house. The two women she had never seen waited in the kitchen or at the curve of the stairway.

Yet she almost never thought, "The dark Maltese landlady lived here on Pretty Bay with a husband and children."

Here the furniture was anonymous. It was impossible to imagine anyone's going out to buy this furniture. The furniture was passing the house one day, and walked in, and arranged itself, waiting for nobody in particular. That was a pleasant notion. She would tell Tom. He liked for her to make up little fantasies. "Silly Caroline," Tom would say.

She had learned not to mention Marie.

At first she had asked innocent enough questions. She had said, "Your wife." At first she had spoken easily of the woman who had lived in Tom's house.

"Are these dishes what your wife used for dessert?"

"Did your wife bother to dust the furniture every day?"

"Where did your wife store cereal and crackers?"

"Please, Caroline," Tom said finally. "You are my wife. You do whatever you want to. This is your house."

Tom said, "We don't have to live here. We'll buy another place if you want to. We can build. Whatever, Caroline."

"You mean you'd leave the house you were born in?" She had spoken easily. She had talked too easily.

"I want you to be happy."

Several times Tom said, "I want you to be happy." It was a sweet thing for him to say. It was the kind of saying that could have brought tears to her eyes. Back then she cried too easily. But she had never cried when Tom said, "I want you to be happy." Tom, for all his charm, could speak quite coldly.

Her blood ran cold, the mystery books were always saying. It was a true saying. A person's blood could run cold, stop cold.

Her blood had stopped cold at the park when she had imagined the child, Becky, dead. If Lewis were to die . . . She could not bring herself to think of Lewis dead.

She said, "I wouldn't dream of leaving the house where you were born."

Tom relaxed. He was pleased. She was determined to please him. Tom had rarely seen her cry.

She had not cried during the frenzy of the last days before the wedding—the frenzy or the lethargy. There was everything and nothing to do. Ellen insisted on taking over the wedding plans. Ellen picked out the dress—an oyster white silk suit, more expensive than anything Caroline Thaxton had ever owned.

They were kind and considerate, all of the Huttons. The twins were beside themselves with solicitude. Ralph, all of them, they couldn't have been nicer.

"You don't want a big wedding, I suppose," Ellen said. "Once you start inviting people, you have to invite everybody. Our wedding was impossible. Had you thought about having just us?"

"Grace. I'll invite Grace Young. She teaches down the hall from me." She felt she should name someone of her own. She could have asked Ellen to stand up with them. Grace was not a particular friend, not really. Sometimes they drove to Columbus together, to shop at Lazarus's. Sometimes Grace invited two or three teachers to her apartment for a casserole—"maiden lady food," Grandmother called it.

"I have just an aunt and uncle. They're far away, and old." They were in nursing homes in Alabama and Michigan. She told Ellen about the nursing homes, because she did not want not to tell her.

"That's too bad," Ellen said.

She could almost not remember their names. "I write to them on their birthdays, and at Christmas." They never answered.

"I'll have Grace. What you say is true. Once you start inviting people, it's hard to know where to stop." She chattered, barely listening to herself. Whom would she have invited? Grade three?

The principal? The superintendent? The paper boy, the mailman?

Grace kept saying, "I'm overcome. I'm absolutely overcome. The maid of honor, oh, my heavens, Caroline. It's just marvelous. You certainly turned out not to be so very buttoned up, didn't you though?"

She was sorry she had asked Grace.

Ellen said, "And the honeymoon. You'll go someplace. Away."

"I hadn't thought. Yes. But it will be a busy time for Tom. He's been talking about how busy they are at the store."

None of them said, "Marie has not been dead a year. The quieter the better."

"We could take a real trip," Tom said. "I haven't had a vacation forever."

She managed to say, "The three of us. Lewis, too."

"He'll stay with us," Ellen said.

"I wasn't thinking." Tom looked away. He almost never lowered his eyes or turned his head in a conversation. But he looked back at her.

"Sure, we could take Lewis."

"I'd like to have him."

"That's sweet of you." Ellen's voice was bright. "But we want to keep him. Tom's such a stick-in-the-mud. That's what you are, aren't you, Tom? Stick-in-the-mud." Ellen's laughter was like glass breaking. "You'll be married here, at our house."

They couldn't have been more gracious.

"Later, the big trip maybe later," Tom said. "England, Europe, all those places."

She said, "There's so much to do now."

All morning she had stood in her apartment, feeling guilty over what she had decided to throw away. There wasn't anything much worth moving to Tom's house.

She said, "School, there's just, I don't know . . ." She wasn't making sense, but the Huttons were kind and gracious. "I'll finish the first term."

"A little trip, then. To New York. Plays and things." Ellen was a good manager.

"That sounds wonderful. But Lewis . . ."

"He will stay with us. The girls adore him. He won't even miss you."

"I hadn't realized there would be so many . . . so many contrivances. I mean complications."

They had all laughed.

"Caroline *Hutton.* Imagine! You're going to be Caroline Hutton. With all that money," Dotty Hicks said in the lunchroom. "Why didn't you tell us sooner?"

She had honestly not thought about the money.

Ellen had wanted an announcement in the *Messenger.* But she had stood up to Ellen. Once she had stood up to Ellen. The twins did the announcing after the Christmas holidays.

"Well, congratulations. My goodness. I mean, best, best wishes," somebody said, one of the girls who taught in junior high.

She had not contrived. She had not killed Marie, whoever Marie might have been.

But it was true. She had not wanted to be an old maid, serving casserole dishes to her own kind, walking on a summer porch, afraid to pass young lovers parked in cars.

Maybe she and Marie had stood beside each other at the glove counter in Hutton's once, once upon a time. But she did not even know what Marie looked like. She would never have known, except for the photograph albums in the bookcases by the French doors.

"Is that your wife, Tom?" she had asked once, just after they were back from the honeymoon. They sat on the couch by the picture window. Lewis had brought out the albums.

"That's Marie." Lewis pressed his forefinger against the picture of a woman standing by a swimming pool. "And that's Marie, and that, and that." The woman held a golf club, she was getting out of a car, she lay in a hammock.

Tom turned the page. "Here's Lewis on his first birthday. He really loved that cake."

"I don't remember it much. But I like cake, all right."

The albums had disappeared. Maybe Tom had taken them to the attic. Maybe he had placed them in a file at the store. She did not ask. "You're my wife, Caroline," Tom said again and again. She wanted to be his wife.

Caroline and Tom, not Marie and Tom, stood in front of the fireplace with Grace and Ralph. Lewis sat in Ellen's new red velvet chair, his legs stuck straight out in front of him, his hands folded in his lap.

"I now pronounce you husband and wife," the minister said, Tom's minister. Her minister, Grandmother's preacher, had left town the month after Grandmother's funeral. Nobody had been found to fill his place. It was difficult to replace a preacher for a mission church.

"And what God has joined together, let no man dare to put asunder."

Tom put his arm through hers, smiling. They had not kissed. "Let's not," she said when they were planning the ceremony.

"O.K., O.K. You're the doctor."

Grace and Ralph kissed her on the cheek. Then Ellen. Then the twins. "Oh, Miss Thaxton," Beryl said. "She means, 'Oh, Aunt Caroline,'" Marilyn said. They were dissolved with giggles.

Lewis stood behind the girls, waiting his turn. She expected him to shake her hand. He reached up to her, pulling her head down. Lewis caught his fingers in the scrap of a hat Ellen had insisted on. It didn't matter. Dear heavens, it didn't matter at all.

Beryl and Marilyn called together, "Be careful." But it couldn't have mattered less. The hat fell to the floor.

"You're my mamma," Lewis said. He kissed her loudly.

"I love you," she whispered.

133

She had not cried, not until that night on the train in their elegant drawing room. Tom didn't like planes. She had never been on a plane. She had never slept on a train before. A train was an anachronism; she was an anachronism.

She undressed in the little bathroom.

"Did you tell him what to say? To say what he did?"

Tom wore paisley pajamas and a matching robe. They were new; the store creases showed. "Tell who to say what?"

"Lewis. That I was his mamma."

"Of course not. We've talked about you coming to live with us. I told him you were his new mamma. He never called . . . He never said 'Mamma' before. His . . . She didn't like the word."

"I think it's a beautiful word."

Silly, silly. Darned fool silly. She was crying.

"Sweetheart." Tom was gentle. He did not take a step, but his creased arms stretched toward her. His hands were fists. She could have laughed, if she hadn't been crying like a fool.

She should have said, "Tell me about Marie." Perhaps that would have been the moment to say, "Please talk about Marie."

Perhaps he would have said, "There isn't anything to tell."

She had not asked.

"Look, honey. I know you're tired. Why don't you go to bed? To sleep. I'll—"

"No, Tom, please, of course not."

She pressed herself against him. "Please."

Tom was kind. Not once that sweet night had she wondered if she was being awkward. The train stopped and started. Behind the windows, fields and towns moved.

Her mind had not thought of Marie.

"I love you, Tom," she said. It was the first time she had said "I love you."

"Sweetheart. Honey," Tom said against her mouth.

In Malta Tom slept heavily.

She thought of Clar. She did not want to think of Clar. She was determined not to think of Clar.

134

It was Sunday. It was the second Sunday in February. He'd almost lost track of dates; he was getting as bad as Caroline, except Caroline barely knew the day of the week. They were a few minutes late getting to the church; he hated to be late. Caroline had gone back for her purse and they'd missed the bus. But it was all right. There were plenty of seats—cane-bottomed chairs, of all things—all over the church. The man was already lecturing. He had an accent, but you could understand him.

The church was beautiful. All the walls were hung with red damask. Lewis gave out a little whistle when they sat down. For that matter, his daddy felt like whistling, too.

The man was going over the history of the place. He said that all Christendom had contributed to this Collegiate Church, amongst whom were Pope Pius V and Philip II of France. The man had a funny way of talking. He said "whilst" four or five times.

The statue of Saint Paul stood over at the left; he was a big fellow, dressed up in gold and green and red.

After the man got through with the history everybody got up —there must have been two hundred people—and they followed the man around to every one of the fourteen altars. There were candles everywhere, and shined silver, and big vases of artificial flowers; it was something to see. The flowers would look fine in a store window at Christmas, felt and sequins and jewels, maybe real jewels. At every stop the man kept talking about the "clothes" of the altars. The altars were dedicated to the different saints that belonged to the different unions.

Maybe if he and Ralph hadn't been born in Ohio, some of the altars would be very important to them. The Tailors and Drapers? The Shoemakers? But maybe you could belong to just one union or one altar. There wasn't any altar for a department store.

There was a stall for Saint Agatha, though. She was the minor patron saint. It was interesting to think about major and minor saints. If he'd ever thought about saints he would have figured that a saint was a saint.

The biggest show was in the part the fellow called the choir. The man said, "This is the column on which the great Apostle was beheaded." Beside it was a silver urn. The man said the arm held the wristbone of the beloved Apostle. The bone was in a glass tube, inside the silver, the man said. There were a lot of jewels. It was remarkable what some people could believe.

But he wasn't knocking it. Saint Paul and his church were really impressive.

The statue was even more impressive when you got next to it. There were big florist baskets all around, with cards telling who sent them. It was like the opening of a store, or an anniversary special, or maybe a funeral. There were candles around the statue, really decorated.

When the lecture tour was over they went up the hill and bought some Turkish delight from one of the carts. Then they had coffee and milk and cheese cakes at the Premier. They were lucky to get a table. After that they walked around and looked in store windows, even though Lewis kept yammering that he wanted to go home.

They were really lucky. It was Caroline's idea. On their way back to the bus she said they might as well walk past the church again.

136

They were just in time. There was a parade of men and boys, wearing black and white, and then some other men in pink with white fur. The men were carrying some of the silver things from the church. Bells started like crazy, and there were firecrackers from somewhere, really noisy firecrackers. Lewis was scared. It was too bad the kid had a scary streak. You didn't want to be mean to a kid just because he was scary. "It's all right, Lewis." He held his hand tight.

The parade was a sight to see.

Lewis pulled at his hand. He leaned over to hear what the boy was saying. "Parade?" Lewis was shouting. He looked as if he wanted to cry. He felt sorry for the kid. He said, "Here, get on my shoulders." In the loud street a person could have yelled out anything, or thought anything. "Hold tight. You're fine."

The kid was heavy.

"I don't see anything."

"Look."

An old man wore an outfit with a long pink train. A lot of people kneeled as he passed. Seeing the fellow made you take off your beret automatically, even though your head was cold. The firecrackers almost split your ears.

Lewis's legs were cold. He was wearing those shorts again, and the blazer. He looked like a real dude. Caroline should have put long pants on him. It was colder than the mischief.

"This is fun, isn't it? Isn't it, Lewis?"

"Yes." Lewis was shivering.

He hadn't really dreamed about Saint Paul. Even if he had dreamed about the fool pageant that happened thirty years ago, he could have figured out exactly where the dream came from. The papers were full of stories about The Feast of Saint Paul's Shipwreck. And being around Lewis made you think about when you were a kid instead of a man. Dreams weren't so complicated as Caroline pretended they were. If a person figured a little, he could name all the people in a dream—who was chasing you, and where you were falling from, and why you woke up in the middle of the night in a sweat.

Last night he had got up and changed his pajama top because he was sweating. He put on the sport shirt he had meant to wear this morning. But he hadn't been dreaming, not about anything he could remember. Caroline put too much store in dreams.

But he didn't worry about her. He wasn't going to worry. They would work things around, with Lewis, and everything. She still felt bad over losing the baby. She didn't really act strange. Every once in a while, sometimes, he had a crazy notion that there was a light behind her eyes, as if she knew something nobody in the world had ever known before. That kind of thing could get in on a fellow. But he was the one that was crazy. They were getting along fine, just A Number One Fine.

The parade was over.

"That was fun, wasn't it, Lewis?"

"A lot of fun."

"We'll come to the Feast Day parade tomorrow. They carry the big statue through the streets."

"I hope it won't be so cold, don't you?"

"We'll wrap up for tomorrow."

They didn't have to wait long for the bus to come. They were the first people on. He sat in the seat opposite Caroline and Lewis. Caroline put her arm around Lewis. "Snuggle up," she said. The kid's cap fell off.

Other people were getting on.

"Who is Saint Paul?"

He wished the boy wouldn't talk so loud.

"You should have learned in Sunday school." He made his voice low. He was ashamed of himself for being mad at the kid. "If my mother had been your Sunday school teacher . . ."

"She would still be my grandmother." Lewis laughed as if he had made a joke.

"Shhhhh. Whisper, Lewis," Caroline said.

"I can't whisper when I laugh."

138

It was all right. People liked Lewis. Almost everybody smiled at him. "An angel," an old lady said, touching his hair.

The bus finally started. The bus said what all the other buses said: "Verbum Dei Caro Factum Est." The shrine thing was a box with a picture of Mary. The picture looked as if it had been cut out of a newspaper.

His mother had been the Sunday school superintendent. He hadn't wanted to be in his mother's department. "This is a cross we both must bear," his mother said. She could make jokes when she wanted to. Generally she was just tired. She did everything people expected her to. Now that he thought about it, though, she complained a good bit. "I've done this, and now I'll do this."

She didn't want him to have the big part in the pageant. "It's nepotism," she said. But the teacher of the class insisted. The class had a name and a pin and a yell. They were named Knights of the King. You got the pin after you memorized so many verses of the Bible. His teacher was named Miss Atwood. His dad liked her a lot. Maybe his mother hadn't been so crazy about her. But you couldn't trust your memory on things like that. Someday Lewis would think about Malta, remembering it different from the way it was.

His mother had found the pageant in a Sunday school magazine. She was a great one for following directions. The magazine said that there should be two blinding lights: "When Paul Loses His Sight, When Paul Recovers His Sight." He could remember the words in the magazine exactly.

The light worked fine the first time.

Young Tom Hutton staggered from the left door, below the choir loft, the door the preacher generally came in from. The preacher was named Reverend Cooper. Tom felt his way to the center of the platform. He was blind. For a minute he couldn't see anything. He was ten years old, and he was in a fool pageant on a Sunday afternoon in Ohio, pretending to be Saint Paul.

Mr. Riggs was in charge of the spotlight. He wasn't very smart.

He'd been a janitor forever, at the church and the store. Mr. Riggs had a lot of trouble getting the spotlight arranged. It was too bright at first. It looked just like a spotlight. His mother had sent Miss Atwood out for a roll of silver paper—the teacher's name was Miss Bernice Atwood. She was good in children's wear. The department hadn't done very well since she died. Of TB. TB ran in her family.

They had made a paper shade for Saint Paul's lamp. When he saw Caroline's lamp it had reminded him of something. Except maybe they didn't have Reynolds Wrap back then. It was hard to remember. Plain paper would have caught on fire. It would have been a sight if the whole church had gone up in flames because of a fool pageant.

Every horizon in Malta was full of churches. If the churches of Malta burned, you would be standing in a circle of fire.

The light worked fine at both rehearsals, Friday afternoon after school, and Saturday morning. But the second light didn't work on Sunday afternoon.

Tom Hutton stood, blind, looking up where the light was supposed to be shining.

It didn't come on, and it didn't come on.

He fell to his knees, pretending to see the light. Maybe he had been a scary kid, like Lewis.

They finished the pageant all right.

"You did fine, Tom," people said.

"You had me believing it all, every minute. I'm sorry about the second light," Miss Atwood said.

"You did all right," Ralph said, "but that old bathrobe looked crazy."

His dad said, "It was a good program, son."

He got a lot of compliments on his performance.

Ralph never could have played Saint Paul when the light didn't come on. Not the way Tom Hutton did.

He was thinking of himself as if he was somebody else. He was thinking about himself and calling himself Tom.

He had been surprised at the parade, even though he knew all about it. He had read a lot. He probably knew more about the history of Malta than anybody he talked to.

Yesterday he had taken the bus from Valletta and got off a long way before Birże. He walked home through streets that curved and turned. If it hadn't been for the sound of the sea helping him find his location, he would have been lost, really lost.

He hadn't told Caroline. Every once in a while he was embarrassed when he and Caroline were alone. It was wrong for a man to be embarrassed with his wife, or his son.

But they were getting along fine. Time was wasting, and they had a lot of things they needed to see.

Yesterday the people had kneeled when the archbishop strolled into the cathedral. The lecturer had said that only the archpriest had the right to be buried in the underground of the church. "No other person has a similar right," he said in his charming accent. "This is rather exceptional."

She had looked hard at the old man. His hair was whiter than plaster. His hair was like plaster.

"You will be buried here," she thought. She was addressing the archpriest, the old man, not herself, not anybody she knew. The rest of them didn't know where they would be buried, not any of them who stood waiting.

She did not know what she had expected the people to do when the figure of Saint Paul was carried down the streets. Surely they would kneel, the thousands.

She was not being claustrophobic. But she wished Tom would not push so deeply into the crowd. "Come on, Mamma," Lewis called from Tom's shoulders.

If she fainted, if the sky fell, if the firecrackers were really cannons . . .

She thought about making the sign of the cross, the way young girls and old ladies crossed themselves when they passed the churches, the thousands of churches.

She had never really liked Saint Paul. Grandmother quoted him more than she quoted Jesus. "Thou shalt not." Women should cover their heads in the churches. Women should not speak in the church. Better to marry than to burn, but better not to marry at all.

Saint Paul made lists. She had tried to love Saint Paul for Grandmother's sake.

The people neither kneeled nor crossed themselves.

They cheered. They clapped and whistled.

Saint Paul was a homecoming float. He was a football hero. He had made the eighty yard run. He was a movie star.

The huge figure under his halo moved toward them, green and red, gold splattered. Men carried him on a litter; she caught a glimpse of the men for only a moment. Saint Paul wore diamonds on his fingers. Light, from somewhere, caught at the diamonds.

"Make way. Make way."

Policemen pushed at the crowd. If they were pushed any tighter together, they would become one person, larger than Saint Paul himself. One person looking at Saint Paul.

She had lost sight of Lewis and Tom. She was not going to be frightened. She was not going to let herself be silly. She would see Lewis in a minute.

People threw confetti. Confetti fell from every window across the street, thicker than snow in Ohio. Some of it was obviously homemade: wads of wrapping paper, newspapers cut into squares, strips from telephone books. Perhaps if she looked hard enough, if she controlled her breathing, she could identify the names of real people who lived in real houses with real ringing telephones.

Saint Paul was vast. He was three times, five times bigger than when he stood in the church among his candles and bouquets.

He did not glide between the lines of cheering people. He did not strew pamphlets: "Thou shalt not, thou shalt not." Pamphlets fell from the sky onto Saint Paul.

Saint Paul minced. He minced beneath the confetti, like a chorus girl in a late movie on television.

143

"Mamma. Hello, Mamma." Lewis was laughing from Tom's shoulders, only five people away from her.

"I'll be up in a minute," Tom called from downstairs in Athens. "Just this one more part."

"All right, Tom," she answered, knowing he would not come to bed until the late show was over, until after the heroine had kissed the hero good night, until after the chorus girls stopped mincing. She did not like the late movies.

Lewis beat his hands together. "Saint Paul, Mamma," he shouted.

Perhaps the parade would mean something to Lewis later, a long time from now, when his parents lay buried—not in the underground of a church, an exceptional privilege—when Tom and Caroline lay dead in, perhaps, Athens, Ohio. It was impossible to imagine Lewis dead.

Saint Paul was almost covered with paper. The Bible in his left hand was hidden; his halo had disappeared among the strips of newspaper; his right hand, raised in benediction, held yellow confetti. He was a prancing girl at a football game.

Tom stood quietly, his hands on Lewis's knees. At football games Tom stood, waving his arms. "Come on, team!"

The men who carried Saint Paul lowered him to the street, almost directly in front of her. The men, six, seven, eight men, stretched. They rubbed the muscles of their arms and legs. They wore white surplices over black robes. Surely they were not priests. They were surely prisoners of some kind, forced into labor. They were convicts, surely, bearing Saint Paul.

Three people—a boy in a white cassock, a real priest, and a man in a business suit—the man was no older than Tom—climbed onto the figure. The boy and the two men pulled at the paper, fluttering the paper down from the halo, the blessing hand, the Bible, onto the crowd.

She lifted both hands to her hair. She was not upset. She did not claw the paper from her hair. She smoothed it away, the newspaper, the telephone book strips, the real confetti.

Saint Paul appeared from his wrappings.

The people shouted.

"Oh, boy," she heard Lewis call.

She thought of saying the child's name. "Lewis, Lewis."

She wondered if Clar stood somewhere in the crowd.

Time was an accordion. The first days in Malta, time had stretched to infinity.

There was time to market, and read, and walk, and take afternoon naps, and write letters, and go to a garden.

She relished writing the letters: people at school, people who had been particularly nice to her, the neighbors she almost never saw at home, Mrs. McCandless, and Mrs. Williams, and Mrs. Raymond, and the others. There was time to wait.

She had never been much of a letter writer. Honestly, there had never been many people to write to. The two years she had been away from Grandmother, at the university, she had gone home every weekend. The year Grandmother was in the nursing home, she had written a few notes; but generally she had managed to take a bus to Lancaster every Saturday morning, to sit by a bed, not sure if the trembling old woman knew who sat beside her telling foolish little stories about the house plants, the children at school, the new buildings in Athens. Grandmother did not seem unhappy. The doctor had been right. The nursing home was the place for her. It would have been impossible to care for her at home.

"Nursing home," she said to herself until the words had no meaning.

Tom teased her. "I'm married to a lady novelist."

Tom wrote painfully. "Hand me the guidebook, will you?" He settled down to write to Ralph, or the minister at the church, or somebody at the store.

She had never received a letter from Tom. That was odd to think about. But she knew what Tom's letters would say: the population of Malta, the merchandise. She did not love Tom less because he knew the height and weight of everything. She envied him. Sometimes Tom wrote on postcards, "Having a fine time." It was a good thing to say on postcards.

She composed her letters to Ellen, sometimes recopying them. She wanted Ellen to like the news from Malta. "Everybody is enormously friendly. The shoemaker came out of his shop yesterday to show me his progress on those old walking shoes I'm having resoled. The girls at the C. and S. ask me how I am getting along with knitting—they have all admired the knitting bag you gave me for my birthday. I went in and showed the girl at Saint Mary's how to roll a ball of wool so that the yarn comes out in the middle. I still work on the sweater for Lewis, two sizes too big, hoping to get it finished before he is seven."

She named names and the prices and relationships of names. She and Ellen would probably be good friends. It was terribly important to keep in touch.

She did not write about the garden. Time was very long.

Tom was organizing them. "Time's a wasting," he said. "You have to see Malta. You might as well be in Athens if you don't see things."

"I love it. I'm loving it here," and, "Yes, Tom," and, "Yes, Lewis is ever so much better. I think the climate agrees with him." It was almost as if Tom were trying to fill all of the days and nights, as if he knew about the garden. But he didn't really know, of course. And there was nothing to know, nothing at all. She had not meant to keep the garden a secret. She had told Tom, "Lewis loves the tricycle paths. Where we go. Sometimes."

Two weeks ago if someone had asked her what Malta was like, she would have told about their curving street beside the bay, the bars, the grocery, the chemist's, the butcher shop, the five tiny stores that sold newspapers and stamps and hairpins; the vendors, the flower man, the baby buggies. Perhaps she would have described the park. She could have told a stranger about the park.

But there were other Maltas. She was learning that there were more Maltas than anywhere.

Tom insisted on her going to the big market in Valletta by herself. "Lewis and I will have a ball. While you're at it, take yourself a couple of extra bus rides. There's a lot to see."

"I'll go with Mamma. I'll help her carry the groceries."

Tom was not annoyed. He laughed. "You'll stay with your old man. We need to get better acquainted."

Lewis knew how to manage people. He smiled up at her. "Daddy and me will have us a ball. I'll go with you next time."

She had been almost frightened. But she got along all right. Everyone was pleasant. A slender English lady with beautiful white hair stood beside her at one of the fish stalls. Her eyes were dark brown; the woman was elegant. She wore a terribly smart suit.

"You were before me," the Englishwoman said.

"No, go ahead. I really don't know what to buy."

The woman said, "I am at your service." She couldn't have been more gracious. "This, and this," the woman said. She began reciting recipes. "I've been here quite a while—two years. One gets on to it."

"Thank you. I don't know how to thank you." She was conscious of her flat Ohio voice.

She had not meant to take an extra bus ride. But she took the Rabat bus clear to the end of the run and back to Valletta. She was proud of herself for managing. Everything was very interesting. But she was glad to get home.

On Wednesday night they went to Saint John's Co-Cathedral for an organ recital. It was strange for Tom to have chosen an organ recital. At Tom's house, in Athens, in the room they called the family room, nine shelves bulged with records. She had played them at first, show tunes, and symphonies, and yes, organ recitals. "You don't mind if I put on some music, do you?" They waited

147

for a roast to finish cooking; it was a Sunday afternoon; or they were reading; or Lewis was already in bed.

"Sure, go ahead." Tom kept on reading. Or he had taken a walk. Or he had gone upstairs. "Sure, go ahead."

She had known, without asking, that the records belonged to Marie.

Ellen said, "Marie bought a lot of records for a while. She belonged to a couple of record clubs, and a music listening group —something at the university. But we're not musical, we Huttons, in-laws or out-laws." Ellen coughed a laugh. Ellen's laughter was never amused. "But you like music, don't you? You really do."

"Maybe I shouldn't play them."

"Why not? Tom has a tin ear. It's your house."

She had stopped playing the records when Tom was at home. After a few months she had stopped playing the records at all.

"The organ recital starts at six-thirty," Tom said. "We'll have plenty of time to get home. The buses run until ten-thirty. It'll be good for Lewis. We won't have to get a taxi. We can eat someplace first."

In the cathedral Lewis listened as if he knew how to listen. Once in a music appreciation course she had learned how to listen to Handel and Bach.

The program notes said, "Handel died blind at the age of seventy-four years. Bach died blind at the age of sixty-five years."

She tried to imagine the person who had written the program notes. She tried to remember the music course.

The arches rose above them. The ceiling held figures. Angels? Prophets? Saints? Jesus? God?

She had forgot how to listen.

Christ soared white over the altar, on a black cross. Pearl? Ebony? She could not see very well. But the Christ did not suffer. If she narrowed her eyes the black cross disappeared. The Christ danced. No strain held him. The black cross was only a theater prop. He leaped, pearl white, above the altar, a dancer. His feet touched only air; his arms moved air.

148

The program was over before nine. The bus waited at the castle.

"I've finally figured out the bus prices," Tom said. "At last." He sat in the seat across from her and Lewis. "It's six cents, except on Sunday and festival days, then it's eight cents. Don't let me forget that. They cheat you every now and then. We've got to be careful."

The bus was almost deserted.

Lewis said something. She leaned down to him. "What, honey?"

"The music was pretty."

"Yes, wasn't it, though?"

"Did you see the man dancing? The picture of the man?"

"Yes. Yes, yes, Lewis."

Almost every day now they rode a rickety bus to the far ends of the island.

Lewis carried a notebook, like Tom's. Tom had bought it for him the day they started "seeing Malta."

The child could read, or his memory was phenomenal.

He kept being delighted with the names of places.

"What's that, Mamma? Read that." Billy Boy Bar was near Sonny Boy Bar, not far from Reborn Bar.

"Write it, Mamma. Write it down in my notebook."

The house with the lavender doors, named My Lady, stood across the street from the white doors of Tom's Place. Lewis was delighted.

"We're about to Shortly Restaurant, and right here, here it comes, Resurrection and God Bless America."

"Shhh, Lewis."

Twice, three times they had eaten downtown, in Valletta, once in a funny place Tom wouldn't have thought of entering in Athens or Columbus.

"It's good food, all right," Tom said.

149

She had not wanted to eat out at all. "Please, Tom. You know I love to cook. I love this kitchen."

"You're on vacation, honey. What's the matter with you? Did I bring you all this way just so you could work over a hot stove?"

Once they had eaten elegantly at the Sheraton, and once at a place named the Bird Cage. Another time they had had lunch at the Hilton. Somebody at a bar had told Tom he shouldn't leave Malta without seeing the Hilton.

She would remember the Hilton as technicolored, purple, gold, glass, a vast sea, rich old people, a few rich young people. The tourists wore summer dresses in the heated lobby. She wore her lined coat. She had almost apologized about her coat to the checkroom boy. She was annoyed with herself. She was not a native. She was a tourist. She wanted to be a native. She wanted to belong to where she lived.

On their Sicily tour every curved road reminded a woman named Mrs. Kantzler of the Appian Way. Every cloister was like that monastery in Spain. "It reminds you of it, doesn't it?" Mrs. Kantzler called back to her. The Kantzlers sat in the front seats of the bus, the deluxe first class seats.

The Huttons had no foreign views for comparison. In Sicily and here, once in a while, she was reminded of something at home, the piece of highway 33 covered with trees, the turn of Woodward and Pine. But she had been determined not to mention the likenesses.

"This is like that place in Palermo? Isn't it?" Tom said.

"Yes, Tom." She had found herself doing it, too. Miss Martin at the bank reminded her of Jamie Tevis at home. The trouble with tourists was that they wouldn't let a place be what it was. More disturbing than their clothes, their voices, was their unwillingness to look at places or people as a single place, a single person. The generalizations were protection. They tied strings to time. The reminding was a way of holding on, a kind of shorthand, building on old relationships in order not to care too much. They were unwilling to look at one arch or one street corner at a time.

But she was generalizing about tourists. "We mustn't generalize, Tom."

"It's really quaint, though, isn't it?" Tom said.

"How quaint," Mrs. Kantzler said again and again.

She wanted to learn. She wanted to be a whole person, whatever *whole person* meant.

Perhaps she was a tourist at home, too. Maybe even the Huttons were tourists at home.

On a Sunday they took a bus to Sliema and got off for a long walk. They walked clear to the Dragonera. It looked closed. But Tom was a good tourist; he was bold. A girl sat at a desk. "Would you mind if we looked around?" The girl was gracious.

The tables in the casino were covered. The place was smaller than she had expected. She had seen casinos only in movies. She had imagined they inhabited areas as large as football fields. But the tables reminded her of . . .

She did not allow herself to finish her thought.

That night Tom had insisted on making love. "It's all right. It's all right," she kept telling herself. Lovers were not necessarily tourists.

They went to the armory. Tom was obviously disappointed in Lewis's reactions. She felt sorry for Tom. She felt sorry for Lewis, too.

"Look. Look, Lewis. How marvelous. How perfectly marvelous," she said again and again.

"Aren't they, though? Look here, Lewis. Look how little those fellows were," Tom said. "Why, you could almost fit in one of those outfits."

They went to the National Museum. Lewis was delighted with the models of Malta. "There's where we are, isn't it? That's exactly where we are. Come here. Come look at this," Lewis kept calling.

"Shhhh," she said.

151

Lewis was strangely interested in the statues and pictures of Jesus. For a moment she had thought of saying, "Come along, Lewis." But she waited with the boy.

"Saint Paul?"

"No. Jesus."

"Is he hurting a lot?"

"I expect so. We'll talk about it. We'll talk about it later." What could she say? What could she say later?

"Did Jesus really look like that?"

"Perhaps. Nobody is for sure."

"My goodness."

Dear God, she thought. She was praying. She was praying about something.

"Look here, Daddy. Here's a lady without any clothes on. Here's a naked lady."

"Sure enough," Tom said. Tom moved to the next picture, a portrait of a man in a breastplate, holding his headpiece in the crook of his right arm. "Look here, Lewis. This looks like *The Laughing Cavalier*. That's a picture you'll be studying about when you go to school."

Lewis returned to the naked lady. He began to giggle.

A distinguished old man in a goatee joined Lewis in front of the picture.

"That's funny, isn't it?" Lewis reached for the man's hand.

"How do you do, young sir?"

"Oh. Oh." Lewis was frightened. "I thought you were my mamma."

"Here, Lewis. Here I am."

"A charming young man," the old man said.

Lewis held her hand tightly. "It's all right, Lewis. It's perfectly all right," she said.

They found Tom in another room, looking at a glass case which held the silver plate of the Holy Infirmary.

Her feet hurt. Being a tourist was hard work. And the place was freezing.

Lewis took both their hands when they got outside the doors. It was warmer outside than in.

"I feel sorry for Jesus," Lewis said.

Tom said, "How about stopping at the Perfecto before we catch a bus home?"

"Oh, boy."

Lewis had cocoa and a sweet. The waiter recognized them. Tom seemed pleased. They talked with the waiter about the weather until somebody said, "*Garçon, garçon.*" It was the goateed gentleman who had been looking at the naked lady.

"Talk about coincidences," Tom said.

"We must have seen everybody on the island by now. At least once." It was strange that they had not seen Clar and Buddy and Becky. "Surely we can't have coincidences any more."

"This coffee is good. Better than across the square," Tom said.

"This is good, too." Lewis spilled a little of his cocoa.

"Don't worry, fellow," Tom said. Tom was kind. He smiled at her across the table. "That's all right, fellow."

One day she and Lewis took the bus to Valletta to exchange books. She lugged home two huge artbooks.

"It's time Lewis was conscious of paintings. I've probably been neglecting his education."

Tom laughed.

"You probably think I don't neglect him enough. Is that right?"

"No, honey, of course not."

"Really, Tom."

"I've told you. I keep telling you. He's important. But we're important, too. We figured that out a long time ago."

"Yes, Tom. Yes."

Lewis loved the artbooks. He learned the names and the painters right away. "This naked lady is named *The Birth of Venus* by Botticelli," he told Tom.

"You do beat all," Tom said.

It wasn't time to get up yet. At home it was only one in the morning. Some nights, at home, Tom didn't come up to bed until after one. At home the moon shone through the branches of the oak tree.

She had waked for a moment, only a moment.

She could turn herself in bed. She could sleep three more hours, four more hours. They got more sleep in Birżebbuġa than they did at home. Tom didn't need much sleep at home.

She heard a knocking.

It was six o'clock. A lot of people got up at six. She had planned to get up early anyhow.

She put on her robe and slippers. Clar, she thought.

But nobody was at the door.

On a Wednesday—a Friday?—they took a picnic lunch to Saint Paul's Bay. Tom had bought Manoel Theatre tickets for the evening. The performance was at six-thirty; they wouldn't miss the bus, Tom said; Lewis wouldn't be up too late; Lewis would be in bed by . . . The numbers, always the numbers mattered to Tom, distances, degrees. Tom did not know that time was an accordion.

She did not really want to see Clar again. There was no reason in the world to want to see Clar.

The theater was a little jewel case. They sat in a box, the middle-priced tickets. She was surprised that Tom had not chosen the cheapest seats, three tiers above them. But she had learned not to question Tom's economies. She was interested in his attitudes, that was all. Interested.

"What wonderful seats," she said. There were eight chairs in the box, but they were alone. They hovered three balconies above the stage, alone. "I've never been in a box before."

"The theater was founded in seventeen thirty-one, Lewis, what do you think of that?" Tom said. "Before Ohio was even settled. Imagine that."

154

Lewis pulled at the lapels of his blazer. She had bought it at the last minute, and not at Hutton's but at the Wee Shop down the street. "We have to patronize our competitors," she told Tom, and Tom had smiled.

The play had been written by a man born in Valletta. It was about nuns and sacrifice and brotherhood, sisterhood. The actors were quite professional.

"You can put some chairs together and go to sleep if you want to," she told Lewis at the end of the first act.

"You go to sleep if you want to, Mamma."

The boy did not sleep during the entire play; he did not sleep on the jogging bus back to Birże, all the way home.

She was pleased to realize that she had thought the word *home*.

After he had said his prayers Lewis said, "I'm grown up now, aren't I? Didn't I grow up quick?"

She hugged him, even though Tom stood in the doorway.

Tom laughed. He was happy. He said, "You grew up in Malta, didn't you?"

"Yes. I go to plays and churches and everything."

She loosened her arms.

Tomorrow they would go to the garden, no matter what Tom had planned for the day.

She sat on the park bench waiting for Clar. "I'm always here," Clar had said a long time ago.

Lewis passed the bench. "Hello, Mamma."

She wondered what she would say to Clar when they met, if they met.

Perhaps Caroline would say, "I've missed you. I've been here several times. We've been awfully busy. We've been being tourists."

Surely Clar would come.

There was no reason in the world to expect her.

Surely.

Clar appeared. She was pushing Becky in a stroller. Buddy rode one of the shining tricycles. Clar did not seem surprised to see her. "Hello, Caroline. Where's Lewis?"

"He . . . he just passed." She swallowed. Her throat was dry. "He's on one of the trails, the paths." She moved the knitting bag to her lap.

Clar flopped down beside her. "How do you like the new stroller?"

"It's lovely."

Becky filled the stroller. The child was huge. Her hair was a beautiful color, auburn, but it was matted. Her hair covered her head like a dirty cap.

"It's new. It changes to a walker. It folds up, too." Clar had on the same skirt, the same sweater with the missing button. But today she wore a vast charm bracelet on her left wrist. "It's wonderful getting on and off of buses. Billy didn't want me to buy it, but my God. It wasn't that expensive. Becky, wait a minute, damn it."

Becky had started away from the bench before Clar could lean over and remove the handles. The child turned to look at her mother. Her eyes were ridiculously blue. She did not smile.

Clar unscrewed the handles and threw them to the ground. "Look at her. She can get around as good as anybody. Look at her go. She could walk if she wanted to, damn her."

"She's large for her age, isn't she? She has lovely eyes."

"She's large, all right. She's hell to carry." Clar settled back as if the iron bench were made of feathers.

Caroline tried to sit more loosely.

"Billy can't understand anything." Clar spoke as if they had met yesterday, or as if neither of them had ever left the bench settled in the bougainvillea. "He's determined now to have another kid. His brother has eight. I told you, didn't I? *His* wife's a good Catholic." Clar laughed deeply. "I wish you could see Billy in bed. No, I don't, either. You'd be embarrassed, and you wouldn't believe it. God, what he thinks up, and it's not just because he was raised a Catholic." She was evidently not too annoyed with Billy. "I guess all men are alike."

She could not look at the woman, but she listened.

Last night Tom and she had made love. It had not been unpleasant. Tom was kind and considerate. She had not mentioned starting the new baby. "Tom, I've been thinking," she had almost said. But she had put in her diaphragm.

"Now just let me tell you. Last night, for instance. Billy

157

wouldn't give me time to get my diaphragm in—I don't believe in pills."

Caroline nodded. She should not have been listening to the woman, and she was nodding.

"They cause cancer—they're worse than cigarettes. I had a cousin in Little Rock. Young. She wasn't even twenty-five. But last night . . ."

Caroline could have said, "I'll check on Lewis, on the children."

She could have stood. "This is your personal and very private business," she could have said.

"You don't have to hear anything you don't want to," Grandmother said. "Evil communications corrupt good manners, Caroline."

She allowed Clar to finish her horrifying story, listening and not listening.

"I don't use the pill, either." She wanted to share a secret with Clar, the way girls in grade school shared cookies from the lunchboxes. Or T.L.s. "You have to give me back a compliment," children used to say to each other, "a Trade Last."

She was telling Clar about the miscarriage. She had never really talked about it, not even to Tom, particularly to Tom. A woman needed to share a confidence. It was good to talk about the baby. "I wanted him too much, I expect. We hadn't been married six months, almost six months."

"Oh, my God."

"I had pains just before dinner. It was time for Tom to come home, right at six-twenty. I was determined to get dinner on the table. And Lewis hadn't been feeling well; he had a terrible cold. I knew I was going to die."

She could tell Clar anything. Clar said, "Yes, yes," and, "Sure enough, of course."

She told it all, the pain, the drive to the hospital, the operating room, the smell of the ether, Dr. McConkey, and the vase of roses in the room when she woke up. She told the story without quite listening to herself.

"Sure enough."

"Tom was nice enough. Tom was sweet. But I know he was out of patience with me. He was in the hospital room when I woke up. He said, 'How's my sweetheart?' and then he said, 'You couldn't quite hold on.' I know he didn't mean anything. He wasn't being cross. I didn't let him know how sorry I was about the baby. He was right. I couldn't hold on. I've never 'held on,' whatever that means."

"Men."

She was telling Clar about last night. She was being delicate, but she told about Tom's matter-of-fact lovemaking. "It's all right. I wouldn't have it—want it—any other way. I know I'm not frigid. I've read all the books. But . . . I don't know." She spoke as if somebody else were telling the story, in another room. Telling Clar a confidence was like dropping something down a well, something you didn't want any more.

The something disappeared. The well was only a mirror.

"Maybe a good marriage is made from not caring too much."

"Your periods regular now?"

"Regular as the moon."

"You'll be all right. You'll have a dozen kids, if you want them. I guess I'm sort of lucky to be able to have kids so easy. I guess we should count our blessings. But my God. Billy! Day before yesterday, no, it was the day before that, in the morning. I wasn't awake yet. Here comes Billy. He's the limit. Honestly. The first thing he did . . ."

She listened. The garden existed for the moments of the experience. She knew she would not be able to record the moments of the experience. If somebody should ask, a judge or somebody, "Tell me what Clar said in the garden, tell me, or your life," she would not be able to remember for the life of her. She had

159

dreamed conversations with Clar. She could not remember how many times she and Clar had met.

When she had married she thought, "I will count the number of times we have made love. I will never forget the making of love." But she had forgot. A person could not count love, even the making at, the acting out, the pretense of love, whatever love meant. "Having sex," Tom said sometimes.

She was not embarrassed by Clar.

Once, at home, Ellen had tried to talk about sex. Ellen embarrassed her. They stood in the kitchen together cleaning up after dinner. Tom had announced the baby during dessert. Ellen could have been a cheerleader. Marie must have been the same.

"Congratulations," Ralph said. "I'm delighted," Ellen said.

In the kitchen Ellen said, "I'm really delighted. I just wish you and Tom had more time, a little more, to get used to each other. Physically, I mean."

Ellen was handing her dishes, two at a time, to scrape, to put in the dishwasher.

"We're fine. We're just all right."

"Ralph and I, we had Ralph, Jr., too soon. We had the twins too late." Ellen laughed her laugh. "That's the way it is, I guess."

"I'm glad about the baby."

She still wasn't used to the dishwasher. She didn't like to use it. But Tom insisted, even for the Haviland. "Mother always did. She said dishes were meant to be used. They never broke any."

"They?"

"Mother. The cooks, the maids. Back when people had maids." He did not say Marie.

Ellen said, "People need time to get used to each other's . . . to each other's persons, bodies. By the time the twins came. . . . If it weren't for the twins, I wouldn't be standing in this kitchen."

She smiled at Ellen. But there was no stopping the dark tight woman.

"They were Ralph's last gasp, as it were. With me, at least."

160

"Ellen. That's too bad. I'm sorry." She had never been more embarrassed.

Ellen handed her two dishes carefully. It wasn't Ellen's fault.

She looked down at the broken dishes on the floor. The pieces seemed to sprout rosebuds.

Tom and Ralph stood at the kitchen door. "Who's breaking up housekeeping?" Ralph said.

"I'm sorry." Ellen held her hands to her mouth. "I was jabbering. I'm sorry."

"Why should you be sorry? I dropped them. I'm clumsy. I'm just a terribly clumsy woman." She did not feel like crying. It would have been easier for all of them if she had made some kind of demonstration.

She stooped to pick up the rosebuds.

"Let me. . . . I shouldn't have." Ellen was about to cry. It was strange to see a woman as cold as Ellen . . .

"It doesn't matter," Ralph said. "Look at Caroline. She's taking it like a big girl."

"Come on, honey. Let the dishes go." Tom held out his hand. "We'll finish later."

"You all go back to the living room. I want to get the rest of them in the washer. If I'm able. I want to do it."

It was not a bad evening, not really. She could bear to think about it. Ellen and Ralph stayed later than they usually did. Generally Ralph began to yawn before they left the table, even at his own house.

They talked about the baby.

Ralph said, "We can always use somebody else in the store."

Ellen said, "Really, Ralph. The poor child isn't born yet."

Tom, patting his stomach, said, "There's life in the old man yet." It didn't sound like Tom. But he'd bought champagne for the announcement, and brandy for after dinner. Tom was easy with Ralph and Ellen. They were all easy with each other.

She had offended them at first. If they were at Ellen's and Ralph's for dinner, she wanted to have them back before she went

161

again. "You have to pay back," Grandmother said. "No, you can't go play with Bertha, not until she comes here." The Huttons were generous. She must keep reminding herself.

Ellen said, "It will be nice having a baby around again." She spoke as if the store were having the baby. Perhaps they were. It was all right.

Ralph said . . . Tom said . . . Ellen said. Surely Caroline had said something.

Before they left she said, "I'm sorry about the dishes. I know your mother treasured them. I've treasured them, too, even if it doesn't look like it."

"She had too many of them. Ellen refused to take them. And Marie got sick and tired of putting up with them." Ralph would not have mentioned Marie if he hadn't been a little drunk. He patted her shoulder. "Don't drink it another thought. Don't give it another think." He was drunk.

"I'll try not to." She could not look at Tom.

They were kind people. They were a race of people, all by themselves, making the past into the present, and then forgetting about the past, at least not bothering much with the past.

In Malta she said to a woman named Clar Tate, "I kept thinking about their mother's buying the dishes and using them for fifty years. They used them for breakfast. Tom's mother trusted the dishes, even with the servants."

She was telling Clar about the evening.

"I cried a lot that night, after Tom was asleep. It's funny, I'd forgot how I cried. I kept wanting to wake Tom up and ask if Marie ever broke any dishes. I guess the Huttons never broke dishes, not the real Huttons, or their servants, the people who belonged with them. I'd forgot how I cried that night."

"Honey," Clar said. "You know you're being a damn fool. Two goddamn fool little damn dishes."

"I know. I know I'm being silly. I try not to be. But they have a . . . a strength. That's what worries me. It's strength."

"They just have money. For a long time. What the hell."

162

"No, it's a strength."

"Religion?" Clar lifted her hands and dropped them to her fat thighs. "That's something else. I wouldn't worry about religion if I was you. I figure religion is like sinus trouble or high blood pressure. You got it or you don't. I'm always telling Billy that. It makes him sore sometimes, but that's the way I figure it."

"I don't mean that. They don't have religion, not like my grandmother's, I mean. They go to church, we all go to church. But it's not religion. It's not supernatural, it's natural, that's what I mean. It's the natural."

Perhaps she would remember the conversation after all, when she was an old lady, if she became an old lady, sitting at the big window in Tom's house, looking out at the oak tree. She would think, "Once I talked to a woman on a park bench in Malta. Once I tried to straighten myself out, talking to a woman." Perhaps the remembering would not make any sense at all. But she spoke easily to Clar, who listened and didn't listen.

"Hello, Lewis. Hello, Buddy," she said.

"Billy calls himself a Catholic. He wouldn't miss Sunday Mass for a barrel of monkeys. And he won't use a rubber, my God, no. But he's not against my diaphragm, when I get it in early enough. Now, that doesn't make sense, does it? Religion's all right. I'm not saying anything against religion."

The old lady by the window, remembering, would be shocked. She would mumble to herself. She would mumble to herself, surprised at the words she remembered. Caroline Hutton was not shocked.

"The things Billy and me do. I like it all right. Not that I would admit it to Billy. But you would tell a friend. You wouldn't lie to your girl friend. Just take three or four days ago, for instance. . . ."

"Maybe because Tom is older. Maybe he doesn't know we're married, really married. Maybe he doesn't know I love him. I do love him." She didn't really know what she was talking about, but it was important to talk.

163

"Love shove. Everybody loves everybody. I love Billy, all right. And I loved a boy in Kansas, and one in Nebraska, and one in Arkansas."

"That's what I am trying to say." She did not know what she was trying to say.

"We're stuck with ourselves. That's what I keep telling Billy. Live and let live."

They were quiet. They were quiet together.

Clar turned the charm bracelet on her fat wrist, once, twice, three times. The bracelet sounded. There were bells on the bracelet.

The sun was warm. In a minute she would have to take off her sweater.

"That's pretty, Clar. That's very pretty. Hello, Buddy, hello, Lewis."

"It's newish."

"I would have thought you had been collecting forever. You have so many . . . charms."

"Just about three, four years. I make Billy buy me something everywhere we go, and we've been all over. Like I said. I swear I've met you in one of those places."

"No, Clar. No, I've never been anywhere."

The charms caught the sun. They flashed, almost blinding: gold, silver, a diamond chip, red, green. A person could be hypnotized by a charm bracelet in the sun. For a moment she had imagined Tom's voice, or Ralph's. Or Lewis's. But Lewis was all right. Nothing could happen to Lewis in the park.

An Eiffel Tower, a cradle, Venus de Milo, a royal guard, a bell, bells, yes, three bells, four.

"Billy didn't buy them all, not by any means. Friends give me things, once they know about my hobby. I appreciate them more than the one Billy goes out and buys. I like for people to give me things that mean something to them. This ring . . ." The bells sounded. With her fat fingers, her deft fingers, Clar picked a ring

164

from the jumble. "A girl friend in Rota gave me this. It was her baby ring. Wasn't that nice of her?"

"Her baby's ring?" The gold circle was thin as a hair.

"No, of course not. Her baby ring. She just had it laying around in a jewel case. I wish you could see the jewelry that girl had, a lot of it real, too. Her husband was in the navy, the submarines, and they didn't have any children."

For a moment she thought of the word *jealous*. Of course she was not jealous of the navy wife in Rota. Clar must have met hundreds of people in her travels. "It's beautiful."

"I try to make friends wherever I go."

"Of course you do." She had to say something.

Tom had wanted to buy her a large diamond ring. She had insisted on the small stone. "I would be embarrassed, Tom."

Tom couldn't understand at first. "What kind of silly are you?"

She would not give Tom's ring to Clar.

She had tried to explain to Tom. "I'm not a young girl, Tom. I wouldn't feel comfortable. I'd think people were saying, 'Look at what she's showing off.' You understand, don't you?" She didn't want to hurt Tom's feelings, but she wanted him to understand. "I've spent a lot of time worrying about money. It will be a long time before . . ."

Back in those days she had kept saying the right things easily.

"You're a silly young girl." Tom kissed her. It was a sweet time. They sat in Tom's car by Dow Lake. Lewis chased yellow butterflies at the edge of the water.

Clar said, "Your ring's very pretty."

"Thank you. I like it. Tom and I chose it together. At Cornwell's."

"I'm not asking you to give it to me."

It was a pleasure to hear Clar's laughter.

"I got plenty charms now."

"I know you aren't. I know you have."

When Clar caught her breath she said, "This is from Clara

Tate, the old woman in London I surely told you about, the one I called up on the telephone. It used to be an earring. She had her ears pierced, a thousand years ago. She sent it to me, Clara did. We corresponded for a while. I like to write letters to people. I'll write you. Clara didn't answer my last two letters. Maybe she's dead. That's something to think about, isn't it? But here's the earring."

"It is delicate. It is very beautiful. I hope your Clara is not dead. Grandmother didn't believe in jewelry. But she let me wear earrings when I was in college."

"Billy says the bracelet is a conversation piece. He's right, I guess. We're talking about it, aren't we? This one he bought me in Rome. The Colosseum. My God, that's the night we started Becky. I guess you pay for everything, one way or another. My God, that man! But you and I don't need a conversation piece to talk about."

"The children. I'm sure they're all right."

"Sure. My God, of course they are. You've got to learn not to worry, Caroline. I'm telling you straight now, as a friend. That's something you've got to learn."

"Becky?"

"What could happen to her? She's too slow for anything to happen to her."

"Maybe we should check."

Clar was laughing. "I forgot to tell you. Billy got stuck in the elevator this morning. I didn't go out to see about him. I was laughing too hard. I had to stuff a diaper in my mouth to keep from laughing so loud he'd hear me down in the shaft. I was changing Becky. I heard him hollering. That Becky!

"The kid who works around the apartment got him out all right. Billy wasn't stuck but a few minutes. That kid's nice-looking. He could put his shoes under my bed any time he wanted to." Clar spoke as casually as if she discussed a bracelet.

"You're joking. You're making a joke."

"Sure, maybe. Who's going to have time to find out, with two

166

kids, maybe a third kid coming on? Billy's scared to death of elevators, but he's too lazy to walk. We're just on the fourth floor, like I said. I told Billy you and your husband were coming to see us, for a drink, or a meal, or something. Billy's kind of funny."

She should have said, "And you must come to see us." But instead, she stood quickly. "I know I'm overprotective, but I . . . I have to check on the children."

Clar had surely seen her stand. Clar had surely heard her say, "I have to check on the children."

Clar was saying, "The fellow at the gate, too. He's a good-looking bastard, isn't he, though? When I saw him the first time I came here . . ."

"Where's Becky?" She looked into the woman's clear blue eyes. She did not say, "Where's Buddy? Where's Lewis?" For a moment she was lost in the woman's eyes. "Where's Becky?"

"Becky? Sit down, honey. She's all right. They're all right. I'm telling you. I swear before God they're all right."

"Oh, Clar." She wanted to be Clar. She thought of saying, "I love you, Clar." She thought about being mad, crazy, like Grandmother at the last.

Becky puffed up the path.

Caroline Thaxton returned to the bench to sit beside Clar Tate. They sat in the sun together.

"See, I told you."

$\mathcal{A}$t the house it was cleaning lady day. He got out before Agatha came.

He had a nice day, nice enough. He got off the bus at Sliema and walked back. He felt pretty good. He got a lot more exercise here than he did at home. He knew this part of the world as well as he knew Athens; he knew almost every wave in the ocean.

He ate three Scotch eggs and drank a couple of bottles of lemonade for lunch at a place named the Green Dragon. He dropped in at the armory again. It was a fascinating place. He didn't talk to a lot of people. He hadn't brought his camera. He didn't know why. He had coffee and a sweet at the Lion and Bear. "Where is the picture machine?" an old fellow named Sam asked him. "I guess I forgot to bring it." He hadn't forgot. "You want to remember Malta." "I'll remember it, all right." "Malta, you like?" "The greatest place in the world," Tom said, and the old man laughed.

He went to the National Museum again. He was glad to see the museum again. A museum was a different place when you went alone than when you went with somebody.

He looked at Lewis's naked lady again. He was the only person in the room. Maybe there was something wrong with Tom Hutton. He would have liked to ask somebody, "What do you think

168

about when you look at the picture of a naked woman? Where exactly do you look? Her crotch, her boobs, the couch she's lying on?" He really wanted to know.

He couldn't ask Caroline. He couldn't ask Ralph. Ralph subscribed to *Playboy* and the *Evergreen Review*; Ralph had the magazines addressed to the store. He kept them in the bottom drawer of his desk. Every once in a while Ralph would show him a picture. "What do you think of this, Tommy boy?"

He hated to be called Tommy.

He and Caroline had had sex last night. She probably hadn't wanted it, either. But she had turned off the bedlamp when he came to bed. He thought she was waiting for him. He figured he ought to do something.

But it was all right.

She said, "I love you, Tom." Lately she was always saying, "I love you." For a while, after she lost the baby, she seemed almost afraid to say the words.

He would have to start reading up on art. He'd made an A in an art recognition test from Miss Falcon in high school. He remembered a lot of pictures he'd learned about: *The Blue Boy* and that girl by Vermeer with a blue band around her head, and the one by Velázquez where the little girl stood with her maids and that big dog, and that picture of apples and oranges on a table with something crumpled white. He could remember the names of the painters, too. But the National Museum didn't have any pictures he remembered.

He didn't like to feel stupid.

It was three-fifty. It was about time for him to head home.

He sat on a bench at Victoria Square. The sun was good.

Two benches down from him, toward the library, an old man fed pigeons. The birds were all around the man's feet; two or three of them ate from his hand. One bird sat on the fellow's shoulder.

He took his little Malta guidebook out of his left-hand inside jacket pocket, the pocket where he kept his billfold. He was so

169

used to carrying all the stuff around he would have felt naked without it.

Iva meant yes.

Le meant no. You pronounced it *lehr*. They jerked their heads up when they said *lehr*.

He was practicing the words to himself when the woman sat down. He was a little embarrassed to be caught muttering, but there wasn't any reason to be.

The woman smiled at him. She had on a white blouse and a blue skirt and a jacket around her shoulders. She was wearing sandals without any stockings. She wasn't dressed warmly enough. She was pretty. Her hair was white, but she didn't look very old. He never was able to figure out women's ages. Caroline was a great one for that. Caroline almost never missed. But he really wasn't very much older than Caroline.

The woman looked over at the man with the pigeons.

He put his book back in his pocket.

"I'm just trying to learn a few words of Maltese," he said. "I'm not much good at it."

She sat straight. "How enterprising of you. The rest of us never make an effort, do we?" She was English, all right. "You are from the States, I assume."

"Yeah. Yes. We're from Ohio."

"I've lived here two years, but I do not know a word."

"Banjo." He was probably pronouncing it wrong, but the pretty woman said, "Very good."

She had a nice smile. It was obvious she stayed out in the sun a lot. But she didn't look dried up, not like Ellen. She had lines around her eyes; they looked like smile lines.

She looked over toward the pigeons again. "They are beautiful."

"Sure. Yes." He hadn't really seen them before. They were all the colors of the rainbow, the way the sun hit them. "Look at those colors."

"Has he been at you yet?"

He didn't know what she meant. He had started to answer something, and then he said, "What do you mean?"

"Sorry. The old chap in the tweed cap. For money. Sometimes he asks for money to buy grain to feed the pigeons. He's not supposed to. They mess up Queen Victoria, and begging is against the law. He has been arrested at least twice."

"No, I've not talked to him."

"He'll be at you."

"I hope so."

She sat back. Her eyes were steady. She had pretty brown eyes. "You respect pigeons?"

"Well, no, not particularly."

"I suppose they are rather a nuisance. But you would give the old man a penny if he asked you? Even if he is narky?"

"Narky? Touched?" He tapped his forehead.

She had a nice laugh, like a little girl's. "That's it."

He didn't know why he did it. He didn't mean to be showing off. But he took his billfold out of the left-hand pocket and pulled out a ten shilling note. He stood up and went down to the old man. He could feel the woman's eyes watching him, but he really wasn't meaning to show off. In Athens Hap Hughes moved dead things from the highway in front of his house—hedgehogs and chipmunks and possums and rabbits, whatever, up to the big hill behind his house. "I feed the other fellows," Hap said. "What with the Health Department and everything these days, the buzzards have a hard time of it." Sometimes Hap came in the store and chewed the rag for a while.

He liked Hap. His dad had liked Hap a lot, too.

"For food. For the pigeons," he said.

The old man stood up. He took off his cap. The air was full of pigeon wings. "Thank you, sir. Thank you kindly, sir."

"O.K. It's not anything." He was sorry the old man had taken off his cap.

"Thank you, sir," the old man called after him. "We appreciate."

171

He pretended he didn't hear.

"That was charming of you."

"No, it wasn't. I just like to see somebody like that."

"Even if you ridicule the English for being sentimental about birds and animals?"

"I don't ridicule anybody. I didn't realize you were . . . sentimental." He really didn't know what she was talking about.

"We are, of course. We write our MP when anything happens to an animal. I write mine. And we have ghastly fits when we think about bullfights. I suppose you attend them, and applaud, and take photographs."

"I've never seen a bullfight. We don't have them. This is the first time we've been over, been abroad."

"Whatever are you doing *here?*"

It was difficult to explain why he and Caroline and Lewis lived in Birżebbuġa. It had been a long time since he had talked to a woman this way, a stranger. But he tried to tell her. "My wife and I, we've been married a little over a year. We have a boy, Lewis —my first wife's boy. It just seemed the right time to leave home for a while. An old lady told me I was getting old." He spread his hands. "I don't know. It's hard to tell."

The woman's eyes were moist. She was wearing eye makeup. Almost everybody did over here. For some reason she looked as if she was about to cry.

"I guess I'm saying something wrong. It's hard to tell."

The woman turned her head. "Please. I am an ass." The way she said ass was different from the word ass at home. "It's only . . . That was quite splendid of you to give money for the pigeons. And to come abroad. I'm sure your wife is very happy." She was laughing again.

"We get along fine."

He told her about Hap Hughes.

"That is a lovely story. You exposit admirably."

"Hap's a good fellow. It's a nickname. Hap stands for Happy."

It was nice to sit in the sun and talk to the pretty woman.

172

"Ralph and Ellen, my brother and his wife, they've been all over. They take cruises. We came tourist class. Ralph said we'd lose our minds. But we liked the boat. And we're having a ball in Malta. We don't do anything much, but it's great."

"Does your brother like Mr. Hughes as much as your dads did?" The woman looked straight at him.

"That's a funny thing to ask somebody."

"Tell me."

"Sure. Ralph likes him all right."

Ralph had told him he wouldn't like trigonometry and Miss Pullen in high school. But Miss Pullen was wonderful. She didn't put A on Tom Hutton's report card. She wrote in, "One Hundred Percent." She had an old-fashioned handwriting. He was crazy about her. He was about to tell the woman about trigonometry.

She was saying, "I adore it here in Malta. I am a widow. I have a flat in Marsaxlokk. I play tennis when I can find a partner. I play bridge once a week at the Imperial with some old ladies—older ladies." She laughed. "Many days I wander around and look. Every place in Malta says, 'Look at me.' The buildings and the sea and the fields."

He didn't know what to say to that, but it was a nice idea. He said, "I know what you mean."

"Do you really?"

"I told you we were having a ball. A lot of days I just take a bus and toot around. There's a lot to do here." He told her about the play and the organ recital and how much Lewis enjoyed them. "He's not five years old, quite, but he really had a good time."

"You don't have a motor, an automobile." It wasn't a question exactly.

She was standing up. She had a good build, for an older woman —he hadn't noticed before.

He stood up, too. The woman was almost as tall as he was, taller than Caroline. He hadn't realized. He said, "It's been nice talking to you."

The lady was holding out her hand. "My name is Gwen . . ."

173

He didn't catch her last name. He had to ask her.

"Pettigrew." She spelled it for him.

"Tom Hutton."

They were shaking hands. She had a good handshake.

"It is a pleasure to meet someone who is not from England. There are too many British here. Sometimes I think no one is left at home."

She was saying, "Life is too brief not to meet the people you admire. It is utterly ridiculous to wait for dinner parties and introductions."

He let loose of her hand. "That's right. If Caroline and I had to wait around for dinner parties . . ." He couldn't imagine going to anybody's house in Malta. It just never had entered his mind.

"You will come to my flat sometime. Perhaps I will get around to inviting you and your wife. And the boy."

"That's mighty nice. You must come see us."

The old man had finished feeding the pigeons. He walked past them. He tipped his cap again. He said, "God bless."

"God bless," Mrs. Pettigrew said. It was nice, the way she said it.

"We'll go to my flat. We'll have a drink."

"That's very nice of you. But I've got to be getting back. They'll be looking for me."

"I'll drive you."

It was the funniest situation he'd ever been in. He couldn't wait to tell Caroline about the woman.

"Thank you so much, but really, my family's expecting me."

"I told you. I'll drive you. You won't lose any time." She had started walking across the square. She was talking over her shoulder. "My automobile is up here. It's a Mini. Black. You will have to help me find it. I always lose it. The license number is . . ." She was walking fast.

It was a real adventure. Ralph wouldn't believe the story.

He got in step with her.

She drove fast, but she drove well.

He felt silly, but he was enjoying himself. There wasn't any reason to feel silly.

"This is a great car. I wish I had one. You don't have a lot of room, but it's a great car." His knees were up against his chin.

She turned right, and left, and right again. "That's . . ." He didn't catch the name. "You must take your wife and son there. It is a marvelous view, all over the island." Her skirt had hiked up, but she didn't seem to notice. He thought about Lewis's naked lady.

Left again, and right. "There is Paola. A lovely church there."

He didn't hear the names of the places. But she was a good driver.

The sky was bluer than blue. All of a sudden it had turned out to be the prettiest afternoon anybody ever saw. At a hairpin curve she said, "I should have told you to fasten your seat belt."

"My dad had several accidents and he was always thrown clear. He said seat belts were dangerous."

"You have surprising turns of mind, Mr. Hutton." He figured she was complimenting him.

She smiled at him. She drove down the narrow road without watching what she was up to.

But it was all right. He felt good, the way he'd felt a long time ago on the Wildcat, at a fair, a long time ago.

"Whee!"

She laughed.

"Here we are." She stopped in front of a three-story stucco building. It was new, but pretty ordinary-looking, right on the street. "Out we go."

She opened the trunk of the car and handed him a couple of string bags, full of groceries. She gave him her purse to hold while she opened the door.

"Pray, come in."

"Golly."

"Do you like it?"

175

The apartment was beautiful. "I didn't know there was any-thing like this in Malta. Or anywhere." He really meant it.

She was pleased. "I am glad for people to like where I live." It was like something out of a magazine.

"Golly, it's so big." He set her purse and the bags down on the counter that divided the kitchen from the huge living room.

"It is only the ground floor. That is all. There are two other tenants in the building. I think there are two. But I can't hear anyone." *Cawn't*, she said. He liked the way she talked. "The building is well constructed."

She walked across the living room to the bay windows—there were three of them. She pushed back a set of white curtains, thinner than spiderwebs. "The bay."

A lot of boats bobbed around outside her windows, little yachts, and the fishermen's boats—the *dghajsas*. He wished he knew how to pronounce *dghajsa:* he would have liked to say the word, but he was afraid to. A fancy bus was parked up the street, two hundred yards or so away. He said, "It's beautiful."

"Thank you."

"And there's a tourist bus. Everybody wants to know where you live."

"They are ruining Malta, the tourists."

"We're tourists. Everybody's a tourist." It was what Caroline said.

She turned quickly. "Yes. Yes, I suppose so." She let the curtains fall. "I am sorry you reminded me."

She was beautiful, too, standing against the curtains. The walls were white. There was a thick green rug. The furniture, most of it, was green. There was a bunch of purple iris in a blue vase on the coffee table.

"You ought to name this place 'The Island.' "

She was a funny woman. She was the kind of woman who made you say things you didn't know you were going to say. Caroline was a little like that, but not exactly. He loved Caroline.

"Yes, I suppose so. I loathe the English, the way they name

their homes—Heroncrest, Ambleside, Thrushes' Glen. But I will no doubt choose a name for the flat. Bide-a-wee. Do you approve of that?"

"I didn't mean anything."

"Of course you didn't. You will fix yourself a drink, won't you?" She motioned over to a table. She had a dozen bottles out, at least a dozen, and glasses, big glasses.

She moved across the room to the other side of the counter. It was a pleasure to watch her walk. The kitchen was green and white tile.

"I'll just have a little bit of sherry."

"You will not want ice, then."

"Yes, I'd like a little ice." He had poured himself more than he meant to. "What can I fix you?"

"I'll tend." She was filling a silver bucket with ice.

"I'm not much for drinking. Ralph does the drinking for our family. I worry about him sometimes."

"You aren't Jewish, are you?"

"Why did you ask me that? Do they take ice in their sherry?"

"You seem a close-knit family. It came to my mind."

"Do you say whatever comes to your mind?"

"I endeavor to."

"You're putting me on."

"I do not know exactly what that means."

"It's an expression."

"There's a saying here. 'It takes six Jews to trick a Maltese.' I heard somebody say it in the market this afternoon. It just came to my mind."

All of a sudden he was really uncomfortable. He didn't know what she meant. And he didn't like jokes against Jews or Catholics —that kind of joke. It was something his mother had been against, too. But his dad was always telling jokes.

"We're Presbyterians. Caroline goes to church with me. She belonged to the Church of Christ." He didn't want to be uncomfortable.

177

"You are lucky, aren't you, though? Happy."

She moved around him. She poured herself a big drink of Scotch. She put three ice cubes in both of their glasses. "American style," she said. "I like it." She sat down on the curving green couch. He thought about sitting down beside her, but instead he sat in the white chair next to the couch.

He tried to think of something to say. She was looking at him over the rim of her glass. She didn't seem to mind the silence.

He said, "A fellow at lunch today—he said Italy wasn't a religious country. He said Malta was the last of the really religious countries. Do you think that's the truth?"

"Possibly." She took a big swallow. She was looking at him hard. "I was twenty-one before I was informed that everyone was not an Anglican."

"That's interesting." He didn't know what he was doing here with Gwen Pettigrew. It was funny. He couldn't wait to tell Caroline.

"You lead a happy life." She raised her eyebrows. It was hard to tell when she was asking a question or telling him something.

"Yeah, I guess so. Everybody has a pretty happy life, I guess." He had been thirsty. He'd drunk over half his glass already. "I've had my troubles, but everybody has."

She was waiting. She had a funny way about her.

But he could talk to her. He would admit, even if he shouldn't, that he could talk to just about anybody. A lot of people said so.

He laughed. "Except my Aunt Irma Anne, maybe. The fellow she was going to marry was killed in World War One. She never stopped talking about him. She kept his letters in a glass dish, tied with ribbons. On the hall table. She kept talking about her tragic life. She loved to be sick. She got as much fun out of a bad cold as most people do out of . . . well, sex. That's what my dad said about her. My mother almost hit the ceiling when he said that. She was my mother's aunt. So . . ." He couldn't think what he had been going to say.

"So?"

178

"So she enjoyed herself."

She was waiting.

"Maybe it's all tragic a little. I don't know. I don't think so."

"I don't like your brother Ralph."

"Well, really now."

"He does not really admire your Mr. Hughes who feeds the vultures."

"That's something you just thought up to say."

"Yes, of course. And if your brother were in this room, I would throw him out. I like Mr. Hughes very much."

He wasn't going to get hot under the collar. Maybe Ralph didn't like Hap.

"Hap learned to play the piano after he was fifty. He got a book and taught himself."

"I told you I liked him."

"Look here." He had finished his drink. She was filling it again. "Hey, that's fine. That's plenty."

"I find you hard to believe, Mr. Hutton. I find you hard to imagine."

Once Marie said, "God damn you, Tom Hutton. You're slow. You're too slow to have an affair." It was a pretty bad argument, and he didn't like arguments. He couldn't really remember how it all started. Marie had invited the golf pro to dinner, maybe that was it. Maybe she had been drinking too much and acting silly. Maybe he'd said something to her after the man left. He couldn't remember.

He had been faithful to Marie. That's what marriage meant. He didn't have any patience with Ralph, running around, leaning up against the girls in the stockroom. That sweet little girl Nancy Roe had told him about Ralph.

He told Ralph. He told him flat out. He said, "Ellen would know what I'm talking about. I figure she knows."

Ralph said, "Bull shit. Bull shit on you, Tommy," even though he generally didn't talk that way.

Gwen Pettigrew was fixing herself a drink again, maybe it was

179

her third one. She sat down on the couch again, but closer to him this time.

"I am not a widow."

"You don't say."

"I am in the process of a divorce, a rather spectacular divorce. I told you I was a widow because I did not wish to frighten you."

But she was waiting again.

"I don't scare easy." It was something to say, but he wasn't sounding exactly like himself.

"You have no reason. I get lonely. I am not interested in sex, not particularly. Perhaps that is part of the reason for the divorce, but a small part. You may relax. My solicitor says I should write a book about my husband. I am considering it. He brought doxies home, all the time. My husband, not my solicitor." She was laughing.

He looked at his wristwatch. It wasn't five yet. "I'll declare."

"My solicitor says I shall have a best seller. My husband had a number of hobbies." She took a really big swig. "Is your wife interested in anything—acting, writing, painting? I understand that American women consume themselves with artistic projects."

"Not particularly. She taught the third grade."

He'd never met a woman like Gwen before. He wanted to get out of the place, but he didn't want to be rude. It was all pretty crazy. He was feeling his drinks a little, too. Just to have something to say he said, "A fellow told me today that if you run over a goat in Malta you have to pay five dollars, no matter whose fault it is. You learn a lot, drinking coffee around the bars."

"I should think that that was rather inexpensive for a goat."

"I don't know what they're worth. Maybe it was five pounds." He was ashamed of himself.

"You do make conversation, don't you, Mr. Thomas Hutton?" She was smiling.

He hadn't quite finished his drink, but he put it down on the

180

table by his chair. "This has been mighty nice, but I'd better be on my way. Caroline'll be looking for me."

"What they say about you is true, isn't it?" She kept smiling.

"I don't know what you mean."

"Nothing. Absolutely nothing at all."

"O.K. That's O.K." He could kick himself. But he wasn't going to argue with the woman.

She finished her drink. "I will drive you home. You must return to visit me another time. I find you rather fascinating."

"I'll catch a bus. The buses are great here. You have good service all over the island." He got up.

She stood up all at once.

"Aren't we nervous, though, Mr. Hutton? I promised I would drive you to your home. What did you do with my purse?"

"It's on the counter. But I mean it about taking the bus. I really like the buses."

"Dear Mr. Hutton." She was standing close to him.

There wasn't any point in arguing with her. "You're the doctor."

They stood beside each other for a minute—for a few seconds; it wasn't any longer than that.

She began laughing and walked over to the counter. Over her shoulder she said, "I was not actually expecting you to kiss me. I think I would have been offended."

"O.K. O.K. That's all right."

He was a goddamned fool, just like Marie said.

On the way to Birżebbuġa she did most of the talking.

He barely listened to her. He couldn't wait to get home.

She was saying, "One is required to wear evening dress at the hotel."

He started to ask her which hotel, but he didn't bother.

"Evening dresses, long dresses, the man in tails. A dinner dress is not acceptable. Once they refused to allow me to enter. I was wearing a rather charming cocktail gown. I had acquired my

181

escort by chance, rather the way I acquired you. He was American, too. Steel. He was terribly embarrassed, too."

"Caroline didn't even bring an evening dress. Who's embarrassed?" They were at Saint George's Bay. He thought about saying, "Who the hell's embarrassed?"

"Not you, Mr. Hutton. Not you, of course."

She turned the corner sharply.

"You can let me out anywhere. We live over there, just over there in the middle of the block."

"I said I would take you home."

"I appreciate it. And thanks a lot. Thanks for the drinks." He was mad at her, but there wasn't any sense in making an enemy. "It's been nice seeing you."

"My pleasure. My particular pleasure."

She slammed on the brakes.

"I'd like for you to come in and meet Caroline and Lewis. They'd like to meet you. We don't meet a lot of people." He was determined to be polite.

"Another time, perhaps. Perhaps I'll be ringing you up for dinner. But don't count on it. That's what you say, isn't it, 'Don't count on it'?"

He was out of the car. He said, "We don't have a telephone." It was a damn fool thing to say. He felt terrible.

"I will write you a note then. Twenty Pretty Bay." She pronounced all the t's.

He couldn't imagine how he'd got himself into such a situation. Caroline would think the story was interesting.

"Another time." The little Mini was moving before he had time to get the door closed. She turned the car around in the middle of the street.

He waved to her.

She waved back.

He couldn't wait to get in the house.

The door was locked. He rang the doorbell, but nobody answered. He got his key out and went in. He called, "Caroline. Caroline."

The table was set for dinner. He went to the bathroom, down-stairs.

Caroline and Lewis had probably gone to a store for something. For some reason he didn't want to be in the house by himself. Gwen Pettigrew was a bitch, and he was a goddamned lucky man.

He went down to the Courageous and ordered himself a glass of coffee. There wasn't anybody to talk to, and he didn't hang around.

Caroline and Lewis weren't home yet. And it was almost six o'clock.

He picked up the *Times of Malta* off the coffee table. He'd read it that morning, but he read it again. He liked the *Times*. You could read it without thinking about it too much. It made Malta seem more like home, and different at the same time. You didn't know anybody who had died or was having babies, but you went through the same weather with them. It was funny. Ohio was very far away.

"The British Council, 6:30 . . . at the University Building . . . at the Manoel Theatre . . ." It was nice to think that you lived in Malta and knew the buildings as well as any place on Court Street.

"At Saint Catherine of Siena maternity wing to . . . Camilleri . . . God's precious gift of a son. *Deo Gratias et Mariae.*" All the birth announcements said *"Deo Gratias et Mariae."*

The house was so quiet you could hear a faucet dripping in the kitchen. He went through the house and turned it off. Caroline was generally pretty careful about faucets.

"Being the *trigesima die* of the death of Dr. Paul Sammut, Ph.D., M.D., all Masses said tomorrow at the Parish Church, Tarxien, Saint Nicholas Priory."

183

"Joseph Agius . . . the seventeenth anniversary of his death. O Merciful Jesus give him eternal rest."

Somebody . . . "Grant him, O Lord, eternal rest."

The letters to the editor were about importation of eggs and mail delivery.

His dad had been dead for seventeen years, at least that long.

"Fondly remembered by his Sons, and Daughters-in-Law," the paper said.

The weather report was like your life. "A weak ridge of high pressure over the central Mediterranean is moving slowly east. Sea: Moderate. Swell: Moderate. Max. Temp. 16° C. Outlook: Little change. Rainfall since Sept. 1 . . ."

He threw the paper on the couch. He picked it up and folded it. He hated a messy paper. Marie always scrambled the Athens *Messenger.*

"Why should you care?" Marie said. "I'm the one who has to pick them up."

Thanks be to God and Mary. That is what the birth announcements said.

It was after six when Caroline and Lewis got in. But maybe his watch was a little fast.

"We're late. I'm sorry, Tom."

"Where have you been?" He had been worried about them, and now he was mad at them.

"We've walked. We've been to a park. The park. I talked to the pleasant woman. The woman with two children."

"I got the same tricycle again."

"I'm sorry, Tom."

"Sure, sure." For a minute he thought about keeping Gwen Pettigrew a secret. It would have served Caroline right.

"Supper—dinner's almost ready. I really have everything almost ready."

Lewis sat on the living room couch and stretched out his legs. He had the damn sky book in his lap. "Once upon a time," Lewis was saying.

184

Tom Hutton stood at the kitchen door and told his wife about Gwen Pettigrew. "The funniest thing happened to me today— the damnedest thing, if you'll excuse my French."

Caroline tossed a salad. She was listening, but it wasn't much of a story. He told all of it, practically all.

"That's terribly interesting. We could ask her over."

"No, not that. I just thought it was . . . interesting."

"It is, Tom. It is."

He went back to the living room to read to Lewis until Caroline called them to dinner.

$\mathcal{S}$he really liked for Tom to come home to lunch. His coming gave a pattern to the days. But he was staying in Valletta again. "This fellow, Edgar, he wants to take me all over his store. I'd insist you and Lewis come, except I don't think you'd be much interested. He has a sort of dry goods store, right down near the library—you know where it is. I met him yesterday. He's been on holiday. He's the nicest kind of fellow. He wants to talk to me about the store."

"Of course. Surely. You must go. Lewis and I will walk around."

"I don't like to leave you."

"Silly, Tom. We've been a thousand places already."

"It's been nice here, hasn't it, though? The very best."

"It's been fine, Tom." How many times had they already said the same words to each other?

"I hate to think about leaving Malta. But it'll be good to be home, too. Everything works out, doesn't it?"

"Yes, Tom."

He kissed her.

"Good-bye, Lewis."

Tom kissed Lewis's forehead. She was proud that Tom could kiss his son.

186

The bus came honking up the street.

"Good-bye, good-bye." They stood at the door and waved to Tom and the bus.

Time got away. Even in Malta, where time slowed, time got away.

She did not mean to be sitting on the wall by the bay every noon, when the children came home from school, in their blue uniforms, their hair burnished, carrying their school cases; most of the cases were made of wood, with tiny metal clasps. Some of the children held hands. The children sparkled. There was no reason to watch them come home for lunch, but she often watched them.

Down the street the men from the Courageous had moved the bentwood chairs out of the bar onto the sidewalk and the street. They sat backward in their chairs, facing each other instead of the sea.

Two young women passed, pushing carriages. Their babies slept. She had almost given up peering into the carriages. The old woman with the green cart passed, crying out something, whatever it was she had to sell from under the dirty cloths.

"Look, Mamma." Lewis wasn't being too loud. He wasn't making them conspicuous.

"Yes. Yes."

He had thrown a stick into the water. A little wave brought it back. The water touched his toes and he squealed. He grabbed the stick.

"I got it. I got it." He ran to where she sat. "I got a little wet, too. Is that all right, Mamma?"

The stick? His sleeve? "Of course, Lewis. Here's a Kleenex. Just roll up your sleeves."

The schoolchildren passed and disappeared.

It was time to go inside for soup and sandwiches.

She sat a minute longer, a little longer. Only two men sat backward in chairs now, talking to each other. A wind had come up from someplace. The sky was gray. She turned, trying to find where the sun had gone. She wondered if the sun had disappeared from the garden. "We'll go in."

Lewis was shivering. "I'm hungry, Mamma."

But before they ate, she washed the dishes in the china closet. Three times now, four times, she had washed all of the dishes.

"That's pretty good sandwiches," Lewis said.

"Thank you. Thank you very much."

"You're welcome."

"Look, Lewis. The sun's come out."

"We could take a walk, couldn't we, Mamma?"

"Of course we could. We will. It's a beautiful afternoon."

"I don't want to wear a coat."

"All right, all right. It's warm. It's like spring."

"It's a beautiful afternoon." Lewis giggled.

"I'll leave the dishes. We're ready, aren't we?"

"I have to go to the bathroom."

"But hurry. We don't want to miss any of the beautiful afternoon."

"I don't even have to take a nap today."

"We'll see."

Lewis walked a little ahead of her. She and Clar and the children had had a pleasant visit. Already she could not remember what they had talked about. She felt buoyant. The sun hung like a searchlight. There was no hurry.

The sun was a searchlight that wasn't looking for anybody. That was a comfortable way to think about the sun. It wasn't a searchlight, of course.

People said *warm* too much. Ellen was always saying, "She's such a warm person," about whoever complimented her on her thinness, or her clothes, or her house, or her children.

But it was a good enough word. Clar was a warm person.

"I want to be a good person," she thought. She was foolish. "I will be good," Queen Victoria said, or something silly. But no-

188

body wanted to be Queen Victoria any more. Caroline Hutton didn't. Queen Victoria was a person pigeons sat on in front of a library.

I want to be good.

Clar was warm. She was open and warm. She was vulgar and offensive and contained and liberated and warm. Clar was a lot of adjectives.

Lewis was muttering to himself.

"Wait for me, Lewis."

He paused, but he did not turn his head. He kept muttering. He was smiling.

"I don't understand. I can't hear you."

"I'm not talking to you."

"Excuse me. I though you were."

"I'm saying son of a bitch."

"Lewis!" She stopped. Lewis smiled up at her. She had almost struck at the boy; she had almost slapped him.

"Lewis Hutton, what on earth?"

His smile was a grimace. "I like to say it. In my mouth. Sometimes I say goddamn son of a bitch."

"Lewis! Wherever . . ." She did not finish her question. "Lewis, no. We don't talk that way. It's not nice. It's not nice at all."

Grandmother said, "March into the kitchen this minute, Caroline. You're going to wash out your mouth with soap. Promise me you'll never use that expression again."

The soap was terrible in her mouth.

She had said, "Gosh darn," that is probably what she had said, something like that. Like God damn. Like Clar Tate, like Caroline Thaxton.

"Lewis, I'm surprised at you." She kneeled to him.

He turned his head.

"Look at me, Lewis. Honey, we don't talk that way." She was in control of herself.

"We say it all the time. Me and Buddy."

"Sweetheart, look at me. There are some things our family

189

doesn't say. We don't take the name of the Lord in vain." She was Grandmother speaking.

"I like to say it."

"Promise me." She stood quickly. She had promised herself a long time ago. "I will never say 'Promise me' to a child of my own." Grandmother had forced too many promises.

Lewis pulled away from her.

"I'm sorry, Mamma." He smiled, showing all his teeth. He could have been saying, "Goddamn, I'm sorry."

They would not go to the garden again. Clar was more offensive than she was warm. A quick and easy companionship with a woman in a public park was not worth endangering the immortal soul. . . .

"Your immortal soul," Grandmother said.

Lewis was running down the street, his arms stretched out.

She had to run to keep up with him.

At the door of 20 Pretty Bay, fumbling for her key, she said, "I love you, Lewis. You know that."

"I love you, Mamma."

Dear God.

She didn't know how to pray any more. "Have you said your prayers, Caroline?"

"What would you like to eat tonight, Lewis?" She had planned on reheating the lamb roast, with gravy, and mashed potatoes, and rutabaga—*swede*, they called it here.

"Hamburger and French fries."

"Very well. We'll manage that."

"Oh, boy," Lewis said as if he had never thought of words different from "Oh, boy."

"And we have marvelous tomatoes."

She would not tell Tom about Lewis's cursing—swearing. She could not imagine what words she could use to tell Tom about Lewis.

Tom would say, "I don't talk that way. Where did he hear it?"

She could not say, "From the strange woman. We have visited

190

in the park, a few times, a very few times. She talks about everything. She faces everything. She has no shame, Tom. I like her. I have liked her very much."

Secrets begat secrets begat secrets begat . . .

Of course Tom wasn't home. She was positive. But she went to the kitchen calling softly, "Tom, Tom." Lewis walked behind her. She went upstairs, into both the bedrooms, the bath, even up the curving steps to the roof. "Tom. Tom."

Lewis was whispering, "Tom, Tom."

"Lewis. Stop that."

The view was beautiful. She turned, seeing all the views. Lewis turned, too. The foolish child began to spin himself around. "Stop that, Lewis. You'll get dizzy. You'll fall."

"I can't stop," Lewis shouted. "It's too fast."

She grabbed at his shoulder. "Stop it."

She held tightly.

"That hurts." Lewis stuck out his lower lip. "That hurt a lot."

"Of course it didn't. It's not good for you, spinning around like that."

She remembered a field. It was dusk. There were daisies. She had been turning very slowly, wishing she knew how many daisies grew in the field. She turned faster and faster. She was falling, but she didn't fall. She whirled until the field and the sky both waited beneath her, or above her.

Somebody picked her up. Perhaps . . . It could have been one of her parents. There must have been a million daisies in the field. She couldn't remember anything else. Where had they been living? Who were they? It had been dusk.

It was afternoon now. The sun hung crooked, at the right. Whoever it was who had picked her up, whoever pulled at her arm, called her name.

"Your daddy's not home. Let's go downstairs."

She reached for Lewis's hand. He yanked away from her and fell backward. He sat hard on the macadam roof.

She took a step toward him. She said, "Honey."

"Look what you did to me."

"Lewis! Really!"

She said, "Careful you don't step on your lower lip." It was a hateful thing Grandmother had always said.

Lewis brushed his hands together, the way Tom did.

Lewis didn't cry. He was a strange child. He almost never cried. He was furious, but he didn't cry. Perhaps he had taught her not to cry.

"I'm going to tell."

"Lewis. Tell what?" She was trembling. She didn't know why she was trembling. "Get on down those steps!"

In the bathroom she ran water into the basin. "Now, wash yourself. Take off your jacket and roll up your sleeves, and wash. Your face, too. You should see your face. Here's the soap."

"You pushed me."

"I did nothing of the sort."

She left him.

Of course she did not expect to find Tom in the other room. She knew he was not in the house. She thought of the third bedroom, if she thought of it at all, as the nursery in somebody else's house, no more belonging to the Huttons than the air over the courtyard.

Agatha had pulled the cretonne curtains closed. The light was vague, like the light of the prehistoric cave they had visited the other afternoon. "Tom. Tom."

She parted the curtains to look down at the bay. The bay was still bright.

"Tom."

In the corner of the room the baby basket still crouched, like a laundry bundle.

She closed the curtains. She moved the basket from the floor to the bed near the window. "There," she said, for no reason at all.

She stopped to look at herself in the three mirrors of the vanity

192

dresser. The light was so dim she would not have recognized herself, if she had not known she stood there.

Tom was always saying, "Lewis has got to learn to get along in the world."

"Lewis has to rub up against all kinds of people."

"We don't want to turn him into a sissy, do we, Caroline? It's hard on a boy to be a sissy."

"Yes, yes, yes, Tom."

"I'm not criticizing. You're the finest mother in the world."

"No, Tom. Yes."

Dozens of times they had made the words together, circling each other.

She honestly did not intend to go to the park again.

Lewis was not without guile.

He was like Tom. He loved to make a story of a day. But he had not mentioned Buddy and Becky and Clar to Tom. He had told only of the tricycle rides.

Lewis was shouting, "Mamma, Mamma!"

The child deserved to be frightened a little. He deserved to be hidden from. Tom was right. She waited on his every beck and call. Perhaps she had been doing the boy an injustice.

"Mamma, I'm yelling at you!"

She counted ten before she opened the door into the hall. She counted ten again.

Lewis stood on the second landing of the stairway. He turned quickly. His eyes were round. He was frightened. But he wasn't crying.

He bounded up to the first landing. She thought he was coming to throw himself into her arms.

He stopped. "Why did you hide, Mamma?" He turned his head sideways.

"I wasn't hiding." Her voice was calm enough. If she cried— it would have been terrible if she had cried. "I was checking on things."

193

"You mustn't tell a story, Mamma." He sounded exactly like herself. He was a terrifying child.

"Tom wasn't in there."

"Daddy isn't home yet. You told me."

She did not lower her eyes. At least she was able to hold her eyes steady.

Lewis lifted his hands. He ran up the steps to her. He threw his arms around her waist.

"How do I look? Do I look nice?"

"Oh, sweetheart." His hair was dripping. He had poured water on his head and combed his hair with his fingers.

"Lewis. Lewis, darling."

To

She had almost overslept; it was after seven. And she had missed the flower man on Friday. She was bound and determined not to miss him again.

She had left her clothes in the bathroom, as usual. As usual she thought of lighting the heater. But Tom liked to light the heaters —that was Tom's part of waking the house. She was trembling, but she got into her clothes all right. It was a usual morning. Except now she was thinking, "one of the last mornings," "one of the last afternoons," "one of the last chances." There would not be many more chances to visit the flower man; another Friday, another Tuesday, and the Huttons would be on the boat to Syracuse, the train to Naples, the boat to New York, the plane to Columbus, where Ralph would meet them. Ralph and Ellen had written very cordial notes. "Hurry home," Ellen said.

"O.K. Home," Lewis had said the first afternoon in Malta.

People already moved up and down the street on Pretty Bay. Somebody was always awake in the world. It was a comforting thought. Somebody was always "looking out."

She tried to look hard at everything. She hadn't looked hard enough at Malta, the streets. The people and their clothes. Did everyone regret not looking hard enough at everything?

She spoke to the British lady who had been buying artichokes

197

yesterday, and the lame man, a couple of the ladies who wore black and always seemed to be coming from church. "Good morning." It was a pleasure to say "Good morning," while Tom and Lewis slept in their beds. "Good morning. I'm back," she said to the flower truck man.

"You got disappointed last week," he said. "I save these for you. Freesias. Freesias is what you want."

The flowers were yellow, orange, red, singing colors, loud singing.

"Two bunches—no, four. They're lovely."

"Yellow, orange, red, madame. Fine colors. I grow them all myself."

She relished listening to the man. He had obviously learned his English from a Scotsman.

She tried to look at the flowers individually. The smell of the freesias made her almost dizzy. The man wrapped the flowers with twine, placed them in a newspaper cone. His movements were smooth. She was, surely, the only awkward person in Malta.

"And the iris. A half dozen of the iris."

"Right you are."

"I feel like a bride."

"And like a bride you look. Cheerio."

At first she thought she had forgot her key. She held the flowers against her breasts, scrambling in her purse. Surely a thirty-year-old woman should be able to learn to manage her keys.

The morning seemed terribly important. This was a morning to do everything right.

She found the key.

"Thank you, thank you," she said almost aloud to someone.

She worked at the sink hurriedly. She was determined to arrange the flowers before Agatha arrived, before Tom and Lewis came down. They always admired her arrangements, but sometimes they were impatient with how long she took. The iris in the green glass vase for the living room—they were fine. There were at least ten vases in the house, all ugly, but ten vases. She trotted into the living room to place the bouquet on the console table. She sloshed water, but it didn't matter. She stood back to admire the flowers against the light blue wall. The green glass caught two diamonds from the transom light. Three of the stalks needed shortening. But she didn't have to do everything right away, not right away.

The freesias were hard to manage, even with the wad of wire she had found the second day in the house. "Oh," or "Joy," something ridiculous, she had said aloud that day.

She tried the orange vegetable dish first, but even the lovely freesias could not redeem the orange dish. And the stems kept collapsing. The mate of the green glass vase wasn't right, either. The flowers looked choked, screaming almost.

Tom and Lewis moved. Their feet sounded above her.

The metal bowl would be good enough. If she could only get the flowers to stand up.

"Stand up, you," she was saying when Tom came into the kitchen.

"Pretty," Tom said.

"I don't have breakfast started. And Agatha will be here any minute."

"There's not any hurry."

"That's good, Tom"

She forced herself to arrange the flowers slowly.

"Pretty," Tom said. "And they smell good."

They were pretty. They were beautiful. It was a good day.

"There's not any hurry. I'll be getting out of your hair; but there's not any hurry."

"That's good, Tom, that there's not any hurry. You're not in the way. You're never in the way."

They had made love again last night. It was good, pleasant. She had been excited. She did not want Tom to know how excited she had been. Tom was a considerate gentleman. She did not want to be unladylike.

199

"Oh, I love you, I love you," she had said, meaning the words, hoping she knew what the words meant.

She had thought for a minute that Tom was going to speak of the night. Tom could have said . . . Or he could have said . . . They could have had a secret together.

"They're pretty," Tom said.

Lewis was at the kitchen door, already dressed. "My, they're pretty, Mamma."

"Breakfast. We've got to have breakfast."

"Did you sleep all right, Lewis?" Tom asked.

"Like a bug in a rug on a log."

Tom laughed. He was always delighted when Lewis quoted him.

At breakfast Tom decided to take Lewis for a haircut, and to see the armory again. Lewis didn't want to go. He never wanted to have a haircut. The idea of a haircut and the armory seemed too much. But she did not say anything.

"Do I have to? Do I have to, Daddy?"

"Sure you do." Tom's voice was firm but pleasant. "You don't want to be one of those freaks, do you? Yesterday I saw the worst-looking guy I've ever seen. His hair was down to here, and his beard . . ."

The child didn't really need a haircut. His hair looked marvelous. She liked it long.

Lewis looked at her.

She turned her head away.

She was sorry that loyalties were so complicated. "It'll be fun, Lewis," she said to her glass of orange juice.

"O.K., O.K." Lewis could be more pathetic than anybody. He raised his shoulders and dropped them. "We might as well get started." That was Tom's sentence, too. She could have cried for the boy.

"Have a wonderful time. Both of you have a wonderful time. Your camera, Tom?"

"I've taken about enough pictures."

200

She wanted to hold them. "You haven't taken a picture of the other room, the third bedroom. You have time for that." A picture would fill a space in her mind.

"We've got to make tracks. I'll get around to it, by golly. We still have time."

"And the courtyard, looking into the dining room." She almost never went into the courtyard. She preferred to hang the few clothes she washed on the roof. The courtyard was always dark. It was difficult to imagine such a space, even a walled space, where no sun could settle.

Malta was a place where nothing happened. Malta was suspended someplace. She didn't know the date. She started to ask Tom. But at least she should know the date. She picked up the Malta *Times* from the coffee table. It was Monday's paper. Today was Tuesday, Agatha's day.

"Good-bye, good-bye."

The sky was dark.

She was tired. She was tired of the cold, bone weary of never being warm enough in the house. She wished Agatha weren't coming. She felt responsible for Agatha. She was tired of feeling responsible. She was tired of keeping, and making do, and holding on—all the admonitions a person gave herself. But she couldn't imagine another kind of living, either. She couldn't imagine living in Athens, Ohio.

She had not seen Clar for two days, for four days.

"Limbo," she said aloud. Perhaps many women lived in limbo. She did not know what limbo meant. It could be the name of a parlor game. Perhaps Tom lived in limbo, too. People could address letters to each other, Limbo, and a zip code.

What was she doing living in a house with a strange clean man and a child who reached for her hand and tried to please her all of the time, almost all of the time?

The doorbell rang.

"How is everything this morning, Agatha?"

"Very well. The same. Thank you, madame."

201

The girl wore new tennis shoes. She almost complimented the shoes, and stopped, realizing that she might be misunderstood. "You have . . . rosy cheeks." Nobody could speak more lamely than Caroline Hutton. She despised herself.

"It is very cold outside, madame."

"I'm glad Lewis wore his coat. He and Tom have gone to Valletta."

She should have said, "We've had breakfast and we're out of your way," something simple. "You can start anywhere."

Perhaps Agatha forced her to ask, "How are your parents?" They stood in the dining room. Agatha untied her scarf.

"My father discovered about the moneys at the bank." The girl's lips were blue with cold. "Every week, for some time, I have saved ten shillings from the pound ten. He is angry. I do not know, madame."

"But that's ridiculous. You're of age, aren't you?" She spoke without thinking, as if a person's age had anything to do with her relationship to her family.

"I am in my twenty-second year."

"If you and your young man want to get married, you ought to go on and get married." She was angry for the girl. "That's terrible." Perhaps she was not angry enough. She seemed to stand beside herself, watching herself pretend anger. If Grandmother had been living when Tom appeared . . . Yes, she was angry.

Agatha was utterly composed, as Caroline Thaxton would have been composed under the same circumstances. At home Mrs. Lovell cried out her troubles: Mrs. Lovell was always getting extra money.

But a person should be able to react to another person's mind as well as to tears. Agatha and Clar stood in different continents. Somewhere Caroline stood.

"I'm sorry. I'm really sorry," she said, as if the girl had cried. "You must take two extra pounds today. I have it, them, right here."

"I do not like to."

"You must."

"Thank you, madame."

Agatha moved past her. The girl headed for the kitchen and her cleaning materials.

She thought of the other Maltas happening, the elegant old English ladies and gentlemen waking in their chic apartments; many people came to Malta to retire. She tried to imagine the room where Agatha's parents moved.

In Malta there were surprises around every corner. But there weren't many surprises for Tom in Malta. Tom knew about a place before he discovered it.

She had discovered The Garden all by herself.

Leaving Taormina for the Sicily tour hadn't been like him, he had to admit. And leaving the tour at Syracuse for Malta wasn't like him. You could say about Tom Hutton that he always finished everything he started. He always ate all the food on his plate and when he started reading a book he finished it even if he didn't like it. But this was a holiday, and there wasn't any reason not to do whatever came to your mind. Changing your mind made you feel good, younger than anybody. A man had to learn to change his mind and not feel guilty, not very guilty. Caroline didn't understand what a big thing it was to change your mind. "All right, Tom," she said. Sometimes he wished she would take a more definite stand. But it was all right. Marie had taken too many definite stands.

He was home early. It was barely two o'clock. Caroline and Lewis were out somewhere.

He picked up the *Times*. Forthcoming Events, Births, Requiem Masses, In Memoriam, Weather Forecast.

He had been thinking about Gwen Pettigrew, just thinking about her. He hadn't mentioned her to Caroline any more—there wasn't anything to mention. He hadn't looked for Mrs. Pettigrew downtown, but a couple of times he sat in the little park in front of the library; and once he gave the pigeon man another ten shilling bill. He certainly didn't wait around the house expecting her to drop by. A couple of times Caroline said they should ask her to dinner. He voted against that, of course, but Caroline had a good attitude. A lot of women—Ellen, for instance—wouldn't have taken to the idea.

"Marsaxlokk," he said to the ticket boy. It was the surly one, with the wen on his neck. "I know I change buses."

The boy seemed to recognize him. He was polite. "Yes, sir. I'll tell you when to get off."

He could have walked instead of changing buses. But he waited for the other bus. He didn't have to wait very long. He was counting on waiting longer. It was a nice day. The fields were full of red and yellow flowers. The sky was full of clouds, like the pictures in Lewis's book.

It wasn't a very long ride.

He rang the doorbell over the printed calling card: Gwendolyn Pettigrew. He hadn't seen the card before.

He felt all right. Gwendolyn was crazy about men who fed pigeons against the law. Lady Gwendolyn.

He rang again, and the door opened.

"Mr. Hutton!" She was dressed up. She had on a hat and gloves and a good-looking yellow suit—you could tell it was expensive. Hutton and Sons didn't sell suits that expensive. Sometimes he had made special orders for Marie and Ellen. And Caroline—her wedding outfit.

Sometimes he had said, just for a joke, "Good morning, Lady Marie," or, "Good morning, Lady Caroline." It was something he'd got from his dad.

"Good morning, Lady Gwendolyn."

"How did you know? Who told you?"

"Told me what?"

"*Lady.* The Lady part." She looked upset. It wasn't a good way to start off a little friendly visit.

"Nobody. It's just something I said."

205

"You're quite mystic, aren't you? Despite your innocent American exterior. Dwight was a commoner, though. Quite a commoner."

He didn't exactly know what she meant: he felt embarrassed. "I see you're going out. I don't want to bother you. I know you weren't expecting me."

"Dear Mr. Hutton. If I had been expecting you, I would be wearing a feather boa." She didn't tell him to come in, but she turned. She started taking off her gloves. "You'll have sherry, won't you?" she said over her shoulder. "With a dozen ice cubes."

He took off his beret and stuffed it in his pocket. He carefully closed the door. He didn't know why he was being so careful and quiet. He followed her down the white hall into the white and green living room.

"Say when?"

He said, "When," almost before she had started pouring.

"You poor alcoholic." But she wasn't being hateful. She was laughing. She seemed glad enough to see him. "You do have a drinking problem, don't you, Mr. Hutton?" She went on pouring. And then she filled one of the glasses with Scotch for herself.

She sat on the green couch. He sat in the white chair. It could have been the other afternoon, almost. She crossed her legs. "And to what do I owe this honor?"

"You told me to come back to see you sometime."

"Of course." She wore a watch on a chain. She looked at the watch. "I get ready for appointments early. It is one of my sicknesses. I have thirty minutes, perhaps three-quarters of an hour." She wasn't so pretty as he remembered, but she was nice-looking.

He didn't exactly know why he was there.

"I would like for you to think I am waiting for the Prince of Graustark. Actually, it's bridge day, old ladies' bridge day. We dress like mad for each other. A countess is calling for me. She is quite ancient. She wears much eye makeup. Crookedly. She resembles the Victrola dog. Are you too young to remember the Victrola dog, Mr. Hutton?"

206

"I remember."

She ran her tongue over her lips. Her lips were paler than her tongue. "I've been meaning to call you and your wife—to dash off a note."

"It's been a week, hasn't it? More than a week?"

"You do sound like a kidnapper. A gangster on Independent television."

"I think you like to bully people."

"Television. You are straight from television. You Americans were born on television."

And then she told a long story about some television people from America that she'd met at the Hilton. He tried to listen to her, but it was hard.

"Quite civilized," she said.

She asked about Lewis and Caroline. "And how have you been improving each shining hour?"

He felt funny—bad. He felt like she was making fun of him. But he wasn't going to back down. He didn't know exactly what it was he wasn't going to back down from. His drink was gone. He kept his hand around the glass, hoping Gwen wouldn't notice.

"Your drink?" she said. "I insist."

Ralph wouldn't believe the story about drinking at two-thirty in the afternoon with Lady Gwendolyn Pettigrew. Ralph always came home with a lot of stories about European women. He never said it straight out, but he implied a lot, and he snickered. Ralph had a bad way of snickering.

Maybe Tom wouldn't mention Gwen Pettigrew to Ralph. The woman had presence. That's what his mother used to say about some people.

She told about a yacht party. It was an interesting story, and then she said, "You came, because . . . ?"

"Because I wasn't afraid to come. I guess that's what I came to tell you."

"Of course you aren't." She was smiling.

"You think I am. You think that's why I came to see you."

207

"I'm quite flattered, as a matter of fact. Perhaps you want to take me to bed. That is my first guess."

He was sweating. He was a damn fool, the way Marie said. He wished he could get Marie told off.

"I'm not a damned fool."

"Well, I should hope not. We all run our chances."

He'd never been in a situation like this. Always he figured things out, ever since he could remember. "Can you imagine a situation in which Tom isn't in full charge?" That's what Marie said, used to say. She meant it, even when she was making fun of him.

He was sitting in Marsaxlokk, acting like a damn fool.

"I didn't marry again just to get somebody to take care of the boy."

But surely that wasn't what he had come to say.

He didn't care what he said to the pretty woman smiling at him over the rim of her glass.

"I'm faithful to her because I want to be." His voice was loud, but he didn't care. He was not sure he was telling the truth. He hoped he was telling the truth.

"We are excited, aren't we?"

"Yeah, I guess so."

She kept smiling.

Something was important. He couldn't figure out what it was. He thought about the Saint Paul pageant, the one in Athens.

She said, "Good Tom."

"I'm not 'good old Tom' to Caroline. She doesn't think of me that way."

"I am sure she doesn't. In fact, Mr. Hutton, I can very well cancel my appointment."

"I wouldn't want you to."

"You flatter me."

"I guess I better be going."

"We have time for another drink before the Countess arrives. We'll drop you off somewhere, in Valletta. You can have a pint

of coffee or two, and then you can trundle along home. By bus."
She was putting her gloves back on. "I should have thought you
would have rented a car by now." Her eyes were little.

He rubbed his hands through his hair. He still had a pretty good
head of hair. His dad had been bald as an onion when he died,
seventeen years ago, whenever it was.

He was all right. He was feeling all right. "When the Victrola
dog comes, I'll say, 'How do you do, Lady Countess Victrola.' "

"Oh, Mr. Hutton." She was laughing.

He stood up.

He hadn't had a vision. Tom Hutton would never claim to have
had a vision. But he understood something. Maybe he would be
able to get around to doing something about what he understood.
It was easier to get along with people who called you "Mister"
and meant it: the man in the cap feeding the pigeons, the young
clerks at the store.

"I guess I'm lucky. I'm a good businessman."

Gwen's eyes were wet again, the way they'd been at the square.
He felt sorry for her. He figured out what she was going to say
before she said, "The Countess . . ." She yanked off her hat and
dropped it on the coffee table. 'I'll tell the Countess . . ."

"You tell her." He was feeling the drinks. He wasn't really in
charge of the situation, but that was all right, too. Not being in
charge was a part of the vision that wasn't a vision. "You tell her
you almost didn't get ready in time because you had company.
Mister Tom Hutton. Damn fool company." He heard himself
saying the words, as if they were being played back to him. He
was talking too loud. "Fool company."

He pulled his beret out of his pocket. "Thanks for the drinks."

She was standing close to him.

In a minute they would have been kissing. He would have been
proud of himself for kissing Gwen and rubbing his hands over her.
It would have been something to tell Ralph. Maybe he would
have been very proud of himself for staying. The doorbell would
ring. He'd be standing there in one of the white bedrooms. He

209

could have heard what Gwen would have said to the old lady in the eye makeup.

It all might have been all right.

But he heard himself saying, "I've been Tom Hutton for a long time."

"Of course you have."

"Thanks for the drinks," he said again.

Gwen's little eyes were beautiful.

That was it.

That was all there was to it. He was probably a goddamned fool.

He waited for the bus on the corner near the statue of somebody. He looked over at Gwen's building. Maybe somebody was standing behind the curtains of one of the bay windows on the first floor.

The bus didn't come and didn't come.

He went into the little bar to ask if he was standing in the right place.

"You are United State," the fellow said. He looked like Dad a little. But he was a big fellow.

"United State wonderful country. Wonderful. You drink with me. You have another drink with me."

Tom Hutton was ashamed. The fellow knew he had been drinking. Nobody ever criticized Tom Hutton for drinking. "My accent. It always gives me away."

"You talk all right. United State wonderful country. What you have?"

"Thanks a lot. I don't want to miss the bus."

"They come all the time, like women. Buses." Perhaps the bartender had been watching Lady Pettigrew's house. The fellow turned to the shelves behind him; he moved his hands in front of the bottles. "Black White, Bell, Teacher?"

"That's mighty nice. Thanks a lot, but no, thanks."

"For the United State?"

"That's mighty nice of you, but not today." He got along just fine with the help. "You really have a nice place here. Thanks a lot. S'long." He parted the plastic strips that served as the door curtain. "You be sure and look us up when you're in Ohio."

It was another fool thing to say. He hadn't even told the man his name. A man bigger than his dad could spend the rest of his life in Ohio looking up somebody that resembled Tom Hutton.

A car stopped in front of Gwen's door. It was a Rolls maybe. He couldn't see very well. Just as his bus stopped, Gwen came to the door.

He didn't look back.

For a minute he thought the ticket boy was the kid from the Birżebbuġa bus. "How many runs do you run?" Nobody else was getting on the bus.

"Where?"

"Where?"

"Ticket?"

"Valletta." He took a two shilling piece out of his pocket.

He accepted the change from the kid. He wasn't thinking very straight. He wasn't expecting change. When Lewis got big— fourteen or fifteen—he might look like the bus boy.

The shrine was full of plastic flowers. And another Jesus. It was just a head. Jesus' eyes were closed.

Maybe he shouldn't have left the green and white apartment. Visions had gone out of style.

Maybe Ralph wasn't so bad, fooling around with the girls in the stockroom. Maybe Tom Hutton wasn't so damned smart.

The scenery was a little different from the Birżebbuġa run, but not much.

He was the last one out of the bus.

He wasn't drunk. Tom Hutton didn't get drunk. But he had trouble finding the Lion and Child.

It was on another street.

On the street he'd already been on.

The fellow at the bar recognized him. "Iowa," he said. A lot of them couldn't tell the difference between Ohio and Iowa and Idaho.

He said, "Yeah. O.K. Fine."

"What you have, Mr. Iowa?"

"Coffee. A couple of cups. Not any cream."

"Joke. You like joke." But the man gave him two glasses of black coffee.

"Everybody say the girls are good in Iowa."

"Thank you very much." He didn't remember the man's name. He almost never forgot a name.

He drank the coffee fast. "Thank you a lot."

He had wanted to find something, maybe. Maybe that's why people went abroad. Maybe you hadn't lost anything. Maybe you wanted to find something. He wondered if anybody ever found enough.

But he didn't want to trade lives with anybody. That was something, maybe. "Let well enough alone," he said, or somebody was always saying.

Caroline and Lewis were waiting for him in the living room. The house was cold.

"We were worried about you."

"Guess where we've been, Daddy?"

"You're all right. You're all right, aren't you, Tom?"

"I'm just fine."

"We had a long walk. We went to the park."

"The same tricycle."

"I went around. I ran into Mrs. Pettigrew."

"That's nice. You must be starved. I hope you had a good lunch."

"Sure, I had a good lunch."

"How was Mrs. Pettigrew?"

"Fine, just fine."

"We're going to have steak for dinner. I'll put it in. It looks like a good one."

"That's good. I could eat a steak."

He said to himself, "God damn it."

"God damn it," he said to himself.

212

"Let's read the sky book."

"Sure, why not?"

"You're all right, Tom?"

"I'm just great. I told you."

"I still need a couple of things. I forgot to get lettuce. And something else. I forget what I forgot."

She stood in the center of the room. He loved her.

"Where's the book, Lewis?"

"It's there. It's on the table."

"Come on. Up in my lap."

"Look. Look up at the sky!" the book said.

God damn it.

He thought of the word *despair*. He didn't know when he had ever thought the word *despair*, like a road sign printed on a cloud in a book.

The next day they took a ride in a *dghajsa*. He had been determined that they all ride in a *dghajsa*. But he'd been so busy, what with one thing and another, he didn't get around to investigating.

He was sorry he hadn't investigated by himself.

He asked a couple of men at the dock how much he should pay for a trip over to Vittoriosa. The fellows were canny. "Arrange with the boatman," they said.

"It will be all right," Caroline said.

"I'm tired, Daddy," Lewis said.

He went to the police station to ask the price, the fair price.

"It doesn't really matter, Tom," Caroline said.

But it did matter. And the policeman couldn't have been nicer. "For all many?" the man asked.

"Three of us, my wife and boy."

"Eight shillings for three," the policeman said right off. "For Sunday."

It was a pretty day. They probably should have tried to find a Protestant church to go to. But, after all, they were on vacation.

213

It didn't hurt to miss church for a couple of months when you were on vacation.

While they waited for a boat to come in, he explained to Lewis about the boats with big eyes painted on both sides of the prow. "The eye of Osiris," he told Lewis. He hoped he was pronouncing it right. It was nice to tell Lewis about the boats; it was a lot better than looking at pictures in the National Museum. The boy was really interested, about how the Maltese pushed their oars instead of pulling them. He told Lewis about how the Roman galleys had had eyes painted on them, too. "They thought the boats could see their way back to port." Caroline was impressed. It was nice. "My, you know a lot," Caroline said.

He could have told them stories about legendary boatmen. He didn't want to show off.

But the fellow who came in to the dock wasn't very nice. He asked for eighteen shillings. When the fellow heard what the policeman had said should be a fair price, he just shrugged his shoulders.

"Tom," Caroline said.

"O. K." The fellow shrugged his shoulders.

Caroline and Lewis sat up front. The man didn't use his oars at all, push or pull. He had an Evinrude motor, a powerful one.

The sun shone like anything.

Lewis said, "Whee," and Caroline called over her shoulder, "Look at the fortifications. Just look."

They were in the middle of the bay. He yelled at Lewis, "That's where we're going."

The boatman said, "You say Senglea. That is Vittoriosa."

"I said Vittoriosa. That's what I said." He had to yell. Caroline and Lewis turned around to look at him. He was ashamed of himself for being upset.

"Senglea."

"We said Vittoriosa, didn't we?" He was really yelling. "I said Vittoriosa, didn't I, Caroline?"

"More expensive."

"The heck you say."

"We can return." The man pressed his hand on the tiller. He was a fairly young man, but he was fat and dirty. The fellow hadn't shaved for two or three days.

He hadn't been so mad since they landed in Naples. It wasn't the price, it was the principle of the thing. He hated to be made a fool of.

"How much more?"

"Eight."

"Half. We'll split." He really didn't like people who said, "It's the principle of the thing." Generally they were trying to drive home a mean bargain.

He was almost scared for a minute. The bay looked as big as the ocean.

Maybe the whole vacation had been a mistake. Maybe he had compromised himself halfway around the world.

But he said, "Four more shillings."

The fellow had spoiled the day. Caroline was embarrassed. She didn't mind being taken advantage of. Maybe that was the difference between men and women. And children. Lewis was probably embarrassed, too.

"Those eyes you've got painted on the boat . . ."

The man looked away from him.

Tom Hutton didn't finish his sentence. He wasn't sure what he had been going to say, anyhow.

At the Vittoriosa dock the man tried to get more money out of him. "Eight children," the man said. "Bad times."

"No, thanks." He was ashamed of himself.

Caroline didn't speak. He wished she had said something. She looked awkward climbing out of the boat.

They walked a little around Vittoriosa. They saw an old Norman house, the outside of it. And the museum was closed on Sunday.

They took a bus home.

He had a bad taste in his mouth.

215

Caroline and Lewis seemed happy enough. They both said they had had a nice time.

He was thinking, "God damn Gwen Pettigrew." He was surprised at himself.

$\mathcal{S}$he and Lewis and Tom had lived in a cold dark house in Bir-żebbuġa, Malta, for almost a month because Lewis, Tom's son, would be starting the first grade next year, because Tom had always promised himself a trip, because she had had a miscarriage, because an old lady had come into Hutton and Sons to buy two yards of elastic, because Tom had seen a travelogue, because somebody in Taormina had recommended Malta, because of a cab driver, because a lame man knew of a vacancy on Pretty Bay. Because, because, because, she told herself, determined to find reasons, pretending to find reasons. She had found Clar and The Garden by chance. Because she and Lewis had walked one morning, right, left, circling. Because. Because of chance. She did not like to believe in chance.

She loved Clar Tate, after a fashion. It was ridiculous not to see her again. Clar was contained. She loved Clar Tate because Clar didn't seem real. And Lewis was destined to have learned swearing words. Words were only words.

Day after tomorrow they would leave for Athens, Ohio.

"Hurry, Lewis."

Lewis saw Becky first. "There's Becky, Mamma."

"I don't think so." They were two blocks from the garden. A child in a white sweat shirt and dark shorts toddled toward the gate. Behind her a woman pushed a stroller. "It's like her stroller. I think it's the right color."

It was impossible to see in the sunlight. The woman and the stroller stopped. The woman turned. She was a vast woman, even larger than Clar. She wore shorts and a white blouse, like the child's. How many times had Clar said, "A woman should be a woman"? A little boy followed the woman.

She heard the woman call, "Get the hell on." She pretended that she had not heard.

"What marvelous eyesight you have, Lewis."

"Thank you."

". . . the hell on here."

"I can hear good, too. That's Buddy's mamma."

"Oh, Lewis." She stopped.

She stopped dead in her tracks, she thought. A book from the British Council said, "She stopped dead in her tracks." It was difficult to choose books in a foreign library. Some days, after wandering blindly past all the shelves, she reached blindly. She felt guilty. But she didn't know what she was guilty of.

She should have turned back. She couldn't imagine why she did not turn back. It wasn't Lewis's fault. She took his hand. They walked faster toward the gate.

Clar and Buddy and Becky waited in front of the ticket booth. Becky stood beside the stroller.

Clar said, "I had a feeling you would be here. In you go, Becky." Clar stuffed the fat child into the stroller.

"It's a coincidence, isn't it? To come at exactly the same time?"

"We're always having coinci dences. I was afraid I wouldn't see you again."

Caroline did not say, "We leave the day after tomorrow." She said, "Hello, Buddy. Hello, Becky. Aren't you a smart girl! I saw you walking."

Buddy stuck out his tongue. Becky stood up and reached her fat hands toward Lewis's head. Lewis laughed.

Clar said, "Don't pull his hair, damn it."

218

"She doesn't hurt."

"Give her a swat. My God. Sit down, Becky."

"We saw her walking." She had to say something. "My, but she's getting active." She wished Lewis would move away from the stroller.

"Too goddamned active, if you ask me. Sit down, Becky. I told you!"

"I wish you wouldn't . . ." But Becky and Buddy were accustomed to their mother's talk. And Tom was right. Lewis had to learn what the world was like. "I wish you wouldn't worry."

"Who's worrying? Sit down, Becky. My God."

Becky's cheeks were rounder than melons. But she had an old woman's face: lines ran from her nose to either side of her chin. It was difficult to look at the child's steady eyes.

Lewis said, "We're twins, aren't we, Buddy?"

Buddy wore a sweat shirt and blue pants. His shirt was filthy, with blood or chocolate. She had not realized that the boys were dressed similarly. "So you are."

"Twins. We're a quartet." Clar pulled at her blue shorts.

It was almost painful to look at her veined legs.

"Me and Becky, too. You're the one that's out of it, Caroline. Where are your shorts? Pretty legs like yours?"

"I told you. I don't wear them much." She hated the sound of her voice.

"These are new. Billy brought them for me. What do you think of that?"

"I'm sure . . . I'm sure they're comfortable."

"Who cares? What the hell. I'm wearing them for a joke, anyhow. It serves Billy right. That man!"

The sun was a Van Gogh sun, the air almost too sweet to breathe.

"What the hell's wrong here, anyhow?"

"Wrong?"

"The ticket fellow."

"Oh, yes."

219

They had been waiting for the ticket man to appear at the half moon of his box. She had not realized what they were waiting for.

Clar rapped against the counter. "Yoo hoo. Hey, there. Hey, you. You got customers."

The box waited as quiet as a roadside shrine.

"Yoodily hoodily. Mister! Hey!"

"You're one, too," Lewis said. He was laughing. Lewis could get along with anybody. He was like Tom.

Buddy laughed.

"Nobody home." Clar spread her hands. "We'll just take us a couple of trikes; three. It's time Becky started. She can ride if she wants to." Becky turned her old woman's face slowly from the boys to her mother. "Stop looking that way, Becky."

She felt sorry for the little girl. Becky didn't have any other way to look from her face, with the lines and fat cheeks. "Maybe they're . . . maybe he's closed. Maybe we shouldn't?"

"Gates open. Trikes here. Why not? The guy's just goofed off. Maybe he's out in the bushes somewhere. A good-looking fellow like him, he must have lots of opportunities." The idea was almost too funny for Clar to think about. "Honestly!" she said, wiping at her eyes.

"This one's mine," Lewis said.

"No, it's mine."

"Lewis." But he was already down the path.

"Don't be a damn fool, Dumb-dumb. Here, take this one. This is for you, Becky. Get on. Ride. You can ride as good as anybody."

The fat child reached toward the handlebars. Her hands were like starfish.

"Climb up. Sit on the seat. My God, Becky."

"She's never done it before, Clar."

"Turn your feet. Press. That's it. That's the girl. Good girl. Look at her. Look at her go. Bye-bye, Becky."

Becky moved away drunkenly.

"What do you think of that, Caroline?"

"She's awfully well coordinated. I wouldn't have thought . . ."

"Kids. They bug you. They'll screw you up if you give them a chance. They're just people, except littler."

"But . . ."

"Look at her. Look at that kid go. My God. She wouldn't be walking yet if I hadn't taken her in hand."

"Oh?" She was sorry she had not turned when Lewis said, "There's Becky."

"Didn't I tell you? Day before yesterday. The elevator wasn't working. I had more than I could carry. I said, 'I'll meet you upstairs.' She raised hell. People came to their doors. But she made it. She crawled partway up, and then she walked, up the stairs, mind you, screaming bloody murder."

"No."

"No, what?"

"No, I didn't know."

"For all practical purposes Becky can take care of herself. I thought I'd told you. I bring the stroller along just in case she gets pooped out. We always have so much to talk about, don't we? That's what's good about having a girl friend."

"No. We haven't met for . . . I don't know how many times we have met."

"I don't either. That's funny."

"I don't at all." This is the second time, the fifth, the eighth, she had told herself, loving Tom.

She could not guess how many times they had made love—she wouldn't dare.

She said, "We should leave money on the counter."

"And let somebody steal it? Of course not."

"But what if the man doesn't come back?"

"Our kids will have free rides, that's all. There's nothing wrong with that."

"No, Clar."

"Come on. My feet are killing me. I've got to have something done about my feet. You're looking mighty nice today."

She looked down to see what she was wearing. It was the black and white hound's-tooth suit. "Thank you. Thank you very much." It had arrived at the store before they left. She did not know why she said, "It's old, but it's comfortable."

"Green's becoming to you."

"Oh?" She was wearing a green blouse and the green head-band. "Thank you."

They sat quietly in the sun together.

Often she felt comfortable with Clar. Serene, almost. She couldn't understand. There wasn't any reason in the world to feel comfortable with the woman who sprawled on the bench, her eyes almost closed, her mouth open, breathing through her mouth.

Clar was interesting, that was all. She would miss Clar. Clar was all of a piece. If Clar mentioned the weather she spoke of it because she wanted to talk about the weather. Clar never made conversation. Everybody else in the world made conversation.

"It's getting good weather, isn't it?" Clar said, as if she had read her mind.

"Lovely." She smiled at Clar. "But the days have always been good here—here in the park." It was like a compliment to Clar. But Clar didn't need compliments.

"It's getting naked weather, isn't it?"

It was all right not to answer Clar.

"I go around naked half the time at home, when the weather's like this. I guess you do, too. You have such a pretty figure."

"No . . . No, I don't."

"I really can't stand the heat. Wait till it gets August. You'll see what I mean."

"We won't be here. I'm sorry." She had not meant to mention their leaving.

"That's right. I forget on purpose. I hate like hell for you to leave. We could have us some good times. The beaches. It's a good place to take kids."

She did not say, "We leave day after tomorrow, in the evening." She said, "Lewis doesn't know how to swim yet. He must

222

learn. Surely this summer. We have a municipal pool at home. And there's Dow Lake. Both places have lifeguards."

"Billy says I've got to stop going around naked so much. He says Buddy's beginning to notice. He'll just have to notice. When it really gets hot I put a sheet on one of the big chairs—they're scratchy as hell if you don't put a sheet on them. And then I turn on the fan. And I spread out there with a big glass of Coke chuck full of ice, or a beer, a really cold beer."

Sometimes it was impossible to listen to Clar. She couldn't imagine why the word *serene* had come to her mind a moment ago. She did not like to think about the woman spread out in the chair.

Lewis had said, "Goddamn son of a bitch."

But she could stop listening to Clar. Other people expected you to listen. Other people waited for answers.

"At the museum the other day . . . Lewis yelled out, 'Come here, Daddy, and look at the naked lady.' " She felt guilty. But she wanted to tell Clar something. She didn't mean to be making fun of Tom. But it wasn't fair to stop in the middle of a little story. "He made Tom come over and look. I think Tom was embarrassed."

It wasn't much of a story, but Clar thought it was very funny. She laughed louder than necessary. But it was pleasant to hear her laughter.

"That's a man for you. Billy would of done the same thing, I'll bet you. Billy's crazy about me being naked. But just sometimes. 'There's a time and place for everything.' That's what Billy's always saying. He's crazy about being naked himself." Clar shook her head. "At the right time and place."

She was sorry she had told about the picture. She was silly.

"To tell the truth, I hate the way Billy prances around, after he's sure the kids are asleep and the bedroom door's locked. To tell you the truth, Billy's uglier with his clothes off than with them on. He is just plain ugly."

She stopped listening for a little while. She was comfortable.

"A woman's different," Clar was saying. "That's what I think. I like to see a pretty woman naked."

Clar's eyes were steady.

"I lied to you one day, Caroline. I've been lying to you."

"I'm sure you haven't."

"Oh, yes, I did." Her voice was as casual as ever. She was not making a confession. She had just thought of something else to say. "I acted like I haven't invited you over because of Billy. Remember?"

"No," she said quickly, surprised at her own lying. "No."

"Yes, you do. I said Billy was funny about company, something like that." Clar smacked her lips, but her voice did not change. "As a matter of fact, Billy's dying to meet you. Every day or so he wants to know when you're going to come see us."

"That's . . . that's very nice."

"I just told him. I said if we didn't have so many of his god-damn relatives underfoot all the time maybe we could have some real company in. He got his feelings hurt. My God, that man must have sixty cousins—at least. Aunts. Uncles. They all love to visit us. They're crazy about me, no matter what I do. They think I'm something on a stick."

"I'm sorry. You shouldn't have."

"Billy said, 'We will arrange a time.' He can be very cold when he wants to be. He said, 'My family is considerate.' That's exactly what he said. I laughed. Billy said, 'Name the day and the hour and I will inform my family to make themselves scarce.' That Billy. What a prick! I just left the room, laughing my head off."

"I really am sorry. That kind of scene . . ." She could not imagine the scene.

"I could of asked you and the kid during the day sometime, if I'd wanted to. But Billy's always goofing off at work—he'd be just as likely to bust in as not."

"I would have liked to meet him."

Clar chuckled. "I was lying to Billy, too. His relatives are all right—dumb-ass, but all right. They don't bother me. It isn't because of the relatives. I just don't want to share you with Billy. I figured it out. You're the only person in Malta I know all by *myself*. I like it that way."

She remembered Clar's eyes that first afternoon, deeper than wells.

"I don't want to meet Tom, either. What do you think of that? Not that I have anything against him, understand."

If once she could be as easy as Clar . . . at a grocer's counter, or talking to Lewis, or in bed with Tom. If just once . . .

"I haven't told Tom." She was whispering.

But Clar had heard her. "What about?"

"About . . . about the garden, our meeting. And the children. I don't really know why."

"I think that's all right. I'm glad. That's the trouble with women. They tell too much. They don't really talk as much as men, but they tell more. I shouldn't of told Billy about this place. My God, sometimes I think I ought to have my brain examined. My God. Christ."

Clar could have been speaking of a forgotten market list or a gas bill.

"I can't believe we've been here so long. In Malta. A month, almost a month. I've known you for three weeks."

"Surely not. It just seems yesterday you were sitting on this bench, looking at me. I knew you were upset, the minute I saw you. I have a sixth sense or a seventh—I always forget how many you're supposed to have. We've had nice times, though, haven't we? You were blue that day, about the miscarriage."

"I wasn't upset. I'm not."

"Oh, well." Clar slapped her thighs. "That's the way the cookie crumbles. Make a friend, miss a friend."

She forced herself to look at Clar. "I don't really know what we're talking about. But it's been good. I'm grateful. The island of Malta."

"Isn't it hell, though?"

225

"No. No, I won't believe that." She was trembling. "I don't want to believe in hell."

"It's just an expression."

"I'll check on the children."

"You do that."

"You remember that first day. You said I hovered too much, something like that. I've been trying. To be more relaxed about Lewis. I love that boy." She stood.

"Sure you do."

"You aren't making fun of me, for checking?"

"You got me doing it." It was another of Clar's jokes. Her breasts shook as she laughed.

The children stood by their tricycles near the green water. The boys were talking to Becky, as if she were one of them. Lewis tossed his head. She heard his laughter over the beds of hyacinths and daffodils. The flowers were lasting forever. Because of the cool weather.

"Spring happens too fast in Ohio and West Virginia," Grandmother said. "Take an English spring—it happens slowly. The flowers hang on." Grandmother had heard a lecture when she was a girl. She talked about English springs as if she had seen one. She had always planned for an English garden, once they got settled, once they had a place of their own, once . . . Grandmother did not say, "Once I am able to keep a job for longer than a year."

Caroline started to call. Her lips formed the letters for "Lewis"; she did not finish the word. She did not make a sound.

For a moment she had thought that Becky turned her head. She imagined Becky's round stare. Glare? It was difficult to determine a word for Becky's eyes. For anybody's eyes.

In the bright sun Becky and Buddy's shirts looked as immaculate as Lewis's. The picture was more beautiful than any picture she had ever seen.

She backed away, to the path. She was holding her breath.

"Clar. Clar, you have to come look."

"I'm mighty comfortable." Clar was smoking.

"The children, our children. They're so beautiful."

"That's nice. Let me finish this cigarette." She inhaled deeply. "God, it's a pretty day. Sit down. Take the load off your feet."

"Maybe they'll go away."

"Relax, honey. Oh, God."

She had sat, but only for a few minutes. Not that long.

Clar said, "When I was a kid I used to think I'd be a dancer. That's a joke for you, isn't it?"

Caroline did not move back in the seat. "I was going to be a missionary for a while. I was eight, I guess. I said I was going to Darkest Africa. I thought it was one word. Darkestafrica. I must have been eight, or younger."

"My folks encouraged me. I took lessons. Once my daddy said, 'I can see your name in lights right now.' I believed him."

"Grandmother said, 'You don't have to start packing yet. You have a little time to make up your mind. But you have my permission. I just hope you don't land up in jail.' "

"They were big fat people. My God, they still are. Maybe they thought I really did have a chance. Daddy calls me Baby. Dear Lord, he writes me letters, 'Dear Baby Grace.' That's my middle name, Clar Grace."

"But I never thought I'd be anything, really. Not a missionary, or a schoolteacher, or a wife . . . or a mother."

"I was going to be everything."

"I was scared. I really thought I'd be a criminal and die in jail. I really did think that. I thought I'd do something terrible, and be sent away. I wouldn't mean to do . . . whatever it was, terrible."

"My God, kid."

"Sometimes I dream I killed Grandmother. And Marie, Marie, too. That's what I dream. When I wake up I pretend I can't remember what I dreamed. I kill a lot of people."

"Look at me, Caroline."

For a moment it was difficult to focus her eyes on Clar's eyes. "Clar." Clar was patting her arm.

"My God, my God, baby."

227

She stood up quickly. Clar's hand patted at the air.

"Aren't we funny, though?" Clar sucked deeply at her cigarette stub. She dropped the stub. "Aren't we a funny pair, though?" She ground the cigarette under her heel. She placed her hands on her knees. " 'Honest confession is good for the soul.' That's what I always say. This has been real nice." Before she pushed herself up she said, "You know, sometimes I think I live here, here in the garden, instead of in that goddamned apartment house with Billy. That's pretty damn funny, too."

She wished she could give Clar something. A charm for her bracelet, for instance. She would have liked to give Clar a charm. "You are my friend," she would have said.

She did not wait for Clar. She hurried the twelve steps, the fifteen steps to the opening in the hedge.

She did not think *homosexual*, a word she did not know. She thought *Grandmother*; she thought *Clar*.

"Wait up!"

The sun was fiercely bright.

One tricycle stood beside the green pond.

"They've gone."

Clar stood behind her, breathing heavily. "Don't sound so upset. It's not the end of the world."

"I wanted somebody else to see them. They were so beautiful."

She looked hard at the spot, as if she were able to make the picture happen again. She felt Clar's breath against her neck.

"My God, my God. My God." The voice was harsh. It was impossible to believe it was Clar's voice. She turned. But Clar's lips moved with the voice saying, "My God, my God."

"What do you want, Clar? What's the matter, Clar? No. No, Clar. You're hurting me."

Clar's fingers bit into her shoulders. The pain was ridiculous. It was more than she could bear. And then the pain was greater. She was being torn apart.

"Oh, my God, Caroline."

She stood alone. Clar was running toward the pond. But the

fire still ate at her shoulders as if Clar had forgot to take her hands away. Clar spread her arms as she ran, her shoulder bag bumped against her hips. She ran with grace, like a dancer, but she was not following the path that bent and turned to circle to the pond. Clar ran through the beds of daffodils and iris. A path followed Clar through the flowers. The fat woman moved like a great wind.

She watched the path form.

She could have hurried her eyes to the pond. But the lengthening path held her, as if she moved down a dark alley to sleep.

She crossed her hands over her breasts, holding her own shoulders, trying to make her own fingers fit into the pain.

If she hurried her eyes, she could see the body at the edge of the pond. The white shirt. The blue shorts. The body was as still as the pond.

She was not conscious of which path she took, the winding one, or the flowers. She was conscious of running. She could hear "I killed Lewis. I killed him this time." She was sure she spoke. It was not the wind against her ears.

The path was long.

But she had moved quickly. She had moved so quickly that she reached the pond before Clar did. It was almost impossible to stop herself. If it had not been for the tricycle she could not have stopped. She would have run into the water. She was grateful. It was strong. The frame bit into her shin to stop her. For a moment she had thought the tricycle was not going to turn over. It took a long time to fall onto its back wheels, its front wheel spinning, above the grass where violets grew.

"Lewis."

"No. Don't."

They were so out of breath that they spoke without breath. It was almost funny to think about. But she did not laugh.

"It's not Lewis," Clar said.

"Help me, Clar."

"You aren't supposed to move them—that's the law. They're strict. . . . You have to leave—"

"Oh, Clar."

It was difficult to see the woman's face. If the wind had blown the woman's face away . . .

"I'm telling you."

"Help me, Clar."

"I'm telling you, Caroline. She must of thought it was a carpet. It looks like a carpet."

"God! Help me!"

The child was heavy. For a moment she had thought she would be unable to move the body. For a moment she thought she herself moved under the water, through waves of scum pounding like pain. A carpet in any house could give way, hurling the house into waves. The carpet at home—Marie's carpet—was the color of wheat. "Help me."

"Becky. It's Becky, all right," Clar cried.

The child was almost impossible to lift, but she managed to pull her to the grass. It was Becky. She had not known it was Becky.

She held the child's feet. She held the child like a wheelbarrow.

Water came from the child's mouth.

"It's the law . . ." Clar was saying.

She let the child down carefully. Carefully she turned her over.

She couldn't find a handkerchief. She pulled a clot of green weed from the child's nose. She ran her hands over the child's ugly face. She ran her fingers through the matted hair.

"I don't know what to do. I don't know. There's something to do, to try to do."

Clar had moved back to the tricycle. She picked it up. She set it on its three wheels. She leaned over to straighten the front wheel.

There was something about breathing the breath of life.

Somewhere she had read something.

The kiss.

She placed one hand on the child's stomach. With her other hand she braced herself. She lowered her head. The child's face was the color of milk.

230

She kissed Becky. She opened her mouth and breathed. She lifted her head. She breathed. Lifted. Breathed. Out. In. Out. In. Out.

"I have not loved enough," she thought, not knowing what she meant.

"I have held to all the carpets," she thought, not knowing what she thought.

Out. Out. Out.

Caroline was able to breathe. She could keep on breathing until someone pulled her away. Until she stopped breathing.

"That's the way you're supposed to do. I remember now. My God. Good, Caroline. Go on. Good, Caroline. My God."

Clar kneeled beside them.

After time, after time and more time . . .

The child's stomach was moving.

Perhaps it was moving, but she did not stop the kiss.

The child, ugly as a fetus, coughed.

Becky opened her vacant eyes.

"That's enough. I know what to do. I remember." Clar was pulling her away. "My God, look at your leg. O.K., Becky. Over we go. That's a girl. That's it. Spit up. Spit it up. That's it."

She walked away from Clar and the fetus, seven steps, eight, twenty-one. She lowered herself to the grass. Under the shade of a tree. She didn't know the name of the tree. She would have to ask somebody.

She lay down.

She would faint. She needed to faint to the sound of the child's retching. She would wake, saying something silly. "What happened?" she would say. "Where am I?"

But she did not faint.

She felt the shape of the grass blades under her shoulders. She smelled the stench of herself. She tasted vomit.

She heard Clar's voice, comforting her ugly child.

"Up we go. That's the girl. Come on. My God, sit up straight. Come on, honey. What the hell were you up to?"

231

Becky began to cry. Her cries sounded like something tearing.

"That's a girl. Shut up now. Come on, shut up. You're all right. Sit up. Sit up straight, goddamn it. What happened to you?"

The child's crying grew louder.

Buddy and Lewis had left the little girl. Lewis and Buddy . . . She would ask Lewis . . .

She would not ask Lewis. He was alive. They were all alive.

She had been asked too many questions. "Did you, Caroline? Are you sure, Caroline? Are you telling me the truth, Caroline?"

She turned her head.

Becky lay naked on the grass. She looked like a doll made of rags. A rag doll, that's what people called them.

Clar was efficient. She pulled a diaper from her bag. The diaper was so white it was blinding. "There we are. And here's your sweater. You got to keep warm. I remember now. Lift your arm. Come on, goddamn it. Here you go. Here. Keep this around you. You can lay back. The grass is soft as a beddy-bye. You're all right."

She heard the sound of tricycle wheels. She closed her eyes for a minute, for a minute more.

"What's the matter with Becky?" It was Lewis's voice. He did not sound guilty. But she would not ask him.

"She fell in the water. She's all right. We just have to keep her warm. I'm telling you, Becky."

"Where's Mamma?"

"Your mamma? She's over there."

She pushed herself up.

She was sitting up when Lewis turned to her.

"You hurt your leg."

"A little." She turned sideways so that Lewis wouldn't see. Then she straightened her leg out. "I ran into the tricycle. Wasn't that silly?"

"Oh, my, Mamma. You better put on some Band-Aid. A lot of Band-Aid. My goodness."

232

"I'm all right." She pushed the palms of her hands hard against the ground. She had almost said, "Give me a hand."

"O.K., you boys. Go get Becky's stroller," Clar was shouting. "Take your trikes and leave them at the office. Come straight back."

Lewis hunched his shoulders. "Mamma?"

"Go on, Lewis. Do what Clar says."

"Go on, both of you. Go up to the ticket office, goddamn it, and get her stroller. Hurry up. Don't just stand there."

"Good-bye, Mamma."

"Hush up, Becky."

Her watch had stopped. She squinted. She turned her head. She couldn't see the watch. Maybe it showed the hour, or maybe it was twelve after something, or twenty. But it wasn't late. The sun stood high.

"What the hell's keeping them?"

The time didn't matter.

"What in the living hell?"

Time and time and time.

Clar was managing.

"Stand up, Caroline. Come on. You can lean on me. Heavy. Heavier than that. I'm strong as an ox."

Becky, the bundle on the grass, moaned.

"Shut up, Becky. You're all right."

Clar was strong, soft and stronger than a bed.

Somebody was crying.

It was Caroline Hutton.

"Does it hurt terrible? Can you bear your weight on it? I don't think you broke anything. Lean harder. Okey-dokey?"

She shook her head. "I'm all right." She was not really crying. Tears fell like rain, naturally, only like rain.

"Sure you are. We'll get us a cab. And we'll go to my place and get you cleaned up. A good hot bath. I'll fix you a nice drink. We

233

never have had a drink together. As good as new. That's a sweet-heart."

"I'm all right. I really am, Clar."

"Sure you are. Come on. Easy does it."

For a moment they stood embracing.

"What in the hell do you think happened to those little bas-tards? Easy. That's a girl. That's a girl."

"Let me. By myself. I can walk."

"Lean on me."

It was Becky who screamed, not Caroline. "You tend to Becky."

"She's all right. Shut up, Becky."

"Please. We've got to start on. I can walk all right."

Clar's arm had been heavy on her shoulders.

She took two steps, three.

"Maybe we should. Those little bastards. If you're all right . . ."

"I'm all right."

It was easier to walk without Clar's arm. If Clar didn't say "Thank you" . . .

She was being unfair. Her mind said, Unfair to Clar. Clar would not say thank you. Clar was all of a piece. Clar didn't need a charm.

"My God, Becky. My God. Stand up. I'm going to carry you. Oh, shit, quit that. Here. Put your arms around me. Come on. Come on, damn it."

All she had to do was to take one step, and then another step, and another.

"Good, Caroline. Take it easy. You're doing great. That's just great."

Think nouns and verbs. Caroline. Step. Step. Caroline. Step.

She had not killed Lewis.

The flowers were beautiful.

She could not imagine what would happen to the beds of flowers when summer came. It would be pleasant if she could ask somebody. But she wouldn't ask. There wasn't anybody to ask.

234

Clar, maybe. Maybe Clar would take her address and write a letter and say, "You should see the garden, Caroline. The flowers are beautiful. There are big beds of . . . And . . ." She couldn't imagine what Clar would write. And there wasn't any point in their writing each other. Everything had already happened that was going to happen.

Caroline. Step.

Clar walked behind her, breathing heavily.

"Hold on, Becky. You can do better than that. Easy does it, Caroline."

Snapdragons, maybe. Cosmos. And roses again—roses bloomed more than once. Dahlias. The little blue flowers—she couldn't remember the name, but the name didn't matter. Daisies, maybe. Daisies tell, daisies won't tell—she couldn't remember what people said about daisies, old people. She could buy a book about English gardens. She could go in to Logan's and ask Mr. Black to order the book if he didn't have it in stock. She could plant an English garden. At the side of the house. Marie hadn't cared much for flowers. Tom said so once. He didn't say "Marie." Tom said, "We've not done much about the yard—we never have." He meant Marie. But there were flowers at home. They must have belonged to Tom's mother. Perennials. Iris, peonies, roses. A few roses.

Step.

She imagined a bouquet of fall flowers. She could pick Michaelmas daisies from the side of the road, going out to the lake. She would take Lewis swimming. It was very important for him to learn to swim. Daisies and roses. Some of the roses would be blooming for the bouquet.

She had not killed anybody, any more than everybody killed everybody.

And chrysanthemums. She had almost forgot about them. She could almost smell chrysanthemums. A fall morning, and fog in the valley out back, down on Ring Street.

"Listen to me, Becky. Goddamn it, I'm talking to you."

235

Spiderwebs. There would be spiderwebs on the grass and on some of the chrysanthemum bushes. They held the dew. They sparkled. They looked like antimacassars. The street was quiet as sleep. A child's good sleep. She was cold, but the day was beautiful.

Already she had lived in Tom's house for one fall. Autumn. Autumn was a better noun.

"What in the fuck? They should have been there and back three times by now. Ten times. Keep up the good work, Caroline. Those kids!"

But it wouldn't be spring yet when they got back home.

Caroline.

Step.

She could smell the chrysanthemums.

Step.

She could ask the man at the ticket window about the autumn gardens.

"I swear, Becky. You weigh a goddamn ton."

Step.

Lewis and Buddy stood by the booth. Buddy was crying. Lewis held his lips between his teeth. He looked like an old man.

Step.

"What the hell's going on here?"

Buddy ran to Clar.

"Don't knock me down, for God's sake. Why didn't you bring the stroller?"

"He wouldn't let us come back." Lewis wasn't crying. She was proud. "He said we stole."

"Oh, Lewis." But she did not step to him, to take him in her arms.

The elegant man stood with his arms folded. He wore a white sweatshirt and navy shorts. The other days—she couldn't remember what he had been wearing the other days.

"Here you are, Becky. There we go." Clar stooped gracefully to the stroller. "Lean back. You can lean back."

236

Becky looked all right. Her color was good.

"Now just what in the hell, mister?"

"My apologies, madame."

"You weren't here. There wasn't anybody here. My God! Picking on little kids, my God!"

Clar was fumbling in her bag.

Caroline Hutton could have said, "Let me pay, Clar." But she did not speak. She had remembered to bring her knitting bag, though. She hadn't left it under the tree. She was glad. Tom was annoyed with her when she forgot things.

"We left one of the trikes down by the pond. It damn near crippled my friend here. But it's all right, the trike. I'll pay for it, if you say so. I'll buy the goddamned thing."

"My deepest apologies. I will fetch the tricycle."

"I should hope so." Clar's face was red.

"One cannot be too careful. A man in charge of a park cannot be too careful."

"Shame on you. I'd be ashamed. Here. You owe me five shillings change."

"Of course, madame."

The man disappeared into the booth.

Lewis was holding to her hand. He almost hurt, holding so tightly.

"Five shillings," the man said to Clar. "I hope you have not been inconvenienced," the man was saying.

"She's leaving pretty soon. What do you think she's going to think about Malta, and the way people act?"

"I am sorry, madame. I am very sorry."

"I should hope. My God!"

She did not say, "Don't, Clar."

"I have made a mistake. I have said I am sorry."

"I should hope."

"Come again, ladies." The man was calling to them. "I hope you will return."

"Don't talk to him," Lewis said.

237

She turned. "Thank you. Thank you very much." She thought of asking about the flowers. "Thank you. Very much."

She was not limping. She did not have to limp. Her leg hurt. A little. Only a little. The pain was like only a remembered pain.

"Shut up, Becky."

The path to the gate was not too long.

"You're all right, Becky."

The path was not too long.

"There ought to be a taxi somewhere." Clar lifted her hand, her forefinger and little finger extended.

Somebody in grade school . . . Somebody had been able to whistle through her fingers. Maybe her name had been Bunny. The sound was so loud that you had to put your hands over your ears.

She had tried to make the sound. Over and over she had practiced. "You aren't doing it right, Caroline," Bunny said. "How will you call for help when you need it?"

She reached for Clar's hand. "No. Don't. Don't, Clar."

"We've got to tend to that leg."

"No, I'm fine. Look. I'm fine. I need to walk on it. I need to get home."

"Oh, come on."

"I'll take a hot bath at home. But thank you. Thank you so much. I need to walk. I don't want to get stiff. I used to fall on skates all the time. I know what to do."

"Come on, Caroline."

"No."

"What the hell?"

"No, thank you. Thank you so much."

Clar's eyes were beautiful.

"Thank you." She was holding Clar's hands. "If we don't meet again," she said in spite of herself. "If by chance, we shouldn't meet . . . Because . . ."

She thought about the hands of her watch and the word *because.*

238

"Bye, Buddy," Lewis said.

"What are you talking about? We'll meet. You'll be back here before you leave. Of course you will."

"But if I shouldn't . . ."

"Bye-bye," Buddy said.

"We'll meet. If we don't meet here, we'll meet in the States, or somewhere. You'll come back to Malta. I never say good-bye to anybody."

"Good-bye, Clar." She let go of the woman's hands.

She had almost leaned forward to kiss the fat woman with the beautiful eyes.

"I shouldn't let you be going home by yourself. My God, girl!"

"Good-bye." She looked down at Becky. She should be saying something special to Becky. The little girl leaned forward in her stroller; she rested her fat cheeks in her hands. "Good-bye."

"Say good-bye, Becky. Go on and say it. You can say it."

Perhaps Becky spoke.

Lewis said, "Come on, Mamma."

She was not Clar. She would never be Clar.

Because . . .

She turned to look back at the garden. It was only natural to look back. Clar and Buddy and Becky were already out of sight.

From the corner of her eye she saw a tallish dark woman in a black and white hound's-tooth suit, wearing a green headband. A little boy walked beside her.

She imagined she saw the woman and the boy.

"Are you feeling good, Mamma?"

"Yes. Yes, Lewis. We'll just have to take it slowly." She was limping only a little.

Tom was sweet.

"My gosh! What happened to you? You're white as a ghost."

Lewis said, "She ran into a trike. She was running down the hill. She can walk all right. She walked good, all the way home."

239

"At the park," she said, "the place we've been going, Lewis and I."

"Becky fell in the water. Becky's the girl."

"I'll get a doctor."

"You'll do nothing of the sort."

"Becky was a mess."

"Do we have any antiseptic?" Tom was concerned. He was not listening to Lewis. Later, if Lewis should mention Becky, Tom would probably say, "Becky? Who's Becky?" Tears started behind her eyes, but she did not cry.

"Yes, I bought some. When we came. One of the first days. Just in case."

"Where is it?"

"In the medicine cabinet upstairs, the right-hand side. But I'm going up, anyhow. I want to take a hot bath."

"My gosh, Caroline."

"I'm fine. I'm really just fine." She was almost sure she was telling the truth.

"My gosh. Look at you!"

"I'm just fine."

"The man at the park wasn't very nice," Lewis said.

Tom said, "You're not to worry about supper." He was frowning. "I'll get it. Lewis and I will."

"Sweet," she said.

"You soak yourself good. You hear me. Maybe we ought to get a doctor."

She had started up the stairs. She did not hold to the railing. She felt almost graceful. "Silly, Tom," she said.

$\mathcal{H}$e wasn't doing very well. Nobody could understand him, after all this time.

"English? You speak English?" the barman said. He was a new fellow.

"Sure I do. I want a glass of milk."

"No milk. Sorry, Mack. Coffee, soft drinks. Beer, whiskey."

"Coffee."

It was pretty discouraging.

He'd been having a nice time before he ordered. A fellow had asked him to sit down at a table with him. The fellow was from Ireland. He'd been drinking, but he had traveled all over. The man said he was tired of the way people acted as if Malta was just a little England. "They have a great culture of their own. You hear more English on the streets of Florence or Amsterdam than you do here. That's the God's truth."

"I believe it." He felt proud, as if somebody had complimented Athens, Ohio. "They have a culture of their own, all right."

By the time he got back to the table the fellow had disappeared. The old man named Tony was sitting in his place.

Tony was delighted to see him. "Where you been, Thomas?"

He hadn't really been avoiding Tony, not much. But he hadn't counted on spending his next to last afternoon with the dirty old man. He probably should have stayed at home with Caroline. But she was feeling good. Her leg didn't look too bad. And she had insisted. "Of course you must go to town. You must revisit places. There may be places you haven't seen yet." As a matter of fact he hadn't been to the Hypogeum or Tarxien. "You're sure you and Lewis don't want to go with me?"

"We'll tidy," Caroline said. "We have a lot of tidying to do."

Tony had lived in Detroit; he couldn't talk enough about what he called "the underclass of Malta."

"They swear ever word, the underclass. They go to church, bet your life. They come out wit' swears mile a minute. They don't say 'God damn,' they make it worser. They say 'Damn God.' They don't say 'Up your ass,' like us Americans. They say 'Up your mother's ass.'"

"Yeah. Sure, Tony. You told me about that." He didn't want to hurt the old fellow's feelings. But he wanted to finish his coffee and get away. The coffee was too hot to drink, though.

"Deat' is a big tragedy in Malta." The old fellow left out most of his *h*'s. He knew what Tony was going to say. He tried to listen to the way he talked. He wished he could imitate him. He wished he was able to tell stories, like his dad and Ralph. He had taken a picture of the old man when they first arrived in Malta.

It was a funny thing. He'd stopped taking pictures.

"Everybody cry, and then they try to keep the body in the house when it time to go to church. Maybe I tell you. You be bury in twenty-four hour in Malta. Mothers and sisters, they always about five sister crying and yelling. We do it right in the United State. We get drunk. We go to funeral. We go home. We get drunk again. Good United State."

"No, Tony." He had been twenty-three when his father died —he'd felt younger than Lewis. He had cried at his mother's funeral. It was terrible sitting in the front row. "Come off it," Marie whispered.

"English, they can't say *h*. We have a tongue twist to show them up. About peaches. They can't say it for nothing." Three times Tony recited the tongue twist.

"S'long, Tony. My wife's waiting for me."

"People's wife wait."

"Yeah, I guess so. But I got to be going." He didn't tell Tony he was leaving Malta. He had already said a lot of good-byes to a lot of old fellows. Most of them called him "Mr. Hutton."

He could have stopped at a couple more places, but he didn't really want to.

He didn't know why he had put off going to the Hypogeum and Tarxien. He had meant for them all to go. They passed the signs every time they went into Valletta. Somehow you never got around to doing all the things you planned. Maybe he had been saving the Hypogeum for last. He'd read four or five things about it: 4000 B.C., underground chambers possessed with fine acoustical properties, sanctuary to consult an oracle, holy of holies, cornices and pillars. He was proud of himself for remembering what he had read in the guidebooks.

Devotees slept and had their dreams interpreted.

He had been dreaming a lot again. He hadn't told Caroline.

"I'm going to the Hypogeum," he told the bus boy. The boy didn't understand him. "I'll ring when I want to get off."

At the place there were a couple of ticket takers upstairs. Three Englishwomen were leaving as he started down. He was the only person in the place.

It was like somebody's basement. He wasn't really sure he had found the oracular chamber, but he tried to look at everything; he followed all the red arrows. It didn't take but a few minutes. He stood on the basement steps for a little while. He was ashamed to go back too soon and face the ticket takers. He didn't want to hurt their feelings.

If ever anyplace needed a public relations man, it was Malta. They needed to pep you up to what you were seeing.

"Good afternoon, sir," the men at the table said together.

243

"Good afternoon. Very interesting. I enjoyed it."

He was disappointed in the Tarxien temples, too. They were just a few blocks from the Hypogeum; he found them all right without asking anybody directions. He was the only person again. Evidence of three Neolithic temples, 4000–3000 B.C., sanctuary, depository, the books had said.

At least this time the stones were above the ground. The sun was warm. He was hot, really hot. And the sky was blue. He took off his overcoat. A bird, maybe just a sparrow, teetered around on one of the big stones.

". . . removed to the National Museum," a sign said. "Much still of absorbing interest exists for the viewer."

There wasn't much. Men put stones together for houses and churches, and the men died, and somebody else built something else on top of the old stones. One pile of stones was pretty much like another pile of stones. Somebody else built something else.

He was glad to get out of the place. The ticket taker wasn't at the door. That was good.

He started back toward the bus stop. There was a new church going up, a round one, as if they needed any more churches in Malta. Next door, at the end of a little parkway, there was an old church with a wall around it. He figured on looking in at the church.

But a hearse stood in front of the gate. He had to look twice to make sure he was seeing right. Malta had a lot of hearses, great big cars with big silver crosses over the windshields. But this was a glass box, pulled by two horses with their manes decked out, tied with red yarn. The frame of the box was gold. There were some cupids on top with pink and green plaster ribbons covering their nakedness. It was like a carriage in one of Lewis's books. Except the ribbons said R.I.P. in big black letters.

The thing was empty.

The horses started off. The driver had on a top hat. Tom Hutton looked hard at the horses and the carriage and the driver. And he kept walking toward the church.

244

There was a side gate. He passed a young girl. She was dressed in black. He figured she wasn't necessarily a part of the funeral. She stood at the edge of the grass. She was looking over at the Tarxien pile of stones. She didn't turn around. He was glad.

Inside the gate there were four or five men chipping away at some tan blocks of stone. They had handkerchiefs around their heads. Over at the left of the path there was one man down in a hole. Maybe it was a grave. He was singing something in Maltese. He wasn't singing loud, but you could hear him all right. His voice sounded good, the way you sounded in a shower.

The other men stopped working. They folded their arms. They were looking over at the central gate. The man in the hole kept singing.

He walked a little way past the man and looked back.

The front yard of the church was a cemetery. Over by the gate a dressed-up priest was making the sign of the cross. There were a couple of boys, like choirboys, and a few men in suits, and three women, two fairly young and one old; they were dressed in black and they had black handkerchiefs over their heads.

A couple of the men stepped forward. There was a casket. The men were raising the lid. The casket was made of two colors of wood.

All of the people looked down. The women dabbed at their eyes, but you couldn't hear anything, not any crying. You could hear the other man singing in the hole, though.

The two men screwed down the lid. They put ropes around the casket and started to let it down. A third man began shoveling dirt. The women didn't turn away.

It was funny about women.

He didn't want to be watching.

He was walking on his tiptoes. He passed the workers, who still stood with their arms folded and the handkerchiefs on their heads. The man was still singing.

The young girl was still standing by the path. She turned and looked straight at him. She looked as if she hated him. She was crying. He thought about speaking to her. He didn't. He walked fast, back to the bus stop. He decided he wouldn't even bother to mention the places to Caroline and Lewis. They hadn't missed anything.

He had to wait and wait. He didn't think about dying, exactly, but he kept thinking the word *death*. He wasn't sure whether you thought about *death* with a capital or a little letter.

After about five minutes a woman came up and stood near him. She was nice enough looking, maybe the way Agatha would look when she got to be forty.

"I get a Birże bus here, don't I?" He was sure it was the right place, but he wanted to make sure. He wanted to talk to somebody.

She turned her head away.

He didn't say anything else, but he felt bad. He kept thinking about the girl outside the church wall. Her eyes had been funnylooking. Maybe Caroline was right about eyes. The girl's eyes were full of hate.

Maybe he should have had sex with Gwen Pettigrew, or tried to. Maybe Ralph was right. "You only live once," Ralph was always saying. Maybe Tom Hutton wasn't so smart as he thought he was. Maybe he was getting old.

"What all did you learn in Malta, Tom?" Ralph would ask. Ralph was always asking, "What all did you learn today, Tommy boy?"

The bus didn't come for eleven more minutes. "Here it is," he said to the woman.

He stepped aside so she could get on first. She went clear to the back. He stood up front. The bus was full of kids in school uniforms, black coats and mustard-colored ties.

He couldn't get the young girl's face out of his mind. He was pretty sure she was the daughter of the man in the coffin who had been driven to the cemetery in a glass wagon.

It was only three o'clock. He didn't want to get home yet.

He got off two stops early. It was cold. A wind had come up.

The waves were twice as high as they had been this morning. The bay was full of boats, more than he'd ever seen out there. He was glad he had worn the lining to his coat.

The Bay View Bar felt good. They had two heaters going. Barney had taken down the plastic strips and closed the door. For a minute he thought about knocking at the door, which was pretty darn silly to think about.

Barney and his sister—they owned the place—were talking to a little bald man. They were talking Maltese, of course. They were shouting. When they saw him they changed right away to English.

'Mr. Hutton," Barney said. The sister said, "How do you do, welcome." She was a thin woman, for Malta. The other fellow said, "Allo."

They had terrible teeth, but they had big smiles, all of them.

"Where you been so long? You have drink with me," Barney said.

"It's my turn. Make it four."

"Not me. Too fat," the sister said.

"Very nice," the bald man said.

Barney opened a lager for the bald man, and two strawberry sodas. The first day, when Tom had refused whiskey, Barney decided on strawberry sodas.

"Your favoritest. Sure enough, we argue over the barometer."

The thing hung over the bar; it was made of paper, a picture of a friar sitting in a chair. It showed his profile. When the cowl covered the friar's head it was going to be bad weather. When it went back, it was going to be clear and sunny; an advertisement for something.

All three of them talked at the same time. Barney and the bald man said the cowl was moving back; the sister said it was getting ready to cover the man's head.

"Very bad weather," the sister said. "All down."

It was nice to stand in the warm room and hear them arguing with each other. Nobody was mad at anybody.

247

"What you think, Mr. Hutton?"

"I don't know, Barney. I never noticed the fellow before. I don't know what's the norm." You could tell Barney didn't know what *norm* meant, but that was all right.

The sister said, "The boats, Italian. You see the boats? They come in for the bad weather."

"They go. Good weather," the bald man said.

"Bad weather." The sister covered her mouth with her hand. She had a couple of teeth missing. Tom didn't even know her name, after all this time.

"Good weather, sister."

He did not want to go back to his own house. Tomorrow he and Caroline and Lewis would be taking a ship and a train and a ship and a plane back to Ohio.

Caroline and Lewis were getting supper. The house was cold as the mischief.

They were glad to see him. Caroline said she felt just fine.

He went back to the kitchen for a drink of water. On the kitchen table Caroline had written a note to herself. "Lamb chops, tossed salad, cheese and pears."

"Look, Tom. I'm writing notes to myself now."

He told her he was getting to like fruit and cheese for dessert.

Lewis said, "We could read together, but I'm helping Mamma."

He got out a couple of guidebooks and read about the Hypogeum and Tarxien.

He'd missed several things at the temples, but that was all right, too.

He didn't take off his overcoat until Caroline called dinner.

He was all right. A man couldn't expect to live forever. And you couldn't do everything.

Caroline was wearing the cashmere robe he had given her for Christmas. He hadn't noticed before. "You haven't dressed all day? You're sure you're all right?" She looked pretty. Her hair was loose around her face.

"Yes, fine. I dressed. I changed and took another hot bath." Lewis said, "You look pretty, Mamma."

He told Lewis he had a good eye.

Lewis wanted to say the blessing. He said the usual, and then he said, "I am glad Mamma didn't break her leg. Amen."

It was a good meal. He did the dishes and Lewis carried them into the dining room, and Caroline put them in the closet.

They all went to bed early. He was tired as a dog. He had a little trouble going to sleep. He kept thinking about the temples.

The wind woke him up. He fumbled around on the little table for his glasses. The hands of the travel alarm said four o'clock, right on the nose. The wind sounded as if it meant to tear the house apart.

He put his glasses back down carefully. They didn't even make a click.

But Caroline was awake. "I'm going to check on Lewis." Maybe she had been awake for a long time, listening to the wind, and maybe being scared of it. He started to ask her something, but he forgot what he had been going to ask her; he wasn't really awake himself.

"That sounds wild." He thought, "The friar's cowl is down. Barney's sister was right." He'd forgot to tell Caroline about the barometer. But he didn't want to get clear waked up. He was cozy warm. He pulled the covers over him. The covers were like being asleep.

He reached out to touch Caroline. He must have been asleep. He fumbled at the covers. Maybe he was looking for his glasses again.

Caroline wasn't in the bed. He'd been dreaming something, about Ralph, maybe, and the East Side School yard. He couldn't remember what the dream was about. He wasn't going to try to remember.

"Caroline?"

He pushed back the covers. He put on his glasses.

The house just sounded cold. He wasn't cold at all. He didn't even put on his house slippers.

But Caroline wasn't in Lewis's room. The boy slept quietly. He was breathing so quietly that you had to lean over to hear him. Lewis was fine.

He couldn't imagine where Caroline could be. For a minute he was scared. It was like being scared in a dream. He looked down at Lewis, not really seeing him. But he could hear him. The boy was breathing all right. It would be a fine state of affairs if he turned out to be as fretful as Caroline, worrying about things you had no right to. He'd read somewhere that married people started acting and looking like each other. That would be hard on Caroline. She was a beautiful woman.

It took him a minute, really a full minute, to remember the other bedroom. He had started down the steps in the dark. He was at the first landing when he remembered the other bedroom.

She stood at the doors that led out to the little balcony over the street. She stood sideways in the center of the opened doors. But she wasn't on the balcony.

The wind was really loud. He could barely hear himself say, "Caroline."

The street light showed her plain as day. And the water beyond her. The water was white. She didn't have her robe on. The wind pressed against her. She could have been naked; at first he thought she was naked, maybe ready to jump naked into the street.

He called her again. He didn't want to scare her. It was good to say her name.

She turned her head slowly. She wasn't scared. "I was just going in to see if you were awake. It's beautiful, isn't it?"

He walked into the room. He stood behind her. He put his arms

250

around her. He cupped her breasts in his hands. She leaned back against him.

He was wide awake. He wished he could think of something important to say to her. He moved his hands. He thought about saying, "We're happy, aren't we, Caroline. We are."

He said, "I hope this settles down before tomorrow. The wind."

She said, "We have plenty of seasick pills."

The water covered the beach. It spilled over the wall onto the street, moving beneath them.

He was picking her up. He put his arms under her shoulders and her knees. He had never picked her up before. For a second he wondered if he was strong enough. He didn't want to be like somebody in a comedy—the man gets his foot caught in a rug, and they both fall down, and they knock over a lamp trying to get up.

She put her arms around him.

He carried her easily, back to their own bedroom.

They were making love. He thought about the waves outside, coming clear across the street, up through their doorway. But he couldn't hear the waves. They had never made love this way before.

"Tom, Tom, Tom," she said. "Tom"

She was whimpering. She wasn't crying exactly.

"What's the matter, honey? Don't cry. Poor kid."

"I'm not crying."

"What's the matter?"

"Nothing. Not anything I know."

It was a good time. It was a fine time.

He got around to saying, "We're happy together. We've been happy in Malta. We know each other better, don't we?" He didn't know why he said that.

"Yes. Of course."

In Athens, Ohio, everybody told everybody else, "Travel is broadening."

"I grew up in Malta," Lewis said.

"I kept house, a cold narrow dark house, but I enjoyed it, and the people were friendly," Caroline said.

"They have a rich culture," Tom said to the minister, maybe to Ellen and Ralph. "We're glad we went. We're glad to be back home."

He started to ask Caroline what she had been doing out on the balcony. But he didn't ask her.

She went to sleep first. He was pretty sure she was sound asleep. She wasn't pretending. Caroline wouldn't pretend. There were a lot of questions you couldn't ask other people.

I didn't learn a goddamned thing.

It took him a pretty long time to go to sleep again.

$\mathcal{A}$ gatha had spent the morning cleaning. They were fortunate that Agatha had their last morning free. They ate lunch together, leftovers, the four of them awkward around the dining room table. They all tried to make conversation. Agatha kept saying, "Yes, madame," and "Yes, sir," even to Lewis. Agatha kept patting her lips with her napkin. It was almost three o'clock.

"You'll have more cake and ice cream, Agatha?" Caroline was standing; she had been up many times during the meal, counterfeiting errands to the kitchen in order to get away from their stilted conversation. She was worrying about giving Agatha the envelope with her moneys. She had put in twenty extra pounds. Tom had suggested ten, but the twenty was fine with him. "Fine, fine," Tom said. She should have given the envelope to the girl before they sat down to eat together.

"No. Thank you, madame."

"You must. We have so much. I can't bear to throw it out. We're having dinner in Valletta." She was ungracious. She sounded like a stingy old woman. "You'll join Tom and Lewis in a little more, just a little more?"

Tom rubbed at his stomach with both hands. He was going to refuse his second helping. "You have to, Tom."

"I want some more," Lewis said.

"If you insist, madame."

But Agatha insisted on doing the dishes. "You have been on your feet too much, madame. Your poor leg. I am going to do the dishes. I am going to finish."

Tom lifted his shoulders. That's where Lewis got the gesture, from Tom. Agatha was stronger than Caroline Hutton. Anybody was stronger.

"It's all done, isn't it? Everything's done. Except the Incidentals." She made herself laugh.

Three of the suitcases and the two new tote bags waited beside the couch. She had laid out everything. Tom had packed. Tom knew where everything belonged. Upstairs the beds were stripped down. All over the house the shelves and drawers had been checked twice. Tom and Lewis had worked hard, too. Tom had made Lewis check after him. It was good practice for the boy. He found a bobby pin and a Wash 'n Dri packet. He was proud of himself. Someday Lewis and a girl would leave a house together. Or a hotel room. They would be on their honeymoon. The girl was pretty. "Have you checked everything twice?" Lewis asked the girl. "We don't want to leave anything we shouldn't."

The house positively shone. But flies circled the rooms.

"Good-bye, Mr. Hutton. Good-bye, Lewis. Good-bye, Mrs. Hutton."

At the door they all shook hands with Agatha.

Always somebody was saying, "Good-bye."

She handed Agatha the envelope. "Our address is here, on the back flap. We would be pleased to hear from you."

"I will write you a letter."

The four of them stood waiting. Tom and Lewis waited as if she were the spokesman for a committee.

"There's a little . . ." But the money would not be little to Agatha. And she had suddenly imagined Agatha's handing the unopened envelope to her father. She had not meant to mention the extra money. "There's a wedding present. It is for you. And your fancy."

"No necessity, madame."

"We wish you every happiness."

"If you're ever in Ohio . . ." Tom said.

"You be sure and come see us," Lewis said.

She wished Agatha would move past them and out to the street. She was ashamed of herself. And so she delayed Agatha's going with foolish words: "Ohio's not too terribly far from New York; you and your husband will probably make a trip to New York," she said. "Let us know how the bedroom furniture turns out." And, "We hate to miss spring and summer in Malta. We hate to leave."

Finally, finally, she let Agatha go, wishing she had never come.

A person could care only so much. Caroline Hutton could care only so much. Always she had felt she should care totally. Love the neighbor, love thy neighbor.

She would not have loved Agatha, not totally, in Athens, Ohio, or anywhere.

She closed the door. Tom and Lewis looked at her, looking like each other.

"It's hard to be a rich American." She had not known what she was going to say.

"Are we rich, Daddy?" Lewis pulled at Tom's hand.

"Not so very. We have enough. What's the matter with you, Caroline?"

"Nothing's the matter."

"You're tired. You ought to take a little walk. It'll be good for your leg. Lewis and I will play catch on the beach. He doesn't need a nap today. We can close up the Incidentals."

"No, Tom."

"Take yourself a walk. You have to unlax. That's what my dad used to say, *unlax*. He got it from Amos and Andy. There's not anything else for you to do. You've done everything."

Tom had told her to take a walk. She had not asked him to tell her. Caroline Thaxton was not a ventriloquist. Once she had prayed to be a ventriloquist. She could have thrown her voice and

255

made a chair talk. The desk could have said something. There had been a ventriloquist at church, an evangelist.

She had prayed until she imagined the desk's saying something, a comfort. "Don't worry," or something, the desk said. Some kind of comfort, over something.

"Did you hear what the desk said?"

"You mustn't lie, Caroline. You're the one."

The desk said something. She could almost remember.

"You must stop lying, Caroline."

"Yes. I'll take a walk. I won't be gone long."

"I'll go with you," Lewis said.

"Look here, fellow. You have to help me."

"You said everything was finished up."

"Go on, Caroline. We're fine."

Lewis stuck out his lower lip. He said, "I'm sleepy."

"We'll have us a game. It's turned out to be a pretty nice day, no matter what the barometer said."

Lewis yawned. "I need my rest." The child turned and ran for the stairway.

"There aren't any sheets on the beds, Lewis." She was whispering.

"Leave the kid alone. He's all right. The nap will be good for him. He's excited over leaving. Go on."

Tom was frowning, but he wasn't cross. She thought of mentioning last night, and the balcony, and the lovemaking—the having sex—whatever the word was. But she didn't know any words to say. She was tired of trying to make words for what she didn't understand.

Most of the fishing boats had left the harbor. "Italian boats," Tom had said. The waves came in fairly quietly, the way they had come in that first day, a long time ago.

A tanker pumped oil at the jetty.

A dog ran on the sidewalk ahead of her. It was the red dog. He wasn't the dog who turned over garbage cans. After you had lived in a place awhile you knew which dog would bother the garbage.

256

The sky was blue and white and gray.

She had turned right, away from The Garden. It was Wednesday. Wednesday was the day they were leaving.

"Evan, you're a disgrace," a stout Englishwoman said. Her husband wore a beard. The woman and her husband stood with another couple, and another child.

"Come on, Andrew. Say hello to Evan."

"Bye-bye," Andrew said. The child wore sandals. He ran toward Evan, splayfooted.

A woman and a man lay on the rocks. It was too cold for sunning. The hair on the man's chest was gray. The woman looked young. Her bikini was orange and red. The man had his eyes open, but the woman seemed to sleep. The straps of her brassiere were pulled down over her shoulders.

The barboy from the Courageous came out of the men's restroom by the rocks. "All right," the boy said.

She walked until all of the houses disappeared.

She turned. She walked past the man and the girl. The boy from the Courageous and the English families had disappeared.

She felt invisible.

She passed their house. The front doors and the inner doors stood wide open. Perhaps she had not closed them when she left. Perhaps Tom had opened them. Tom did not mind the circling flies.

No doubt she would have found The Garden if Lewis had been with her. To Saint George's Bay, left, right, left.

She was running.

Left again, right, straight, and left. They had visited The Garden enough times to have found it in their sleep. In her own sleep.

She was breathing almost too heavily to ask, "A park? The Garden?"

The old lady with a baby buggy did not understand her.

"It's close. You cawn't miss it," an old gentleman said. "Right up the way." He pointed with the stem of his pipe. "Right and left, and turn again."

"I don't know. I'm a stranger here," a woman said. "Are you from the United States, by any chance?"

"No, no, I'm sorry."

She did not find the garden.

She turned.

Perhaps she had not really been looking for it.

She had been taking a walk, to unlax.

She made herself walk casually. Once, a couple of times, she was afraid she was lost. But she found her way all right. She didn't know exactly how long she had been gone, but she was home in plenty of time.

Tom and Lewis sat on the couch. Tom was reading the cloud book to Lewis.

"Hello, Mamma." Lewis jumped up. Tom stood, too, almost as if she were company.

She said, "I had a good walk."

"Is it time to go down to the boat, Daddy? Almost time?"

Tom looked at his watch. "Almost. We'll get us a good dinner. We can get on early. We'll get us a good night's sleep. We'll be raring to go when we get to Syracuse."

"Syracusa," Lewis said.

The four suitcases, the two blues and the two browns, and the new tote bags waited beside the couch.

"I don't think we've left anything," Tom said. "I guess you always come back with more than you brought," Lewis told the girl in the hotel room, or Tom was talking.

"You're bound to leave something," the girl said. "No matter how hard you try. Maybe you bring back different things."

She was crying.

"Mamma, did you hurt yourself?"

"I'm just fine." She turned. She pressed her chin hard against her shoulder, wishing she had hurt herself enough to bleed.

"Does your leg hurt, Mamma?"

"Caroline?"

"Mamma. Don't, Mamma!"

258

"You're tired. You're bound to be tired."

She couldn't stop forever. Lewis had almost never seen her cry, and now she was crying forever.

Or she had stopped crying.

"What on this earth, Mamma?"

"I don't know. I guess I'm tired. Excuse me."

"Here, Caroline."

She took Tom's handkerchief. "I just don't know."

Perhaps she would never be able to lie to the boy, or to Tom. Perhaps she would always be able to lie to them. Sometimes always.

"My gosh, Caroline. You scared me."

She was laughing, quite naturally. She felt graceful. She laughed as if she were a lady at a picnic, or a reunion, some kind of a reunion, or just at a dinner party at home in Athens, Ohio.

72 73 10 9 8 7 6 5 4 3 2 1